The Getaway

by

Leopold Borstinski

1956

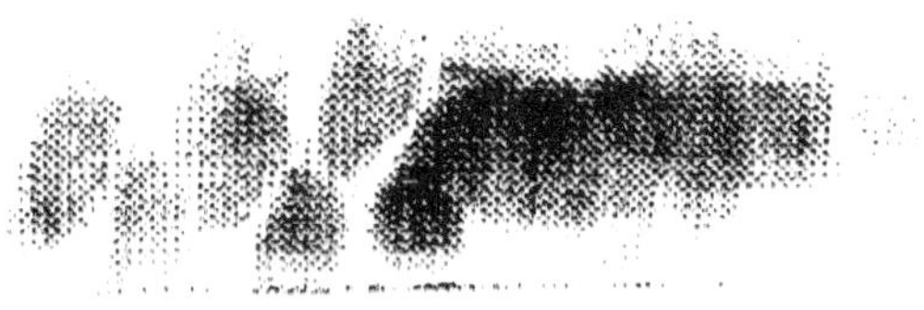

1

MARY LOU BELLE'S father died when she was only eight so her mother, Alice brought her up, along with her two brothers and two younger twin sisters. The eldest sibling was six and the youngest were born three years later. Times were tough in Texas for everyone and Alice's lack of a man to support her made life even harder for her family.

Tied to tending her young offspring, Alice rarely left their side and her only escape was the baptist church around the corner from her home. In particular, she leaned heavily on the kind words and understanding ear of Pastor Neil.

In 1956, Mary Lou turned fourteen and he started to look after the kids for Alice on Sunday afternoons so she could take some time to devote to herself and not just to the family. She spent these invaluable hours in the bar with her girlfriends sipping Long Island iced teas where she listened to them complain about the men in their world.

Pastor Neil brought along board games for the children to play. First, he showed the youngsters the rules, then he would sit and let them have their fun with snakes and ladders or checkers. Because of the age difference between herself and her brothers and sisters, Mary Lou sat back too. Apart from her one male teacher, Pastor Neil was the only constant man of any significance in her life and she didn't want to squander that time with children's games. This father figure was all she had and they enjoyed each other's company. She liked the fact he didn't spend Sunday afternoon talking about god like all the other priests felt the need to do.

Just before Mary Lou's next birthday, he asked her if she'd ever seen God's Trunk and she confessed she had not. While the youngsters were playing their board games, they wandered into her bedroom and he showed her his Trunk and got her to touch it. Within three weeks, she was so used to God's Trunk, Mary Lou would stroke it until its sap would rise and rush out of it. She made him very happy.

On her fifteenth birthday, he bought her a large bar of chocolate, which he told her she did not have to share with anyone—just like their secret times together. He asked her if she'd started her woman's bleeding and she confirmed she had.

The following week he encouraged her to take off her panties for him and over the next month instead of touching the Trunk and releasing its sap, Pastor Neil got Mary Lou to let him put his Trunk inside her Rosebush.

The next school year came and went. He kept up his visits and Alice leaned more heavily on him. He would pop over of an evening during the week and they would talk. Sometimes she would cry and he would give her a hug for solace but always he would listen and be respectful of her, something her long-dead husband failed ever to do.

Mary Lou's school career bumped along near the bottom but she finally made some real friends and could engage in honest conversation with people her own age. Being seventeen, many of the girls were putting out for their guys, describing their sexual explorations in lurid detail during Monday recess. This was the point when Mary Lou discovered her Sunday afternoons with this man were not normal by any stretch of the imagination.

She knew her mother wouldn't believe her. She eavesdropped on Alice's conversation with him one evening and they talked about getting married. They planned to move the family to the Pastor's house next to the church.

Mary Lou packed a bag she found at the back of the cupboard by the front door and stole a knife from the kitchen and hid it under her bed until Sunday arrived with a thud in her life.

As always, the kids played their games while her mother got drunk in a bar. Pastor Neil took her into her room and sat on the edge of the bed. She kneeled down between his legs while he pushed his shorts down from under his cassock.

Then without a word, she grabbed the knife she'd placed so carefully at exactly the right position and stabbed and sliced at his groin. Blood poured everywhere and he rolled off the bed, writhing in agony. She reckoned she had carved his dick clean off.

She took the bag out of her wardrobe and stuffed her last few possessions into it. Then she turned back to Pastor Neil, picked up the knife she'd left on the bedside table and plunged it into his throat. As much as she wanted to watch that man suffer, Mary Lou Belle didn't stay to witness him bleed out. She walked out the room, out the house and out of that town— never to return.

The Getaway

TUESDAY JUNE 17, 1968

2

FRANK LAGOTTI DROVE his white van south at high speed down Hollins Ferry Road in the suburbs of Baltimore, ignoring any red lights trying to impede his progress. Next to him sat Brian and jammed under their feet where two black bags stuffed with banknotes, which a short while ago had been resting in the vault of the First Bank of Baltimore, Lansdowne Branch.

Even though he'd extracted the cash from a bank, Frank was not a happy man. He had left two of his gang dead on the ground, but what really made him angry was his girlfriend had not kept her word to him that morning.

Police sirens wailed behind them; they had exited the bank minutes earlier and the cops were already chomping at their heels. The noise remained in the distance and Frank couldn't tell if they were gaining on him. Foot flat on the gas pedal, arms rigid-straight attached to the steering wheel, he stared ahead and continued to fume.

Brian sat in total silence, an occasional glance towards Frank the only discernible movement in his entire body. Surviving the raid was one thing, but they weren't clear just yet. He was lucky to be alive although there was no guarantee that state would continue. As a reflex action, he checked his guns were in their correct place in his coat, having refilled the chambers in case of need.

"Check mine."

Frank passed his revolvers to Brian who repeated the process and returned them to his boss.

"I think they're fading."

"Maybe, Frank."

The men sank back to silence as the wagon sped along the road heading for a barn which was the gang's rendezvous. Frank was right, the sirens were disappearing: must have taken a wrong turning because even though Pete the Wheels spent a lot of time souping up their vehicles, the van was no competition for a police car in a high-speed chase.

That was why Frank planned to set charges along the telegraph poles near the bank—to make it real hard for the police to follow them. But they hadn't blown and the cops were behind them now. Brian tried not to dwell on the events that had gone down in the bank. He knew he needed to keep his wits about him and remembering the blood pour out of Andrew's chest was not the way to go.

"Hop into the back and tell me if you can see anything."

Brian loped over the shift stick and landed on the mattress he'd found so uncomfortable on their route into Lansdowne. He shuffled to the small window at the rear of the van. He peeped out and stared.

A lot of dust from the van's tires and an empty scene: road, verge, fields. Amazing how quickly the suburban sprawl gives way to the countryside. The land was flat and the road was straight so the tarmac looked like it fell away at the curvature of the Earth. Just at that point. Brian thought he spotted a glowing light, flashing red, but he couldn't be sure. He stared again, but the sunlight was at precisely the wrong angle for him to be certain.

"Well?"

"Give me another minute. Might be something, might be nothing."

Frank knew Brian well enough to allow him the time to decide—he was a professional. He rode shotgun for many jobs before this one. If the man demanded a moment, he needed it.

Tick tock.

"And?"

"There's a red light on the horizon. Not catching us up but not going away."

"Hang on, I'll give ourselves an edge."

Frank waited two seconds and then flung the wheel hard right, forcing the vehicle to career off the road, onto the dirt and into a field. He gunned the vehicle as it made its way over the bumpiest field in Maryland. The steel reinforcement attached to the chassis kept the van in one piece. It headed straight for a clump of trees and bushes. He skidded it to a halt, facing the road a thousand feet away.

Five minutes later a single cherry top sped past staying on the road. Both men had guns drawn and had stepped out the van ready to let rip if anything left the safety of the highway. They stayed a minute to make sure the blue and white didn't return and hopped back into the van.

"Gonna stay here all day?"

"Nope. But if we're not being chased, we don't have to drive like we are."

Brian thought about that for three seconds then nodded understanding and, by extension, his consent. Not that Frank was asking for it.

Nothing appeared. Not from the left or the right. There was the occasional chirp of a bird and the rustling of leaves in the breeze but apart from that: zip.

Another ten minutes of silent waiting. Frank put the van into gear and drove at a sensible pace back to the highway. Then he rejoined the road and traveled at five below the legal limit. He was right: if you travel at high speed, every cop will want to stop you. If you drive legit then they'll arrest you for a bust tail light. And Pete already checked them the day before.

Fifteen minutes later, the destination loomed in the distance. There were no automobiles out front but he expected that. Pete and Brian parked the vehicles away from the line of sight from the highway.

Frank turned off the road and idled the vehicle round the side of the barn. There were three cars, filled with gas and ready to go. All were family saloons; nothing to raise an eyebrow of a hero citizen: a white Galaxie, a blue Falcon and a red Ford Torino. Brian noticed they remained in the exact location where he and Pete set them up the previous night.

There was one exception: a black Cadillac parked at the end, blocking all three vehicles from exiting the makeshift parking lot. Stood next to the saloon were two men Frank and Brian recognized.

Paul and Luigi were there to collect the take for Frank's Shylock and money-laundering uncle, Frank Senior. Frankie to close family and friends. Nothing was out the ordinary so they stepped out the van to greet Frankie's heavies.

WHEN MARY LOU sped out the back of the bank lot, she contained a maelstrom of emotions. Her Barracuda took her away from the man she thought she loved and back into the arms of a man who'd have worked out she'd betrayed him.

South onto Hollins Ferry Road and her thoughts were with Carter. He'd spent months telling her he would clear his gambling debt to Uncle Frankie by stealing from the bank on the day the gang was due to appear. Then he hatched a plan to steal from Frankie too. Instead of fleeing for her life, he was meant to be sat beside her with a bag full of cash.

When he was a no-show, Mary Lou figured the smartest thing was to head to the barn and see if Frank got to the money. This would have been perfect were it not for one small detail. As she drove away from the First Bank of Baltimore, she noticed the silence. She might have placed the explosives on the poles near the bank but with all the stress of the morning, she'd forgotten to set the timers. Frank would be pissed.

If that wasn't awful enough, Mary Lou had no notion why Carter hadn't appeared. Frank might have singled him out and done who knows what. She couldn't let herself pursue that idea for too long as it made her want to cry. If Carter was a sap, so be it, but he deserved nothing bad to happen to him.

She remembered the words of advice she'd received repeatedly. Drive under the limit. Don't jump any lights. Don't give the cops any excuse to pull you over. You're just a single girl in a powerful sports car out for a tour of the countryside.

Far off in her rearview mirror: a flashing red light. Mary Lou's heart sunk and her stomach tightened. Her bowels churned. A blue and white gained on her every time she checked its position.

"Steady, steady. Keep your nerve."

Within a minute, she caught sight of the face of the driver clear as day, his car tucked in behind hers. She took her foot off the gas just for a second to give him the opportunity to pass her more easily, which he did. Hers was the only vehicle in the vicinity so he gunned his Chevrolet and sped off in front. Five minutes later, it had gone beyond the horizon. Almost instantly, so it felt, the barn appeared and Mary Lou slowed down and passed the building by six hundred feet or more.

She let the Barracuda glide to a halt hidden among some undergrowth next to two trees. If anyone was already at the meeting point, she hoped they wouldn't have heard her arrival. She popped open the glove compartment and took out a small snub nose Pete had left for her in case of any trouble. He was a great getaway driver. Despite that, Mary Lou reminded herself the guy had been a creep every time he'd been anywhere near her and she should cut his throat before they were through.

She opened her door as quietly as she could and kept it ajar. She scampered out of the undergrowth and ducked from one tree or bush to the next until she made her way back to the barn.

The building itself fell into disrepair a decade before and the far wall had collapsed several years before then. The wooden structure contained a window on each of its short sides and a door and two windows on the remaining front wall. These were just shutters now: the glass shattered and fallen away long ago.

Mary Lou pushed the side shutter and revealed the derelict and empty building inside. There was a fence running down the middle to tie up farm animals and she made out pens on the far side. She barely lifted the shutter a few inches, so her view onto the back was limited. The automobiles were out there somewhere but she couldn't see them. Mary Lou closed the shutter to make sure it didn't slam shut and sneaked along the wall toward the rear. At the corner, she espied the three cars but saw a fourth black one parked in front of them all. Strange, that wasn't part of the plan.

She inched her head out further and recognized two men leaning against the far side of the car: Luigi and Paul, Frankie's goons. She shivered because they creeped her out. Old school mafiosi in the making. Uncle Frankie was connected for sure.

The white van appeared which was strange as Pete drove a Chevy Impale, not that lump of a thing. Mary Lou craned further and witnessed two men get out, not the four who went to the bank. The others could be in the back but she'd thought they'd all want to head the fuck out of Dodge, as Frank used to say.

First she recognized Brian. He'd been in the passenger seat. Due to the morning's sunlight, the other guy was in the direct path of the sun so all Mary Lou could see was his silhouette. Five seconds later, she saw Frank's face and a tear rolled down her cheeks. He was safe.

The men stood and talked a while. She couldn't hear a single word because they were too far away. Then they pulled out guns and fired at each other.

3

"LET'S BE CAREFUL out there, Brian. Frank Senior won't be happy with the way things have turned out so far."

"Okay, Frank."

The men slipped out the van leaving their doors wide open. Frank eyed Paul then Luigi and they both stayed leaning against their limousine. Relaxed.

Frank took two steps toward them, stopped and Brian mirrored him.

"Hey boys."

"Hi, Frank."

Paul had never spoken so much to Frank the whole year since he was out of the jail. Luigi remained his usual silent self.

"Radio said you robbed a bank this morning."

"Yep. Shows there are some things you can believe on the radio."

"Big haul?"

"Big enough, I reckon. Not like we've had any time to count it."

"Got it with you though?"

"Yes. It's safe with us."

"What about the others? Four of you walked into the bank. That was the plan. There's only you two and your goomah's missing."

"Plans change. Andrew and Pete didn't make it. No idea about Mary Lou."

"Any loose ends?"

"Nope. Both bodies in the getaway car and we torched the fucking lot."

"That explains the van."

"It brought us here… So you haven't seen Mary Lou? She's not been here?"

"Uh-uh. No sign of the skirt."

"And did you bring some seed money? Frank Senior promised us cash while he laundered the take."

"He did."

"So you got it?"

Frank became tetchy. Why was Paul so casual when Frank hoped they'd be on their way within minutes of arriving?

"Sure. You in a rush?"

"Paul, we've robbed a bank and the police are swarming all over the place. Can we get a move on?"

"Thought you might want to wait a while for your blanket warmer."

"She knows the score. Be here or don't and take the consequences."

Frank looked around as though mention of her would make Mary Lou appear in a puff of smoke.

"Let me grab your working capital."

Paul lifted his body off the Caddy and opened the front passenger door, while Luigi stood upright. Brian turned to go into the van but Frank glared at him until he stopped. Brian edged nearer the door without noticing himself do it.

As Paul spun round, Frank spotted a black barrel and whipped out his revolver and aimed it at Paul. A flash and a roar as Luigi's gun let rip and Frank hit the dirt. He rolled over and hid behind the driver's side door.

Bullets flew and amid the whizzes and bangs, red spurt out of Luigi's left shoulder but he didn't go down. Instead, the ox stood there and blasted towards both himself and Brian. Frank aimed at Luigi's heart and squeezed out a shot. It landed square and true and Luigi crumpled in an instant. One down, one remaining.

"How you doing Brian?"

No answer.

"Brian?"

Nothing.

Frank hunkered down as slugs continued to fly in his direction. He checked his revolver: two left in the chamber. Patted his pockets and found he had no spares. Rolling under the van, he got close to Brian's body which was lying face up. One pool of blood around his stomach, another round his forehead. Two good shots.

Frank dragged the corpse behind the passenger door and checked each of Brian's coat pockets. There was a box, but it only had three shells in it. He stuffed them into the chamber but he knew it wouldn't be enough. He squeezed off one shot at Paul and missed. Paul responded with a dozen slugs which flew over Frank's head and around his feet. No time to think.

Paul scampered round the other side of the Cadillac and Frank couldn't figure out where he was. Another burst of fire aimed where Frank was squatting so Paul still had him in his sights. Frank rolled back under the van and stayed there. Five seconds. Ten seconds. Silence.

This was not the OK Corral and he had too few pills for any kind of gunfight. Either Frank needed to be nearer to Paul or he should wait for Paul to come to him.

The space between the cars gave little room for any sneaky maneuvers and there was an open field further out. Get into the barn and scoot round the wasteland which had grown up since the place became derelict? Not a great idea.

Stay put and wait? A hail of bullets landed around the driver door as Paul assumed Frank had gone back to his original side. Perhaps Paul didn't have as good a line of sight as Frank thought. Didn't mean the new plan should change though.

All he could think about was his breathing which sounded like a hurricane to his ears. He focused on looking at both sides of the van to wait for Paul's calves but the sound of his hair swooshing the dirt was far too noisy. An earthquake in his head.

His bright idea quickly turned the space below the vehicle into a death cell. He realized that now. There were no more stray bullets. No more bursts from Paul at all. Frank strained to hear Paul's footsteps, but the wind picked up and the rustling of the trees took over from any other noise.

Two feet appeared just out of reach from Frank's head, facing towards him. He aimed his revolver at one calf and squeezed the trigger. Click. The damn gun jammed. He tried a second time. Click. Nothing. Damn. Paul bent down and Frank saw an eye looking right at him with the guy's semi-automatic pointing straight to his forehead.

A SINGLE SHOT rang out and Paul slumped to the ground, parts of his brain flying to the left and landing on the van door.

"You okay?"

Mary Lou's voice echoed under the wagon with genuine concern but with an edge of fear.

"You alone?"

"Yep."

"Okay, I'm coming out on the other side."

When Frank got up, she held her gun in combat position and continued to point it at Paul.

"Relax, Mary Lou."

She ignored him and Frank stormed round and stood next to her. Then he placed his hands on hers, gently. Her fingers clasped the snub nose more tightly until he kissed her on the neck and the tension in her arms eased off. He took the gun off her and they walked away from the van until he'd made sure Mary Lou stayed with her back to the carnage she'd created. Then he pocketed the piece.

"Thanks."

"You're welcome."

They kissed and hugged even though Frank still hadn't figured out what happened at the bank and whether she had betrayed him.

"You hurt?"

"No. You?"

"All good."

Frank surveyed the scene.

"Where's your car?"

"Down the road a ways. You got any of the money?"

Frank ground his molars.

"Yes. We took the entire haul. Eventually."

"Huh?"

"Tell you later. Now is not the time. We gotta get out of here."

A siren wailed in the distance. Faint but wailing nonetheless.

Frank sprinted to the open van and leaned over to grab the two bags under the front seats and yanked them out.

"Which car?"

Mary Lou shrugged as they all looked the same to her.

"Blue one."

Frank traipsed over to the Falcon and opened the driver's door then halted.

"What about your Barracuda? It'll be faster than this thing."

"Yes but it stands out. That's why Pete chose these family cars for us."

They'd go further in the Barracuda but it turned too many heads.

"Okay, you're right. Bring it over here and we'll deal from there."

Mary Lou ran off leaving Frank to scavenge through the Caddy. A semi-automatic, several boxes of shells, but not much else. He lifted Luigi and Paul's wallets. They had a hundred bucks on them, which was now in his coat pocket. Before getting out of their vehicle, he shunted the shift stick into neutral and pushed it but got nowhere. Instead he dragged the two bodies into the back of the wagon. Then he kneeled down by Brian.

He put his fingers on Brian's neck. No pulse. Frank took the cash from Brian's wallet and threw his body into the van too. He looked around for the gas cans left in advance by the gang. Mary Lou appeared inside the sports car and Frank gestured for her to park in the field behind the barn.

"We've a couple more guns and a pile of shells. And about two hundred bucks spending money."

"I've only got a few dollars on me."

"Same as me before I swiped the wallets."

Mary Lou noticed the feet sticking out the back of the van.

"What do we do first?"

"Help me push the Caddy towards your Barracuda."

Once they had the two cars close to each other, they scurried round the barn looking for the gas cans. Meanwhile the sirens felt like they were getting louder. Every minute, one of them would hold their head up, ears pricked, trying to gauge the distance. Always failing.

Mary Lou walked into the barn and cried out.

"Found them!"

Frank hunkered over and counted six black cans.

"Come on. Dowse the Caddy and Barracuda and I'll make a start on the others."

She walked away to follow his instructions until he gave out a shout.

"Stop! What are we thinking?"

Mary Lou swung round and scrunched her face up.

"We gotta be better than this, Mary Lou. This is gasoline we're about to splash around. Why don't we move the Falcon away from it all so when we fire up its engine, we don't make ourselves a bonfire?"

She slapped her forehead with her palm, nodded and drove the Falcon round the corner. Now it was visible from the road if you were traveling slowly enough to notice it, hidden under a tree. Mary Lou returned and slopped gas all over the remaining cars until all the cans were empty and thrown inside the vehicles.

Frank pulled out a match, struck it and threw it on the Caddy which lit up in twenty seconds. Orange flames licked across the bodywork and flowed along the interior leather. The yellow tongues grew in size until the wind blew in just the right direction causing a spike to transfer to the Barracuda until it, too, was a ball of reddish melting.

He passed the matches to Mary Lou and picked up both black bags.

"Light 'em up, babe. I'll be in the Falcon."

Mary Lou took the matches and watched him disappear round the corner. For a second she wondered if he would drive off without her. What had happened to Carter, Andrew and Pete?

She shook herself out of her reverie and threw one match into each of the cars and two into the van. Only once she was certain the flames had taken hold did she walk away. Mary Lou looked back to see the clothing of the bodies catch light.

"It's a goddamn crematorium in there."

She ran to the side of the barn to watch Frank revving the engine of the Falcon. Mary Lou jumped into the passenger seat and closed the door.

"Let's get the fuck out of Dodge."

Frank slammed his foot onto the pedal and the car skidded around, the back end swerving right then left until the Falcon reached tarmac and its tyres found some grip.

"Easy, Frank."

He laughed, gunned the saloon along the highway for about two minutes and slowed down to below the speed limit.

"We're out for a drive to enjoy the countryside."

"You said it, Frank."

"If the police stops us, it'll be for a blown sidelight. The guns are in the trunk. So's the take. There's nothing of interest in the glove compartment. If a cop pops the hood, we're dead. Do whatever you need to prevent that from happening. Understood?"

"I got it, Frank."

"Good."

Frank switched on the radio and swiveled the dials until he found his favorite station.

"WFTX 96.4 FM, where you're never more than 60 seconds away from quality Rock 'n' Roll."

Both hands on the wheel, he tapped along to the songs while Mary Lou sat there sinking into the passenger seat. His silence bore down on her because she thought he'd want her to explain about the explosives, if nothing else. And she knew the robbery itself was still too raw for her to ask what went wrong.

Meanwhile, Frank was desperate to not think. He walked into the bank at 09:01 with a balaclava on his head exactly one hour ago. The security guard was dead, two of theirs were gone. No three: Brian. And Uncle Frankie sent Paul and Luigi to kill them.

That was before he could figure out what to do with the woman sat next to him. The lack of explosions meant she sabotaged the whole job to take the money for herself and Carter. But she hadn't been out there in the parking lot to go with the chump when Frank left the bank. So what was exactly happening? And those sirens were only getting louder behind them.

He Lagotti had no clue and, as far as he was concerned, the best thing right now was to drive and hum along to a bunch of songs. It had not been a good morning. In the rearview mirror, a plume of smoke rose from the barn. The flames must have reached the building itself. Halloween had come early this year.

4

FRANK TAPPED AWAY at his steering wheel and focused on keeping just below the speed limit. He avoided the freeway in case there were any cordons but there were too many alternate routes for the cops to prevent a felon from fleeing the scene.

The plan had always been to head off in the wrong direction from their intended destination and Frank saw no reason to deviate from this sensible decision—even though that siren was getting louder.

He kept checking in the mirror for some sign of a red flashing light but there was nothing. A few cars and the occasional truck behind him.

"Any idea where the siren's coming from?"

"No. But if you listen carefully, only sounds like one."

"You reckon?"

"Yes, Frank."

Mary Lou opened her window to get a better fix. A blast of cold air entered the cabin due to the speed of the car. Her hair flapped around and whipped her face. Frank's short back and sides unaffected by the airflow.

"One for sure—unless they're so far away…"

Frank was certain the cop was getting closer, but there wasn't even the dust trail from a high pursuit vehicle behind them. Nada.

Mary Lou shook her head and shrugged.

"Wind your window back up. If we can't hear the siren, then I might as well listen to my music."

"Okay."

He carried on tapping and Mary Lou put both feet on her seat, turning her body into a ball. And the car stormed along despite traveling at exactly five miles an hour below the limit.

"How far east should we go?"

"Long enough so that if any local recognizes us, they report to the cops we were heading for Philly."

"How long you reckon that is?"

"Another hour tops. Then we can head north and round until we are on a straight line for California."

"California? Wow."

Frank sucked in air. He didn't want to have this conversation now.

"Not planning on heading to the west coast then?"

She stared at him.

"I had total faith in your ability to take out the bank. We spent enough time preparing for the robbery to be sure we'd carry it through right."

"But?"

"There were complications for both so us, I'd say. Me before you hit the entrance and for you once you'd told everyone to stick 'em up."

"Complications. Nice description. Yes, there were problems inside. No one knew where the money was. Not even the bank manager."

"Crazier things have happened."

"Did Carter tell you he would run off with the take?"

Mary Lou's eyes widened as Frank had nailed the situation perfectly. Carter was their mark inside and she'd been playing him for months. Squeezing him for information, spending time with him, sleeping with him. Falling in love with him.

"He spoke about it but I didn't reckon on him going through with it. Talked big but acted small."

"Is that why you didn't mention his plan to rob the take from under our noses? Not even a word. Not once."

"He didn't name a date. Said it to impress me. Nothing more than that."

"Then any idea why he chose the exact day we came in to lift the money?"

"Well, it was the largest amount of notes in their vault for months. That's why…"

Frank's eyes showed he wasn't buying a word she was saying. To be fair, she was skating close to the truth but withholding certain key facts. Like she was planning to run away from him. Or Uncle Frankie's involvement in the whole deal. That could wait until later. Much later.

"Not now, Frank. It's too complicated and I doubt you're happy with what I've said, judging by your expression."

He nodded in agreement.

"But at some point you need to tell me what happened in that bank. There's next of kin to call."

"Pete had no one: he was a cantankerous little shit who had no friends and no family. And don't spare a tear for Andrew. He's the guy who blasted a hole in Pete's head."

Mary Lou sat and stared at Frank with a stomach cramp reflecting the pain of his words.

"Now is not the time."

"For sure. We can talk later. Let's get further away from the scene of the crime. There's a lot to figure out."

"You said it."

The siren got nearer but still only a handful of cars and two trucks. And a plume of smoke receding in the distance. The noise was loud and Frank listened hard. Mary Lou was right: there was only one noise blaring out. Nothing in the rearview mirror. He looked at the road, at the mirror and noticed beads of sweat dribbling down the side of his face.

"Put your legs down. If this goes belly-up, you don't want to be crushed by the dash."

Mary Lou sat properly again although Frank's comment didn't help her anxiety levels, which were through the roof.

There was a bend up ahead which shifted the highway about eighty degrees right. A clump of trees stood at the inside line of the road's curve. As if from nowhere, a blue-and-white hurtled toward them and then past heading back into Baltimore. Its red light flashed and the siren wailed. Frank recognized the driver from the car which overtook the van earlier. He relaxed.

"Looks like we're not the ones being chased."

She leaned over and planted a kiss on his shoulder—she couldn't reach his mouth.

THE MILES STRETCHED out behind them until Mary Lou thought she'd been to this place before. When Frank pulled into a faded parking lot next to a tumbledown building, then Mary Lou knew for sure. He'd taken them to the disused factory where they'd held their meetings as a crew.

"What we doing here?"

"You'll see."

Frank drove round the back of the rundown warehouse. Originally it stood four storys tall but now half the building was a pile of rubble and the surviving bricks comprised a series of small rooms missing walls, ceilings and, in two cases, floors.

They had used the only space with functioning walls, complete floor and ceiling, which was located in the middle of the space. The location was obscure and even if someone followed them to the site, finding the room was a trial in itself.

They both walked round the fallen bricks and Mary Lou trailed Frank into the room they'd been in so many times before. A sole chair lay on its side, which Uncle Frankie used while everyone else stood around. Four feet away from it was the flat ground Frank had drawn a map of the bank.

He went past the seat and headed towards the far wall. She couldn't tell quite where he was going, but he certainly had a destination in mind. He halted in a corner and counted fifteen footsteps heel-to-toe. Then stopped and faced the whitewash.

Mary Lou watched him squat and pull out a brick to reveal a gap containing a box. He dragged it out of the cavity and flipped open the lid. Inside: papers. He passed two items up to her.

"Here's a passport with a fake name and a matching driving license."

"How long have you had these?"

"Long enough."

Frank smiled up at her and winked.

"Got them sorted a month after I departed the Baltimore State Penitentiary. Never knew when they might be useful."

"You said it. What else is in there?"

Frank slammed the box shut and crammed it into the cavity.

"Never you mind."

He stood up and shoved his passport and photo ID into his pocket.

"Does that mean we're going to leave the country? I thought we were off west."

"Never hurts to have a plan B. And these will give us options if we need then."

Mary Lou flipped over her ID to find her new name: Claudia Starr. Sounded like a porn actress.

"Who's Claudia?"

"You."

"No, silly. I mean who d'you know called Claudia?"

"Nobody. It's just a name."

Mary Lou nodded, but she found it hard to believe.

"And I'm Karl Todd."

"Hi Karl.

"Hi Claudia."

They both laughed a little and then headed to the Falcon.

"Can we get a bite to eat? I'm starved."

Frank sat there for a second.

"I am too. I know a place a few miles down the road. Brian mentioned it to me. We can go there then head west."

"Cool."

Out the parking lot and back onto tarmac. Stubbornly remaining under the limit, he drove off, still avoiding the expressway. Thirty minutes later they understood why the interstates were built. Straight lines with faster traffic. If they weren't concerned about police cordons they would already have been tucking into bacon and hash browns.

Instead, they made their way safely along the back roads. Whenever a blue and white crossed their paths, Mary Lou froze in her seat. Frank appeared more relaxed, but he always stopped tapping on the steering wheel until the cop car faded into the rearview mirror. While there was stress in the automobile, there was nothing but rolling hills and the great outdoors beyond the Falcon.

Mary Lou noticed they traveled under the I-95 as they passed the exit and entrance ramp signs. A minute later they went by a gas station on the right and twenty seconds further on, a diner appeared on the left: *The Joppa-de-Doopah*.

They parked and she stared at the ramshackle venue. It looked like it hadn't seen a lick of paint since 1945. The slime of oil seeped into every corner of the lot and the brickwork. There was a large and one small building. The smaller one clearly was an outhouse and the larger was filled with light, tables and women wearing waitress uniforms. You didn't need to be a genius to figure out what went on inside the Joppa-de-Doopah. Even though the smaller outcrop from the diner appeared basic in the extreme, Mary Lou knew she needed to use the facilities before she ate.

"You go ahead. I'll catch up with you in a minute."

"Huh? Oh, sure."

She was taking a risk: Frank could drive off and leave her stranded but she'd already tested him with the same quandary at the barn and he had waited for her. So the chances were he'd do the same again.

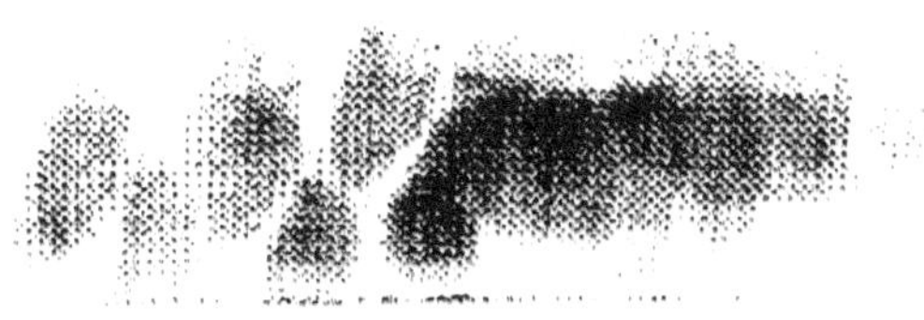

5

WHEN SHE PUSHED open the door marked with an enormous 'W', Mary Lou held her breath. There were two mirrors above cracked sinks and on the other wall were a pair of cubicles. Only one had a lock.

Given the amount of grime on the faucets, she decided against washing her hands and went into the diner to find Frank in a booth by a window. She sat opposite him and realized they could see the entrance to the lot as well as the Falcon. No surprises there.

"What d'you kids like to wrap your lips around?"

The waitress's voice carried over the two feet tall menus which she'd earlier deposited on the table when he first arrived.

Without looking at her, Mary Lou asked for coffee and a glass of water. Frank ordered the same. She lowered the laminated menu in time to see a middle-aged woman waddled off to behind the counter to prepare their drinks. She was no spring chicken. Mary Lou eyed her up and down. The woman's blouse was too tight for her; each button was about to burst. Perhaps because of this, one too many buttons were undone. Or she did it to get more tips. Most of the clientele were men, who'd left the expressway for a bite to eat and an ass to ogle.

"Thanks."

"Call me Lucy."

"Thanks, Lucy."

"You're welcome, fella."

She turned to Mary Lou.

"He's a big hulk of a man, isn't he? You better hang on to him. Take my word. You lose sight of him for one minute and I'll be all over his bones. No offense dear."

"None taken."

They ordered too much food and Lucy left them alone for a while. What she lacked in subtlety, she made up for in efficiency. Soon they tucked into their feast: bacon, eggs, hash browns, toast, home fries.

There was no conversation, just chewing and slurping of coffee. Frank and Mary Lou both deep in their own thoughts, playing over the last two hours and projecting into the future without knowing what would happen one moment to the next.

"What went down in the bank, then?"

He put his silverware down and folded his arms.

"It was a fucking mess. That's what happened. The money had gone from the vault. No kidding."

"Jeez."

"I had to break a few heads before I believed the bank staff when they said they didn't have a clue."

He replayed the images in his head of him torturing the manager, slicing a cashier and cutting her tit.

"We were walking out with nothing when something didn't look right in the state of Maryland. One pinhead couldn't keep his eyes straight. Kept on looking below his desk and I figured he'd stashed the cash. In the two black bags in the trunk. That was your Carter."

Mary Lou continued to stare at him but said nothing.

"Maybe you know what the fuck he was up to. You can tell me in a minute. Brian was standing next to me but Andrew was nowhere. We exited the bank and found him outside, by Pete's driver's door holding a gun. He'd shot Pete in the head. The interior of the vehicle was a fucking mess. You never want to see what that car looked like."

Frank sank the rest of his coffee and Lucy came over for a refill and walked away. He watched her return to the counter and turned his gaze back on Mary Lou.

"So I shot him dead. Couldn't have a killer in the crew. One minute it's Pete, the next it could've been any of us. Then we met up a few minutes later."

He sipped the now hot coffee and drank a mouthful of water.

"The cops chased us out of Lansdowne. Any idea why?"

Mary Lou nodded.

"Because you failed to the explosives. Why?"

"It might be hard to believe but it was an honest mistake. I placed them all, but I got flustered and just plain forgot to flip the switch to set them off. I told you all I wanted nothing to do with the bombs but y'all insisted."

"You forgot?"

"Yep."

Frank remained silent for five minutes, staring at Mary Lou and sipping his coffee. Eventually, she broke the tension.

"Carter had the money, but he was in the bank?"

"Yes. Hidden under his desk, like I said."

"Any idea what he was doing with it?"

"He was gonna rob our bank. Actually, he had robbed the place, if you think about it. But he had missed a key element of any robbery: he forgot to get away."

Mary Lou let out a nervous laugh and he carried on staring. She had known Carter would steal the money for a while before the job but, for whatever reason, instead of leaving before Frank arrived, he had gained a yellow streak down his back and hadn't stolen anything from anyone. Shifting the cash from one part of a bank to another meant nothing. And she had been planning on spending the rest of her life with this sap.

"It's the little things that count."

"Any idea what your Carter was gonna do this morning?"

"First, he's not my Carter. Just plain Carter. Second, no. If I had known he would run off with the money then I'd have met him and we could have bushwhacked him with no one going into that damn bank."

"And you hadn't schemed with him to steal the take away from us?"

"Frank? Listen to yourself. Please."

He continued to stare and then it was Mary Lou's turn to sip at a coffee mug. To her, it was only a partial lie. Once Carter failed to come out the bank then she was telling the truth. Until then, her plan was to follow the money. She was attracted to both men and, although she'd selected Carter, Mary Lou knew Frank was a decent man. Didn't mean he would believe her.

"Listen. If I wanted you gone, I'd have let Paul and Luigi do you in at the rendezvous. But I saved your life."

She allowed those four words to sink in because his staring was annoying her. He had good reason to be angry over Carter but he should show some gratitude too, she reckoned.

THE PROBLEM THEY both faced was simple: neither trusted the other enough. In the last few hours, Mary Lou and Frank had supported the other but the bliss they felt yesterday before the heist had dissipated into thin air. She had withheld vital information before the job and understood he was wary of her.

When those detonators failed to blow, Frank was well within his rights to hunt her down and throw her out the window. That's what he'd done to his last partner when a robbery went sour. Mary Lou plain didn't know if he was just biding his time, waiting for the right moment.

"Where do we progress from here?"

"I don't know. We could split up the money and go our separate ways."

"Is that what you want Frank?"

"Me? No, but I understand if that's what you wanted. I wouldn't choose that to happen but I'd get it."

"I don't wish us to split either."

"Then where shall we go from here?"

He smiled because he understood the double meaning to his words. He had only intended the geographical question.

"West like we said a year ago?"

"That's been the plan all right. Cali-forn-I-a. I've always wanted to see the Pacific Ocean."

"With our new passports, we could always head to Mexico. Swift shuffle over the border and then we vanish."

"Sure could. I love the sound of the weather they have down Tijuana way but neither of us speak Spanish."

Mary Lou thought about how much she'd hate to move south. She had spent her entire life trying to escape from those murky depths of the country.

"There's also Canada, Frank."

"It hovers over us and enough people have gone over the border to dodge the draft, we know we could slip through the customs barrier no problem. But man it's cold up there and I don't fancy that. If we will relocate the least the place should offer us is a warm environment."

"So does California sound the best option then?"

"Does to me."

"Me too."

Mary Lou reached out her hand and Frank squeezed it, briefly. They were far from reconciled but there was still enough connection between them to carry on together. At least for a while.

"But there's a problem with the cash, isn't there?"

"We're stuck with dirty money and we have no idea how much we have."

"Do you think Paul and Luigi got greedy or were they following Uncle Frankie's orders?"

"Good question and right now I don't know. He's always been kind to me even though there's no blood tie."

Mary Lou bit her tongue. There was more to Frankie than a benign step uncle.

"Should we go over to Frankie and sort things out?"

"Any other day, I'd say yes. But if he called a hit on us then we shouldn't be going into the lion's den. Besides, we need to get out of Baltimore and out of Maryland as soon as."

"Where can we launder the money instead if we're not touching Uncle Frankie?"

"We must make a detour."

"Huh?"

"Vegas. I know a guy who knows a guy out there. And worse case, we can hit the wheels."

"Are you serious?"

"I've got some connections out there. It'll be fine."

"And after Vegas, on to California?"

"For now, but we can decide for sure later. Depending on how much heat is after us, we might have to head over the border—north or south—before coming back or leaving forever."

"But we don't have to worry about that right now."

"Not at all, Mary Lou. Without laundered money, we might as well make a break for Canada now because at the moment all we have in those black bags are bunches of paper. They are useless to us. If we pass any of those notes over, the cops'll be all over us within thirty minutes. Make no mistake: we can't do anything with those notes until we've got them washed and dried."

"I understand, Frank."

Lucy strolled over and refilled the mugs which killed the conversation at the table.

"No need to stop just 'cause I came around. I heard just about everything over the years in this diner. There's nothing that'd embarrass me."

"We were just trying to decide where to go on vacation. Which do you prefer: Mexico or Canada?"

"I've never been to either. Never left the States. I reckon the heat of Mexico'd lead to some sexy nights for a woman and a man like you two."

"What are we like?"

"Young. In love. You know."

"Do we look like we're in love?"

"Sure do, hon'. Are you married?"

Mary Lou glanced at Frank.

"No, we're not."

"Oh kids. If you love each other, then do it right. I've been hitched twice but I'm single at the present."

"No guy to keep your bed warm?"

Lucy chuckled.

"No, hon' but I have a man aiming to heat my mattress tonight."

Now it was Mary Lou's turn to chuckle; Frank didn't respond.

"Can we have the check?"

"Sure thing, babe."

Lucy pulled out a pad from her apron and wrote out the total on the bottom of the chit. She placed it face down in front of Frank and went away.

"Why did you encourage her so much?"

"Just being nice."

"But you've basically told her where we're thinking of going."

"Sorry, I didn't think."

"You said it. Think before you talk next time, okay? We can't afford any slip ups."

6

FRANK LAGOTTI SENIOR switched the radio off just before ten. No news for ages and the music annoyed him. He returned to his office, sat down behind his desk and took his mind off the bank robbery by focusing on his favorite pastime.

He pulled open the top right drawer of his bureau, picked out a girlie magazine and opened it. Leaned back in his chair and stared at the pictures. This was his morning routine and the heist had disrupted it.

Frankie told himself the robbery was a win-win for him. On one side of the coin was step-nephew Frank. He'd funded the boy and his crew, knowing the place would be fat with cash and was ripe for picking.

The other side was a deal Frankie'd made with one of the bank employees who'd run up a hefty gambling debt whose marker Frankie had purchased. He gave the schmuck a choice: spend the rest of his life paying back his bill or take the money out of the safe.

Frankie set Carter up to grab the greens the morning of the heist. He told himself the only way he could lose was if the coin landed on its edge. And what're the chances of that? Whatever the probability, he sent out Paul and Luigi to extract the take from Frank and head back to his auto repair shop.

The fact the radio announced the robbery meant Carter owed him forty thousand dollars and a huge explanation. Frankie would deal with the mook later; there was more than enough time. He had told Frank he'd need two weeks to launder the take, which wasn't exactly true. An arrangement had already been reached with a connection and within twenty-four hours the cash would be returned. Frankie intended to use the rest of the time to invest the cash and make a little on the side.

What concerned him was the time Paul and Luigi had been gone. Their primary orders were to bring the money back at whatever cost. If Frank bought it that was an acceptable loss, he'd said to Paul. With the guy toast, he could keep the whole take for himself as none of the rest of his crew would come after him. Apart from Pete the Wheels who was a homicidal maniac. If his two did for Frank, Pete was a dead man walking. He'd cap the crazy fucker; great driver but a sociopath for sure.

If Paul had misinterpreted his words, who knows how Frank might react. He could be volatile at times. Either way, Luigi would do whatever Paul told him to do because he was a fine bodyguard but not one of Nature's natural thinkers. A simple soldier though.

Frankie's concentration was distracted by a particular image of a naked body stretched out before him on the page. He turned the publication sideways to not strain his neck. A true connoisseur of free creative expression, Frankie liked the shape of her tits.

Of an evening, Frankie would pursue his artistic interests at the *Kitkatt Club*, a venue he acquired as a result of a different failed attempt to pay off a gambling debt by some other degenerate. This strip joint did good business thanks to its location near the expressway. It also served as a great place for Frankie's R&R—he never paid as he was the owner.

His mind drifted even further as he thought about the girls he had banged there. Some wild nights. Mrs. Lagotti made him breakfast but asked no questions where he'd been. They had been happily married for decades and the source of their happiness was Frankie's porn collection and titty bar. He and his wife hadn't been intimate with each other for over fifteen years and that was how they both liked it.

Frank Senior preferred younger flesh; much younger. And the Kitkatt Club was a feast of fresh naïve pussy ripe for plucking. Those girls made a lot of money and earned every dime. It was the American way.

A foot slipped off his bureau and this knocked Frankie out of his reverie. Despite himself, Frank Senior jolted upright and his mag fell on the floor. He threw it back into the desk drawer and stormed into his anteroom. There was only one person there: Anthony, who was sitting forward in his chair playing cards, chewing a matchstick.

"Any word, Anthony?"

"Nothing."

"Why's the radio off? How do you know what is happening?"

"You switched it off, so I reckoned you didn't want me flipping it on the minute your back was turned."

Anthony was right. That boy was brighter than Paul and could handle himself better than Luigi, who was an aggressive fighter who'd give no quarter ever.

"Okay. Put it on, we might learn something about the heist and if they got away with it."

Very disappointing about Carter. Next week Anthony will pay him a visit. Until then Frankie wanted to get his hands on that money. He looked at the clock and he gave up on waiting.

"Anthony. You have reliable guys you can call on now?"

"Guess so… yes."

"Bring them over to the rendezvous. You and them. As soon as you can paint a picture, find a payphone and tell me."

"Right boss."

Anthony made two calls and promised Frankie he'd phone with information about the money. Paul and Luigi could wait until later.

"Sure thing."

Anthony put his playing cards back in their cardboard packaging and placed them neatly in a drawer. Then he stood up and left the auto repair in search of the take.

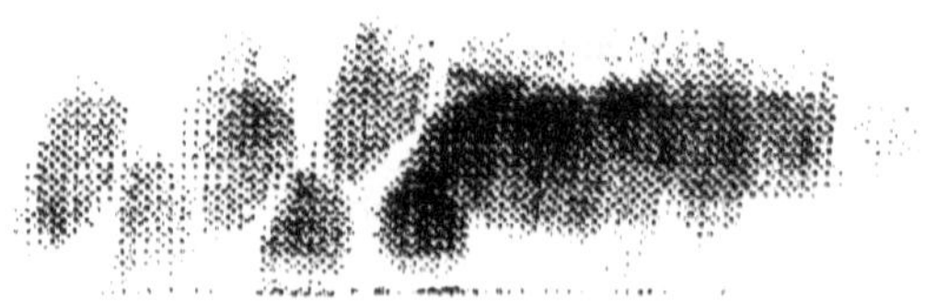

7

AFTER ANTHONY LEFT the premises, Frankie returned to his office and spent some time examining the visual poetry of his girlie magazine. He made a mental note to pop over to the Kitkatt Club on his way home tonight. He needed the relief on offer from one of the girls.

Frankie settled into his chair and the day passed uneventfully. The place was quiet: no vehicle had been in for repair since the day he took over the auto shop. Visitors came and went but none had any car business. An hour later and a knock at his door.

"Enter!"

Anthony walked in and stood waiting. Frankie always forced everyone to wait at least a minute when they entered the room. It was his way of reminding you of the power he held over you. Tedious.

"So?"

"We found the barn but we couldn't get too close."

"Why not?"

"The place was ablaze. Flames forty feet in the air. Too many fire trucks and blue-and-whites for us to get near the joint."

"Okay. You've told me what you don't know. Got anything more useful for me?"

"We talked with the rescue servicemen and there were several cars set alight. They reckoned that was the cause."

"Did they say how many vehicles had been torched?"

"Three saloons and a van, they said."

"Any bodies?"

"Yes. They found some incinerated remains in the vehicle but they aren't too sure exactly. The inside was like a crematorium."

"Jeez."

"Three or four corpses for certain, but they need to sift through the bones to count up accurately."

"Do you think Paul and Luigi got themselves cremated?"

"They ain't nowhere to be seen and there are bodies turning to ash in that van. I reckon two will be Luigi and Paul."

"Rest in peace. Let's get some flowers sent over to their widows."

"Right, boss."

"If our two bought it that means the money is still out there and that step nephew and his skirt are on the lam."

"We asked about, but no one had heard or seen anybody else. A cop remembered seeing the van and a couple of cars on the road before the barn burned. And they mentioned passing a blue Falcon."

"That's them. Frank gave way too much detail for me and listed all the vehicles Pete had acquired for them to use."

"What now?"

"Wait outside. I need to make a few calls. Are the people you've brought in reliable?"

"I trust them."

"With your life?"

"Well, I'd trust them with my money overnight. There's no one I'd trust my life to."

"Trusting them with money speaks volumes and is good enough for me. I'll call you when I'm ready."

Anthony shut the door behind him and Frankie sat at his desk seething. Looked like that step nephew of his skipped town, possibly with his girlfriend in tow—depending how many bodies were in that van. The other possibility was that she had survived and the rest of them were goners. Either way, he and his men would find the survivor and extract the take from them—whoever they were. And a bonus if they wind up dead.

Carter let him down and Frankie would have smiled had he known the man was fighting for his life in hospital suffering from gunshot wounds to the groin—administered by Frank after he took the cash off him and before he left the bank.

Instead, the Shylock was planning his own revenge for the gambler which involved a workshop vice and a lot of pain. This train of thought only increased his anger because he was dealing with the loss of his money and two doses of betrayal on top.

Frankie's sister remarried after her husband met an unexpected end when a mechanical digger crushed his stationary car with him in the driver's seat. Her second fella played poker with Frankie before they were hitched and, to his regret, he felt he had introduced them to each other.

The problem with Giuseppe was five-card stud. He had a series of tells you could read a mile off and many did. This meant him a loser and like gamblers before and after when he lost he often would double up hoping to turn things around. When the deadbeat had borrowed to the max from everyone else, the only person left to get cash from was his brother-in-law.

So Frank Senior spent ten years keeping this guy afloat to ensure his sister lived in the lap of luxury she deserved. That annoyed the moneylender daily, but what hurt him more was Giuseppe's son from his previous marriage.

The schnook was short of brains and long on mistakes. Frequently Frankie had organized work for him—a variety of crews hitting different venues—but he got caught more times than was good for a professional.

And the boy had the family name. How? Maria had reverted to the Lagotti moniker after the car crush and then refused to change it when she remarried. Frankie regretted the age in which he lived and the bra-burning feminists who inhabited it.

Then his step nephew decided he preferred his mother's name to his own and used that instead. Frankie ground his molars as the memory of these events raised his blood pressure even more. He hoped Frank's body was on the funeral pyre and that Mary Lou had survived. He could have some more fun with her if Anthony caught her alive.

The money became his focus again. That and an amazing ass which appeared in his field of vision as he flipped through more of the pages of his magazine.

What annoyed Frankie most was he had no handle on the amount of the take. The radio DJ had been vague at the start and then his update implied there was a big haul. Frankie knew the heist was large because they'd planned it that way. In his mind, he imagined a pile of notes and counted them out. His fear was that the news was exaggerating the size to beef up the story.

While the accuracy of the radio was not Frankie's primary concern, the fact there was talk of a six figure sum was very important to him. And if he could listen to the broadcast, so could his boss back in New York—and that built up expectations he couldn't meet. When the Five Boroughs wasn't happy then bloody retribution often ensued.

THE BEST THING was for Frankie to place a call. He didn't need to look up the number as it was tattooed to the inside of his eyelids.

"Is Charlie available? It's Frank Lagotti… Sure."

Charles Pentangelo was a made man for the Bonanno Family, who controlled much of the significant criminal activity in the Five Boroughs.

Frankie was left holding the receiver for several minutes. The six minute wait stretched to eternity.

"Charlie! How's that wife of yours and your wonderful children?"

"All fine, thanks Frankie. And how is Mrs. Lagotti?"

"She's cooking me up a storm."

"Great news. What can I do for you?"

"Wanted to give you an update on a matter I mentioned to you a couple of weeks ago."

"Oh yes, how is that proceeding?"

"Good and bad, hence the call."

An audible sigh.

"Talk Frankie."

"Is it okay for us to speak on this line?"

"Sure thing."

"They got the money out. That's the good news."

"And the bad?"

"I sent my men out to collect the take but something went wrong. My people are dead and the holders of our cash appear to have flown the coop."

"How big is the yield?"

"That's not well defined right now. We were waiting for a large haul but the only count I have comes from the radio so it's not reliable."

"What do you intend to do about it?"

"I will send a different crew to chase after the cash. So far what's left of the gang have been careful. They've burned evidence and kept under the police radar."

"Are they smart?"

"I wouldn't have said so. My step nephew is not the sharpest tool in the box."

"But he's been clever enough to steal the money from a bank, wipe out your people in a puff of smoke and still evade capture."

"Yes."

"So perhaps you should have the decency to give him the respect he deserves."

"Yep, it's the trouble with family—from the wrong side. It's a bad business but I shouldn't let it cloud my judgment. My apologies."

"Accepted, Frankie. How reliable is this second crew you are planning to send after them?"

"They are fine. I trust them—with my money if not my life."

Charlie laughed and Frankie was pleased to steal Anthony's words and turn them into a joke to lighten the mood.

"But what about with my money? That is the question, isn't it?"

"Of course."

"Just messing with you. We all have a vested interest in your success. Any help required, say."

"Thanks, Charlie. I wanted you to know what was happening. We are still only a handful of hours since they took the bank, so it's early days."

"Sounds like you are trying to tell me our money may be in the wind."

"It is possible. Hence my call."

"I appreciate you calling me. You were correct to do so: always pass on bad news quickly."

"That's what I expect of my people and I wanted to offer you the same curtesy."

"How certain are you that this second team will succeed where your first crew failed?"

"Pretty sure. Paul and Luigi were fine upstanding guys but you could never accuse Luigi of having too many brains. God rest his soul."

"Luigi? Shame, I knew his family well, but no one shall mourn his passing—not even his wife."

"That's for sure."

"Sounds to me you've underestimated your step nephew and overestimated your own people. Don't make that mistake again, Frankie. These errors can compound each other and become dangerous."

"I understand. But you need to know I won't be able to offer tribute tomorrow as I originally indicated."

"I figured that out myself, but again it is good to hear you voice these concerns instead of pretending they aren't out there."

"Thank you. I do these things because I respect you."

And because you'd whack me if I didn't.

"Once you have a reliable figure, tell me. And once you have the money, call me too."

"Of course."

"I ask a second time, is there anything I can do to help?"

"Not right now. They've left a trail of destruction in their wake but they're still on the road."

"The radio said there were deaths at the bank even before they torched that barn. Was it a rendezvous point?"

"Yes, it was. The good news is that Frank shared the plan with me in great detail as I was funding the venture. Once he's circled away from the Baltimore area, he will head for California. It's what's driven him to keep going all these months."

"I'll have a word with our west coast contacts and get them to prepare a welcoming committee."

"You need not do that just yet. They might not have left the state."

"You and I know they'll wave Maryland goodbye. The question in my mind is whether they will actually strike out for California or pick anywhere apart from there."

"I may have underestimated him as you say, but I saw his eyes light up every time he mentioned that state. If they leave Maryland then they'll head for the west coast."

"So be it. California will be the destination."

"Trouble is it's a long way from here to there."

"Frankie, send your people off on the trail at your end and I will handle any of the other details."

"Okay, Charlie. Thanks again."

"It's what I'm here for."

Click.

FRANKIE CALLED ANTHONY into his office.

"Pack your toothbrush, you're gonna be on the road for the next few days. Come back with the cash."

"Frank and the girl?"

"Get me my money. If they hand it over to you, then that's fine."

"And if they don't?"

"Find me my money, anyway. Two more dead bodies won't make much difference given the trail of blood they've already caused."

"Okay, boss."

"And if you find them alive and you want to keep them in that state then do so. I'm happy to have a conversation with them. But if you have to shoot them between the eyes, do it. There is no need for any of us to be precious around them."

"Sure thing."

"But remember, do not come back without the take and make certain your crew doesn't dip their fingers in the cash. Every dime is mine alone."

Anthony nodded and closed the door behind himself. This gave Frankie an opportunity to return to his porn journal and soak in the exquisite beauty of the naked girls on the pages.

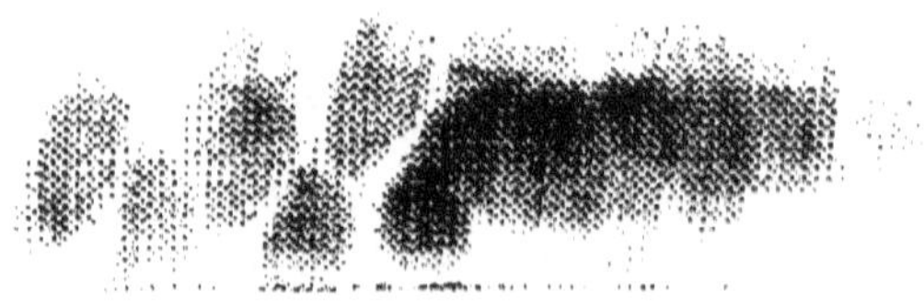

8

MARY LOU AND Frank walked out the diner and back toward the car.

"You drive for a while, okay?"

"Sure thing, Frank."

She adjusted the seat and the rearview mirror, fought the shift stick into first and pulled out of the space.

"What route are we taking? I have no idea how to get to Vegas from here."

Frank laughed.

"Neither do I. Hang on a minute."

He shut his eyes for five seconds and then opened them. Frank described how they'd go cross-country to Frederick off to the west and join the I-70 for a straight run to Pittsburgh. Beyond that was another day. She nodded.

"Let's hit the road."

She punched the gas pedal and they squealed out the lot.

"Take it easy, babe."

Mary Lou eased off the pedal and took the vehicle down to a sensible pace.

"Five miles an hour under all the way, right?"

"Got it, Frank."

Her voice contained no annoyance. Calm personified. He settled into his seat, folded his arms and focused on the road ahead. No mistakes, Mary Lou. No need to get pulled over by some lazy cop with a quota to fill. Before they'd stepped back into the Falcon, he'd walked round to check all the lights, a task he'd perform every stop they made from here to California. If they got that far.

"This sounds totally crazy, but I missed you today, babe."

"When?"

"From the moment we said goodbye and split up this morning. I didn't want you to go."

Mary Lou reached over and squeezed his knee then took it away for a gear change.

Ever since he got out of the penitentiary this time last year, their relationship had gone from distant to extremely close. Frank discovered how to be a loving human being. It had been quite a journey, but he was getting there.

"We've had a bumpy ride, but after our Miami trip things were good between us…"

"But?"

"But after this morning I don't know. I told myself that what happened with you and Carter stayed with you and Carter, and I haven't asked questions any more."

There was a silence in the cabin as they both recalled the argument they'd had on this same topic—only in a different car.

"What about Carter and the money? You didn't explain."

"It was complicated."

"Just tell me. I want to know."

Mary Lou sighed a deep heavy outpouring of breath.

"Carter has a gambling problem: he loses way more times than he wins. And Uncle Frank holds a forty thousand dollar marker on him, so he gave him a simple choice: take the money or spend the rest of his life paying off the debt. Refuse either option and finito."

"So…"

Frank was taking his time putting the pieces of the jigsaw together for himself. Mary Lou helped him out.

"Frankie ordered Carter to remove the cash from the bank on the morning of our hit. Either Carter followed his instructions and got Frankie the take or we did. Whichever way, Frankie wins."

"Uncle Frank?"

"Yes your uncle, Frank."

The words sank into Frank's skull. The man had always been so good to his ma and the family. To turn on him like this while pretending to only have his best interests to heart.

"And the barn was a double-cross?"

"I reckon. If Carter had succeeded, I'm sure he'd be buried in a field by now. He didn't even own a gun."

"And you held this back from me because…?"

"I couldn't see how you'd believe me. I doubt if you do now."

"The double-cross I believe. Paul and Luigi fired first. They were operating under orders. Paul wouldn't have been dumb enough to steal from Uncle Frankie and Luigi was plain too stupid."

"I just didn't know how to tell you, hon'. And the explosives?"

"A terrible mistake. I forgot. The stress of tying the damn things to those telegraph poles did me in. It took longer than I thought and I was so obsessed with getting them all done that flipping the switch flew out my head."

"And you expect me to accept that?"

"It's the truth. You believe what you need to."

"A cop car followed us out of town because that C4 didn't blow."

"What happened?"

"Was way behind for miles, then it kicked up an extra gear and passed us."

"Huh?"

"Yes. They must have been expecting something more like your Barracuda for a getaway vehicle and not a white van."

"Pete was a smart cookie."

"And a pain in the ass the rest of his waking hours."

He stretched out and rested his left hand on Mary Lou's thigh below her black miniskirt, occasionally stroking her skin as they talked.

"ARE WE BEING honest, Frank?"

"I've been. Yes."

"I'm scared, here in this car. With you."

Mary Lou felt Frank's fingers stiffen, which made her even more nervous.

"Because you see me as someone who's failed you, I can't be certain you have any faith in me at all. On top of that, the last job when you lost confidence in somebody they took a trip out a window. And you've already whacked Andrew today."

"He'd clipped Pete before we'd got away."

"Frank, I'm not saying you were wrong to take him out, but you have to admit you're a dangerous man to be around."

His fingers relaxed, but the stroking stopped. Mary Lou kept both hands on the wheel.

"And that makes me nervous. Especially when I look at what happened at the barn."

"What went down there?"

"After it was all over and you hopped in the car, I had no idea if you were going to drive off and leave me."

"Of course I wasn't, babe."

"But that's not how it felt. You were angry with me and you've said yourself you can't figure out if there was anything between Carter and me. So how am I supposed to know?"

The stroking started up again.

"It crossed my mind. It's true."

"If I was going to double-cross you, wouldn't I have struck a deal with Uncle Frankie or got Carter out the bank and run off with him or… beats me. There are a thousand ways you can punch someone in the face but only one way to kiss them."

"And do you love me?"

"I did this morning. Now I'm building up a wall so I don't get hurt by you. But I did earlier today."

This lie tripped off her tongue with remarkable ease. A week ago Frank was the one—or at least he was after Florida. Then the idea took hold in her that Carter was a better catch. That he had a stronger chance of getting the money and she should go with him instead.

Carter found the cajones to remove the cash from the vault but didn't leave the bank for whatever reason. That was the moment she stopped trusting him and loving him. If a guy can't do a simple thing, like keep his word, then he was not a man at all. Besides, Carter was always going to lift the money for Uncle Frankie but it was only the day before she discovered the game Frankie was playing with all of them. And she was right. Frank would never have believed her. The proof only existed at that point in Carter's words.

"Remember. Carter was just someone to get the crew into that vault and out without obstruction. What I did, I did. But for us."

"I know."

"Do you?"

"Not sure, to be honest. I want to believe you but there's so much up in the air right now. And what you're saying about Uncle Frankie."

"None of this easy."

"Nope."

Mary Lou kept them at a steady pace and passed through Cockeysville, a small nowhere town with a crossroads, shops and people who notice a stranger's car flying past even if it's not stopping. Both hands gripped the wheel and only relaxed when they were back on empty roads with fields or dirt either side of the road.

"You never answered my question."

"No? Which one?"

"Were you definitely going to wait for me at the barn?"

The hand stroked her again.

"When I left you with the matches… I was angry and I wasn't sure if you were with me or the take."

Mary Lou sighed. He was right and he was wrong. When she exited the parking lot at the bank she was following the money but by the time she arrived at the barn she was following Frank. That's hard to explain though—even to yourself sometimes.

"And when I appeared at the car?"

"You were there and I waited for you."

"Sure. But why?"

"Like I said before. I cared about you; I care about you but did I trust you at that precise moment today? Don't know, but I wanted to."

"I shot Paul so you would live. If I was so intent on getting hold of the money, and nothing more, then I'd have let him take you out and then clipped him. You were a sitting duck, Frank. Without me, you would be a corpse."

Mary Lou's words scratched deep inside Frank. This was the first time he'd had to consider today's events. She was kinda right but did that mean he could forgive her for what she did with Carter?

He ought to because he inserted her in the situation with the financial adviser. However now he'd seen the guy, so up close and personal, didn't remove the image of the two of them naked together from his mind's eye. It hurt each time it flashed across his brain. Yet part of that self-same thought—with Mary Lou's body in it—turned him on. The lust he felt for her was real and consistent. It was fucking her again that kept him going in prison. At night. Those lonely nights. After his first stint inside he understood why some men became fags in jail.

His hand moved up her thigh and under the skirt almost reaching her panties. She grabbed it and dragged it back nearer her knee.

"You won't be getting anywhere near that until we can trust each other."

9

SILENCE FELL OVER them as they experienced the isolation of their own thoughts. Without admitting it to themselves or the other person, they both had been in the wrong and both had right on their side.

Mary Lou carried on driving, catching the occasional sign for Westminster forcing them to make a wide arc, leaving Lansdowne and the city of Baltimore behind and heading towards Frederick and the expressway beyond.

As they left Westminster, Frank tapped her thigh.

"Pull over, now!"

She slammed on the brake and drove off the road.

"What is it?"

"Saw me something of use."

Frank popped the trunk and grabbed what looked like a stick and ran back two hundred feet. Through her side mirror, Mary Lou watched as he took a screwdriver to the rear plates of a rusted carcass of a car standing with flat tires in a ditch. He replaced the Falcon's plates with his newfound spoils and dropped the old ones into the trunk.

"Pennsylvania plates. Spotted them as we flew past and soon we'll need them. Besides, if anyone has somehow figured out who we are along the way, this'll throw the cops off the scent."

"Paranoid but beautiful."

"That's me."

Mary Lou carried on down the highway, five miles an hour below the speed limit.

"Should we have waited until we crossed the state line for the new plates?"

"No, we're close enough to not raise suspicion from passersby. This way we look like we're returning home."

"There's a thin line between appearing to go home and looking like we are on the run."

"Sure but I can't see how the cops'd even know they were chasing a man and a woman, let alone knowing what we look like or what kind of car we're driving."

"Wasn't expecting this to be the getaway, Frank. I imagined the cars crammed with the crew laughing and celebrating."

"You and me both. We don't even know how big the take is. We have two bags stuffed with notes but that doesn't mean I have any idea how much we're talking about. How about you? You were in those vaults often enough."

"They brought in half a million yesterday to distribute to other branches so it's a lot. I shouldn't say this so soon but…"

"Our share of the haul has gone up in the last few hours. I know. Only thing is that without Frankie's connections and family discount, it will cost us more to clean the cash."

"We need to take care of that trunk. Should we bring the money inside, Frank?"

"It'll be safer where it is. The most likely problem we'll encounter is a traffic cop and those bags must be out of sight."

"Sure. Makes me nervous though."

"Yeah. It's quite a sum. Shame we can't spend a single cent of it yet."

"Really?"

"Not. One. Dime."

Frank squeezed her knee in time to his words to reinforce their importance as the Falcon continued on its journey from Westminster to Frederick. Dusk approached and as the light faded, more houses came next to the highway and eventually the outskirts of a town formed round them. She flipped the headlights on and three minutes later a neon sign appeared up ahead.

"Pull into the motel, babe."

She stopped the car near the reception and he walked inside. As she hung around the bank and Frank had worn a balaclava, he reckoned his face was less likely to be recognized than hers, even though he spent so much of his time walking the streets of Lansdowne these last nine months.

Five minutes later he emerged with a key and Mary Lou moved the car to park it outside their room. They dropped their two bags of cash on the bed and drew the curtains so they could open them and count the money in private.

They split up the notes into their respective denominations and then they each counted every pile. This was a simple way to spot errors and ensure they would agree on the final amount. Five hundred and fifty thousand dollars. Even losing most of it to whoever laundered the money, they could still live out their days like royalty.

Once they discovered the total, they put the notes into the cases, careful to keep the money split evenly.

"I'm hungry."

"Me too."

Taking the bags with them, they walked round the corner and along half a block where a fast-food chain had dumped a building. Thirty minutes later they were in the room filled with burger, fries and a shake. Mary Lou brought back her drink as she couldn't finish it at the burger bar.

"The trouble with you and me, Frank, is that we've known each other for a long time."

"Met in '62."

"We've both been through a lot of shit over the years."

"And?"

"And we've always been there for each other. Even in the bad times. Now the trust between us is breaking down. You think I'm in love with Carter and I think you're ready to dump me for the money. Right?"

"More or less."

"Today has been one hell of a day but we're never moving back to Lansdowne and you are never returning to your family. What has past is long gone. We only have what we've brought into this room: you, me and the take. If you're not satisfied with that then we should separate now because it will not get any easier if we stay together and the other wants to leave."

"Do you want to split, Mary Lou?"

"No. That's what I've been saying to you this afternoon. I choose to be with you. I chose you over Carter because you are the better man, Frank Lagotti. In the car I got to thinking how much we need each other. Not just to escape the cops today but how you fill me up. How you are a part of me."

"I don't want us to split up either."

"Then we shouldn't."

"But I gotta tell you I find it hard to think about what the two of you got up to."

"Then don't think about it Frank because I can't spend the rest of my life apologizing to you for extracting information from Carter Reinfeldt. It's what you wanted me to do and you never said there were any restrictions on how I should go about doing it."

Frank nodded. They both sat on the end of the bed as there was nowhere else for the two of them to perch. He returned his hand to her leg, just as though they were still sitting in the car.

"And I won't keep asking you if you'll drive off and leave me. If we're with each other, it has to be because we want to be."

"Mary Lou, you're right. If we trust each other then we depend on each other. And if we don't we've got nothing."

She nodded in return and kissed him on the lips.

"Let's go to bed."

He undressed first and snuck under the covers still in his shorts. She came out of the bathroom and removed her blouse then her skirt as he stared at her rose tattoo which peeped out from her pubes and headed up until it nearly reached her belly button. She slipped off her bra and panties and lay beside him.

Frank threw his shorts onto the floor, rolled over to face her and wrapped himself around her body until his groin moved just below the rose. Mary Lou didn't push him away.

CHARLIE PENTANGELO PUT the phone down on Frank Lagotti Senior. He had already listened to the radio to know the robbery had taken place and had been waiting for the call so he could press the button on the money laundering. The last thing he wanted to hear was the take was on the lam.

Ordinarily, Charlie would have shrugged this off but the news broadcast had mentioned a heist value much higher than any sum Frankie had offered him. This meant either Frankie was withholding money from him or that the bank was involved in an insurance scam by overinflating its claim.

If Frankie was hiding money that was the same as stealing from the Bonanno Family. The punishment for that crime was anything from having your hand cut off through to death, depending on the sum involved. If the bank was lying to the insurers then this created its own set of problems. While Frank had selected the First Bank of Baltimore for logistical reasons to make a heist most successful, he had picked a financial institution where the Bonannos had made a series of investments.

Banks inflate figures only to hide losses and this sum was big. The implication was clear: if the bank was claiming more than had been stolen in Lansdowne that was because the amount was gone elsewhere and needed to be recouped. Chances were that was Bonanno money which had been silently lost.

The Getaway

Charlie made a mental note to instigate some enquiries about their First Bank of Baltimore investments. The chief executive would receive a phone call and that should straighten matters out.

The other outstanding issue was that Charlie's cash was in the wind and if Frankie was stealing from him, then he couldn't be trusted to recover all the take and deliver it for laundering. That meant only one thing: Charlie must recapture the money himself.

Pentangelo picked up the receiver and made a local call.

"Hi there."

"I told you not to phone me."

"This is an emergency: I need your assistance in a small matter."

"How small?"

"Some objects of mine have gone missing and I'd like you to help me find them."

"The usual recovery fee?"

"Of course. And given the importance of the materials to me, there'll be a healthy bonus if you succeed."

"And the location of the items is known?"

"Not precisely but we know the individuals holding them right now. My people will fill you in with the details. You'd better pack a suitcase; it'll take a few days to track them down."

10

TED GOODWIN HOPPED out of his vehicle and walked into the Lansdowne branch of the First Bank of Baltimore. The call had come through at five past nine and by the time he arrived, there was a police line in situ and he had to fight his way to the front: the numbers of passersby who'd stopped to stare was remarkable for an ordinary Tuesday morning.

He flashed his detective's badge and the officer let him duck under the tape and go into the bank. The first thing he noted was the sheer quantity of blood—it looked like the robbers had smeared red over the floor and the walls. A uniform stood near the door as a defense in case someone crossed the line.

"How many dead?"

"Two out back we reckon but the bodies turned to ash when they set the van alight."

"Injured?"

"Three in hospital and the rest in shock."

"What happened to the three?"

"The security guard was pistol-whipped and was unconscious when they took him out. Another man shot in the groin and one cashier… Well, they slashed her breast, sir."

"Where are the rest of the staff?"

"Right now we have them all in the manager's office, but it's pretty cramped. Doubt if we can keep them there much longer."

The Getaway

"Until we've got enough vehicles to take them back to the station, let's hold them where they are. It won't be long and they're out of the way."

The officer nodded and Goodwin moved tentatively around the bank trying to figure out what happened and when. Once they interviewed the staff, they should have a reasonable picture. Goodwin spotted Sam Parrish squatting next to a pool of blood, so he scooted over.

"Hey Sam. Here before me. What you see and what you got?"

"Yeah, I was round the corner buying a coffee."

"Did you get here before they left?"

"Nah. The cashier only pressed the alarm after the perps had exited via the back door."

"And then they killed two out the rear?"

"Yep. It's all strange. From what one cashier was saying: the money hadn't been in the vault but an employee, Carter Reinfeldt, had taken it."

"Say again."

"Sounds crazy, but it definitely happened."

"Any news on the identities of the bodies in the parking lot?"

"You're kidding, right? Have you been out there yet? They torched a sports car and stuffed what we think are a pair of corpses inside before they lit it."

"How are we so sure there's two if the car's been in flames?"

"There were twin bursts of gunfire. One happened when at least two of the gang were in this room and the other burst occurred after they departed."

"Are all bank staff accounted for?"

"Yes, so the bodies are likely to be crew members, not civilians."

This case would take a while to crack. Dead 'uns, money stolen from bank staff who'd pilfered it from the bank.

"And the vault?"

"Clean as a nun's conscience."

Sam pointed to a security door next to the counters. Goodwin followed the finger and entered the staff-only area. Cashier desks to one side and a corridor in front. As he walked along the narrow space, Goodwin noticed a kitchen and a locker room.

At the far end, by the exit was a staircase leading downwards. At the bottom of the stairs: a wall filled with deposit boxes and on the opposite side behind bars was the safe itself. It was open and there was no sign of the large denomination notes. None of the security boxes appeared disturbed.

The gang come down here to take the money. At least one guy upstairs to maintain order over the staff. Possibly more. Someone's hit the safe before you so you'll be spitting venom by the time you get back up top. Then you torture people to find out where the cash is.

Goodwin couldn't understand it: two hits on the same bank on the same day. That was a new one. So unlikely it couldn't be true, could it?

What next? You scream for the money and the staff look blankly at you. Reinfeldt knows but doesn't say and lets a woman get slashed for her troubles. Gangs rely on bank staff to hand over the loot in a breath because it's covered by the insurance. Policy would demand they hand it over but still Reinfeldt refuses. How did he give the game away?

Strange fact number two: if they were professionals and they had the money, why shoot Reinfeldt? Why the unnecessary violence? They'd be able to interview him in the next day or so—assuming he survived. The chances were he was part of the gang and had tried to double cross them.

Detective Goodwin sauntered upstairs and popped his head into the locker room and kitchen, but neither appeared to be the source of anything interesting. The boys would have a look-round before they left.

Ted made his way out the back into the parking lot. He gagged with the stench and covered his mouth and nose with his handkerchief. The last fire wagon was heading off to leave a husk of a car—black, charred—and a large puddle of water hiding any forensics that might have been on the ground.

He peered into the remains of the automobile and made out two bodies —one dumped across the front seats and the other at the back. Doors were open, but the fire had done its worst. Shards of melted glass lay on the floor. They came prepared to burn evidence: no matter what happened for two people to get killed, they were expecting to destroy a vehicle here. And why were the pair dead? An unsuspecting civilian bumped into the waiting getaway driver, perhaps. That doesn't explain the second body though. Strange fact number three.

Goodwin walked out the parking lot onto the street and made his way left, then same again two hundred feet later, to arrive at the front of the bank. Into his car and back to the station to interview the staff before their memory for details faded.

TED SAT AT his desk and stared at his typewriter. Most bank jobs were simple affairs: some men enter a building, take the money and leave. End of story. But this was peculiar around the edges and plain weird in the middle. His phone rang and he carried on focusing on his typing. The ringing continued until he snapped out of his thoughts and picked up the receiver.

"Detective Goodwin."

"The staff from the robbery have arrived. They're in the interview rooms."

"Thanks. I'll be right down."

Goodwin headed over to meet Sam organizing drinks and food for the witnesses.

"How are they shaping up?"

"Fine under the circumstances. All seem eager to help but it's hard to tell if they know anything."

"What we got?"

"Bank manager, assistant manager, deputy manager, cashier. Other cashier, the security guard and financial advisor in hospital."

"I'll take the bank manager and the assistant. You take the deputy and the cashier. First one to finish gets the donuts."

He winked and walked off to bring Joshua Hunkerton into an interview room. Food and a coffee arrived a few minutes later and Goodwin waited for the guy to settle down. He sat with a straight back and a dignified air the whole time.

"How're you doing?"

"I'm fine. Shaken, you understand and obviously concerned about poor Miss. Galtieri and Mr. Grimble."

"The cashier and the guard?"

"Yes."

"You didn't mention Carter Reinfeldt."

"Well, it looks as though he was involved with those people, so forgive me if I'm less worried about that fellow."

"We'll come back to that later. Let's go over the events of the morning a piece at a time, starting with your arrival at the bank. What time was that?"

They burrowed through the minutiae from Hunkerton's breakfast rituals through to the moment just after nine when three men wearing balaclavas entered the building and announced the start of a stick-up.

Hunkerton was in his office. The gang came in and forced him at gunpoint to join the others in the middle of the floor in the customer area. One of the crew made them lie face down and the other two left to go to the vault. A few minutes later, they returned empty handed. The leader was furious and threatened him to say where the money was.

"I didn't understand. I had opened the safe as usual at eight in good time for some smaller denominations to be taken upstairs by the cashiers. I was dumbfounded. I'm sure that made the felon more angry, but I plain had no answer. That is when he walked over to Miss. Galtieri and…"

The bank manager sank into silence as he recalled Frank taking a knife and slashing open her breast to force Hunkerton to spill his guts. But he had nothing to say. And the blood…

"Then what happened?"

"They looked like they would give up. Him and the fellow who had been with us earlier."

"What about the third guy?"

Hunkerton squinted to improve his memory.

"I don't recall him being in the room at that point."

"Go on."

"The leader strode over to Mr. Reinfeldt and demanded the money from him. It was as though he knew him but Carter didn't do a thing. So the man upturned Mr. Reinfeldt's desk to reveal two bags. He took them and made to leave but then he stopped, turned round and shot poor Carter in the…"

Another introspective silence as the image of the red pool forming around Carter's groin returned inside his head. And the screaming. Carter had lapsed into unconsciousness before the robbers had gone out of the staff corridor.

"Did you hear any shots?"

"Only after they left. Two, I believe. Then a roar and Mrs. Pieck was brave enough to move and press the alarm."

Goodwin checked a few more details and then was done with him. Meantime, Sam had interviewed the deputy manager, George Hunkerton.

"Related by any chance?"

"Yes Ted. My Hunkerton is the son of yours. And I figured out why such a small branch needed an assistant and a deputy. My Hunkerton couldn't find the end of his nose."

"Good that nepotism is alive and well in the banking industry."

"For sure. And we're not even in Alabama. But the goofball had one useful thing to offer. While they were being minded, my Hunkerton heard a single shot go off."

"He's certain of this?"

"Told me he'd already pissed himself when the gang came into the bank and he was trying to hold it together by listening to anything happening outside the room. And he definitely caught a gunshot while two of them were in the building."

"So one left early and clipped the fourth?"

"That's what I'm thinking."

"But why?"

"Beats the hell out of me."

"What did your little Jimmy have to say about Reinfeldt?"

"Not much. The guy had a roving dick and problems at home but George knew nothing about the money."

"Trouble?"

"Reinfeldt transferred over to the Lansdowne branch after he slept with a young floozie at his previous office. Now he was carrying on with a customer. Been seeing her for months, apparently."

"Where is she?"

"Not clear as yet but I'll work on it."

"And was anything else happening at home?"

"Dunno. He and his wife have no children but they weren't happy. Not getting along. That's all I got so far."

"Let's keep going and catch up later. The girlfriend might tell us if Reinfeldt was mixed up with the gang. One of the uniforms can put together a description from all the staff. If we're lucky, we'll even get an address."

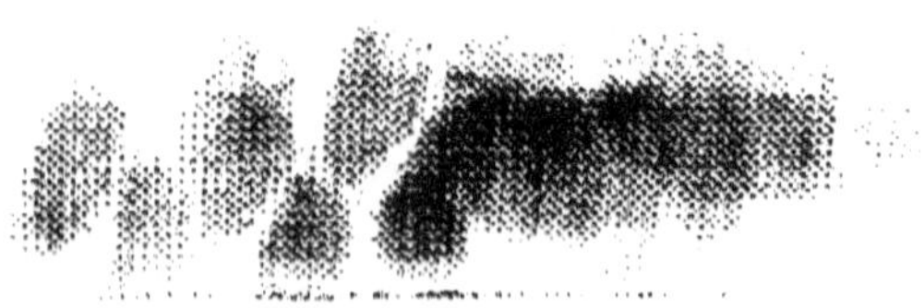

11

FORTY-FIVE MINUTES later a blue-and-white called in a blaze on the outskirts of town. The uniform had been chasing a suspicious vehicle when the smoke hurtled into the air. He'd swung back to find a barn on fire and steel shells billowing flames.

Goodwin left Sam to finish the interviewing and hightailed it northeast of Lansdowne via the scenic route to Philadelphia. A pair of melted cars in an hour were too much of a coincidence in a day filled with them. This marked the trail of the gang out of town.

When he arrived there three uniforms in front of the barn and two fire trucks. Smoke was still visible, but no flames were in view from the highway. What once had been an outbuilding lay in seared carbon on the floor, one corner of a wall refusing to collapse. Behind this mess was rough ground containing a melted vehicle with another blob of former cars standing on the edge of the field.

Goodwin strode around the devastation at the front and reached the vehicles, where uniforms and a medic were hard at work.

"Hey, doc."

"Hi Ted. Quite a morning."

"Telling me. What you got?"

"Three bodies all piled into a van and torched. The fire service arrived in time for them to douse the crime scene in gallons of water. But at least the corpses are partially intact. By which I mean there are clearly three

Caucasian males thrown in the back of that vehicle: all shot. The boys have already searched for shells in the vicinity."

"Thanks, doc."

"More for you once these fricasseed felons are back to the lab."

The detective winced at the pathologist's gallows humor. Goodwin was facing a major robbery with violence and five dead souls. Word from above was that the take had been over a million. Unimaginable. What was a small-town bank doing with that much cash in its vault?

Who knew? Someone had piled those bodies into the van and had sufficient gas to burn the fucking lot up in smoke—just like at the bank. They had been prepared and there must be at least one of them still alive. Chances were they were in a vehicle this minute high-speeding out of Baltimore and, most likely, out the state too.

Without a description, all he had was person or persons of unknown gender and racial profile. So he had nothing to hang his hat on. Just a trail of carnage running parallel with the I-295. Trouble was they were only ten minutes away from the 895 which meant the person or persons unknown drove from the vicinity east or west and he'd have no way of knowing in which direction to try. This would need to be a mighty wide net to cast.

Instead of focusing on the great unknowns, Goodwin examined what was visible to him, in front of his nose. Eye witnesses reported seeing a white Ford Econoline leaving the bank area after the robbery and he was standing next to the shell of a van right now. There was a saloon, a once-feisty sports car and a beast of a Cadillac. He recognized the logo lying on the floor.

Presumably the saloon and Barracuda were used by crew members now deceased but the Caddy? It didn't fit. Perhaps the inhabitants came to meet the crew. If bullets flew that meant there was some disagreement and discussions went south from that point. So he either had the gang in the back of the van and the owners of the limo ran off with the money or vice versa.

A glimmer of good news for this crime scene was the collection of slugs found by the uniforms. There were five different calibers bagged up and ready for inspection. Five guns and only five people in total: anyone holding a knife to this gunfight would be first into the back of the van. With three dead, there were only one or two at large.

His best bet was a search for a single vehicle with two inside. What kind? Dunno but probably a saloon. What do the people look like? Arms, legs, torsos, a head each and a million dollars in the trunk.

Goodwin scuffed the scorched earth with his foot and came back to his car. He sat inside and knew this was not enough information to keep his boss happy.

When he returned to the station, his prediction proved accurate.

"Goodwin. Looks like you got jack for me."

Lieutenant Fred Hester stared at Ted over his glasses while seated at his desk. Goodwin remained at attention.

"Tomorrow's headlines will say the Baltimore Police Department knows zip about a million dollar heist. No description. Nothing. We don't even know how many are alive in the perps' gang."

"They are professionals, sir. Covered their tracks well. In our favor is Reinfeldt in hospital, who stole the money before the crew hit the joint. Doctors say he's survived surgery and when he regains consciousness, we can interview the hell out of him."

"Is that the only lead?"

"There's also his girlfriend who visited him most days these past nine months. Even though uniforms stayed at the bank all day, she hasn't appeared. Sounds like she's hit the road. If she doesn't show tomorrow then she has gone for certain."

"And what about today? I can't believe your best idea is to hang around and wait a while."

"The chances are they've flown the coop. I think we should call on the resources of the FBI, sir."

NO POLICE FORCE likes to seek federal assistance. It's almost written into the Constitution, but Lieutenant Hester had little choice. They had a violent armed robbery and an enormous haul to chase down with no tangible leads to work with. The press was baying at the Mayor's feet and soon they'd be clamoring for his blood. It was the natural way of things. Hester gave the order for Goodwin to place the call.

"Outside line, please."

He dialed the number and waited until a girl on reception answered. He explained his mission and she put him on hold.

"Phil McNamara. How can I help?"

"Detective Ted Goodwin of the Baltimore Police Department. We need your assistance."

"I thought we might get a call from you. No offense, but our Intel informed us you've quite a case on your hands."

"Well, yes."

"Look, I know asking for our support wasn't easy and I don't want to tread on anyone's toes, okay?"

"For sure."

"I'm in the area so why don't we meet in an hour's time. Does that work for you?"

"Sure, Phil."

"Gather what you got and we'll take it from there, Ted. See you at your station house in an hour."

The Getaway

Sixty one minutes later, Phil McNamara arrived at Goodwin's desk. The piano had stopped playing the minute he entered the building and you could hear a pin drop within two hundred feet of where McNamara stood.

Goodwin hustled him into an interview room and fetched him a coffee. And brought a cup each for himself and for Sam.

"Thanks for coming."

"Don't mention it. Just to be clear: I'm not here to take over your case. I'm here to offer you resources you can't access so we can catch the bad guys."

"Okay."

He knew not to trust Hoover men: their reputation traveled before them but this guy appeared reasonable—at first glance at any rate.

"What do you need from us right now?"

"We're sitting on a lot of burned corpses and no identities to attach to them so anything to help with that…"

"You got it."

"And we have a poor description of a girl who is a person of interest with no address for her."

"Give me what you have and we'll see if we can figure something out for you."

"Right. Also, it doesn't take a genius to work out they ain't staying in Maryland."

"One step at a time, Ted. Once we have a better idea of who we are looking for then yes, I'll get sufficient men on the ground to search for them interstate. We don't have enough to wipe our asses right now. No offense intended. Just saying what needs to be said."

"None taken. My boss isn't the least bit happy to see you—as you no doubt know. But Sam and I are fine with anyone who can help us catch these guys. They slashed a woman in the tit for Christ's sake."

"How's she doing?"

"Twenty stitches and she'll be on the road to recovery in a few days. Her biggest issue at the time was the amount of blood she lost. Next week, the docs tell her she's scarred for life."

McNamara nodded and allowed everyone's thoughts about Theresa Galtieri's tit to hang in the air for ten seconds. Then he sighed and carried on.

"They'll get theirs. Robbery with violence at a state bank, murder in the first degree, arson. Sounds like the gas chamber to me."

"Phil, now who's getting ahead of himself?"

Goodwin smiled at McNamara, who returned the favor.

"You're right. Just want to get to the end of the journey."

Sam had been silent until then, allowing his older colleague to take the lead.

"Do you need to pitch tent here or are you in the local FBI store?"

"Here would be good. I used to live in Baltimore but moved away five years ago."

"Where are you staying?"

"In a nearby hotel. Don't worry. I'll be okay. This is how I spend my life —on the road living out of a suitcase."

"The least we can do is take you out tonight for a bite to eat and a drink."

"Sounds like a mighty fine plan. Is there somewhere with a phone to call the cavalry?"

WEDNESDAY JUNE 18

12

MARY LOU WOKE first and enjoyed the time to stare at Frank and feel the warmth of his body next to hers. He appeared to be back on her side. She only hoped his words would translate into action and he wasn't about to double cross her. There was a lot of cash in those bags and people make bad decisions because of money.

She dozed twice and finally remained awake. Frank had rolled over to face her and had draped an arm on her hip. It slithered down to land between her legs. His eyes were shut, but he was conscious. Mary Lou took his fingers and placed them on her groin.

One of Frank's eyelids opened and stared at her, soaking in her head and upper torso—all he could see without moving his neck.

"Sorry babe, but we should get going."

"I know."

He removed his hand and kissed her rose, got up and threw on their only set of clothes.

"We can't wear these things all the way to Vegas."

"Better buy some more."

They checked their cash and realized they had enough for gas and some diner meals but not much else. A thrift store would be handy and if they couldn't find one, they'd have to be creative.

Back to the diner for breakfast with their bags and into the car for Frank's turn to drive. Before he hit the expressway, which ran round the edge of town, they drove until they found just the right place.

They could tell by the quality of the eaterie in what part of Frederick they'd landed: there was a lot of grease and not much else but the coffee wasn't bad. A store with clothes for next to nothing was an inevitable consequence of the local demographic. Frank and Mary Lou hopped into the place and grabbed jeans, a tee-shirt each and underwear. They each threw one top into the shopping basket too for some variety. He also found a jacket to hide his handgun and back to the motel so they could change before the journey.

"We've spent too long here. We'll need to make a move before people notice we're hanging around."

"Sure. A sweep of the room before we go. Let's not leave any incriminating evidence behind—like a black bag or two."

Out the door, into the car. he hit the gas pedal hard until they joined the on-ramp for Pittsburgh.

ROCK 'N' ROLL continued to spit out the speakers and Frank drove and tapped on the steering wheel in time to the warped blues of the music. Over the years Mary Lou had got used to Frank's taste though it was far from her favorite. She was a Country and Western girl.

On the hour the news cut into the musical extravaganza to reveal the FBI had been called in.

"We've dead people strewn all over Lansdowne. That was inevitable even if you ignore the size of the take."

The broadcast carried on to say the haul was over one million dollars.

"Brilliant. The bank's doing an insurance fraud! Why else would they lie about how much we stole from them?"

"Don't know but it will not be good."

"Yep. Let's make some distance between us and Maryland. Then we'll deal."

"Sure Frank."

He drove for ten miles, both sitting in silence while the world flew by five below the speed limit.

"We need to get off the freeway."

"Why's that?"

"If the FBI are on our trail, they'll man the largest roads so we should avoid them while the Hoover men put up road blocks."

"Good point."

Two miles later and he left the expressway. He didn't want to turn up at a gas station to buy a map because that would make them too visible.

The Getaway

Instead Frank used his vague memory of the countryside and a careful eye on the signs to help them wend their way to their destination.

Vehicle after vehicle in Frank's rearview mirror looked like a G-man to him. The cropped hair and inky black color of the car conspired in his mind to equate to an unmarked FBI team. He would take extra side roads to lose them and they'd stop following him but another unmarked car appearing further down the route would only feed the fire in his head.

"Do you think they've found us so soon?"

"No idea. I'm just being cautious."

"The only way to catch us is if someone saw you and I leave the barn, but there wasn't anyone for miles around."

"Apart from that cop car that screamed by."

"Yeah, but it didn't stop us—twice. If they were doing something, they'd have pulled us over then."

"I s'pose."

"And they don't have either of our descriptions and you swapped the plates. Frank, they've got shit."

"We still need to be careful."

"I know. All's I'm saying is that losing FBI cars that aren't there is slowing us down. Take it easy, hon'."

Despite her words, he kept off the expressway and rattled along the narrower roads in and out of towns with no names. The Falcon trundled out the other side and they headed towards the next place further down their route.

One hour later and the vehicle edged into yet another conurbation— only this time it was the outskirts of Frederick, announced by the usual signage: 'Welcome to Frederick'. Frank drove past a used car lot and a diner stood immediately after on the right-hand side.

"Let's pull in here. If you're correct about the Feds, we can get back on the expressway and be in Pittsburgh before midnight."

ANOTHER MEAL COMPRISING a burger and fries. Frank ordered a coffee and she took a vanilla shake.

"Is this all we're eating?"

"You still hungry, babe?"

"No, I mean there's more to life than flipped burgers."

"Mary Lou, once we get to our destination we can eat steaks for the rest of our lives. Right now, we need to keep under everyone's radars, so that means coming to a lot of crappy diners and having the shit food. That way we fade into the background, never to be noticed or remarked upon."

"Sure, Frank."

"But places like this do sell good homemade desserts."

Mary Lou's eyes lit up and she ordered a piece of key lime pie as soon as she caught the waitress's eye. The dessert gave Mary Lou a frisson of nostalgia for her childhood. There wasn't much for her to remember that was positive but the treat of her mom baking key lime pie for Sunday afternoons before her father died enabled a small ripple of happiness to echo on her face.

"We'll take turns at the wheel, okay?"

"Of course, Frank. As long as we are creating some distance between here and us, everything'll be fine."

"There's more to it than leaving Maryland. We must sort out something with our packages."

Both pairs of eyes pointed below the table to reinforce the circumspect language Frank chose whenever civilians surrounded him and he needed to talk business. Once his look returned above the ceramic surface, he glanced around the room to check everyone—if they'd reacted to his words and if anyone appeared too intent on their conversation. He eased back into the seat of their booth until he slumped onto his coccyx. Mary Lou realized the rest of the world was eating, sitting and chatting as the afternoon degraded into the night.

Like every diner in America, there were truckers on their own taking a pit stop before the next leg of their cross-country haul. Frank noticed they always sat at the counter—almost as if they wouldn't allow themselves the comfort of a booth or a normal table. There was an occasional couple, chowing down before they heading home to destroy their brains on beer and game shows hosted by men who used to be comedians.

One exception to this scenario sat next to Frank and Mary Lou: a mother and her child. The child was three, maybe four but no older.

"Sit on the seat like a good boy."

A pair of feet appeared on the shared backrest between Mary Lou and the kid. She twisted as she noticed small movements in her peripheral vision. The legs disappeared and were replaced by his head. The boy was staring straight at her.

"Eat your burger like a good boy."

The skull bobbed down and resurfaced as soon as Mary Lou turned away to resume her conversation with Frank. She looked back at him and he vanished for a second time but she was not in the mood. She scowled at him until he cried and leaped off the seat to perch next to his ma on the other side of the table, far from Mary Lou.

The woman hugged the boy and stroked his forehead. With his mother's attention secured, the tears stopped flowing.

"You shouldn't bother the lady. Remember: nice things happen to boys who behave nicely."

Mary Lou eavesdropped on this maternal advice and pondered for a second. Was that true? What did it say about her time with Frank?

"You all right?"

"Yes thanks. Just thinking is all."

"Don't make a habit out of it."

He winked and squeezed her hand. She smiled back, knowing he was not demeaning her. The trust between them was building.

"We will need to hit the road. Are you okay to take a turn behind the wheel?"

"Yeah. I prefer it to being a passenger."

"Me too. Watching America fly by is no fun, is it?"

"Nah. Do you think we'll make it?"

Frank looked into Mary Lou's eyes, boring a hole straight through.

"It won't be easy but we have an advantage: we've no idea quite what our route will be. So no one else can predict it either."

Mary Lou nodded.

"You reckon they're after us?"

"You can bet on it."

"Everyone?"

"Everyone who's breathing. Yes."

Mary Lou imagined the Feds and Uncle Frankie sending out their hordes to capture them.

"But we'll be okay?"

"We're ahead of them now. All we have to do is keep going and once we clean up our act, we will be home and dry."

Frank emphasized the word 'clean' to ensure she understood what he meant. Mary Lou felt better hearing his reassurance but she could not tell if he was only boosting both of them up before the first of a long series of car hops.

"Home and dry."

She mulled the phrase over her tongue to hear how it sounded out loud. She didn't remember a time in her existence when she'd felt home and dry. So the idea this state was around the corner from her seemed alien.

"Will we have a home one day?"

"Sooner than you think. Once this is behind us, we can settle down and start a whole new life for ourselves."

She took Frank's hand in hers and stroked her thumb over the back of his fingers. They leaned forward over the table and kissed.

"You love birds good or you want the check?"

The waitress waded into their moment and dissolved it to nothingness.

"Check'll do."

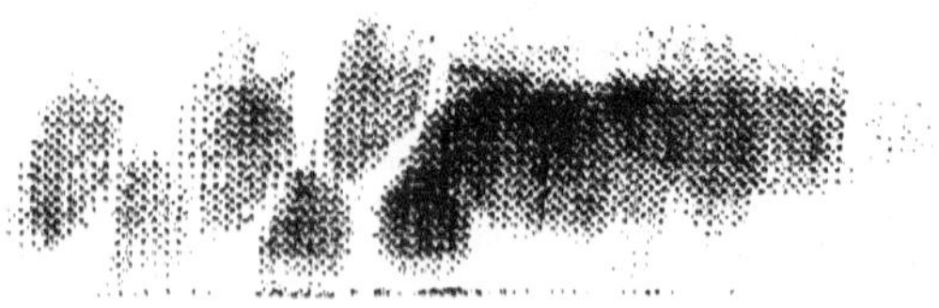

13

ANTHONY FACED TWO major problems with following Frankie's orders. First, he had no guys to bring with because Luigi and Paul had been incinerated earlier in the day. Second, he had no idea which way Frank and Mary Lou were heading.

The initial problem was resolved with a quick call or two. Mickey agreed to help as there was money attached to the deal and he had nothing else on the cards the next day or so. Bobby was harder to track down because he was in greater demand. While he was a paid goon like Mickey, rumor had it that he was a mob hitman, so he was tough, tenacious and took no quarter. Precisely the dude you want on your side when you're chasing across the country to kill people and get your hands on their pile of cash.

Anthony waited three hours for Bobby to finish a job he was on. If he was on your team, you needed patience and not to ask too many questions on his whereabouts. If he wanted an alibi, you gave him one. By late afternoon he was free and Anthony gained his attention. A large amount of money as a finder's fee proved sufficient to motivate Bobby onto Anthony's crew.

His two new recruits met Anthony on the outskirts of town at the Kitkatt Club because nobody asked questions in a strip joint. The lights were low and Anthony could get a discount by having a boss who owned the flophouse. There had to be some advantages to living in a crap heap like Baltimore.

The Getaway

Anthony positioned himself at the back of the auditorium so there were no tables behind them: no one to notice them arrive or leave. He ordered a bottle of scotch from the big-tittied girl who wandered by holding a tray and only wearing a pair of purple panties.

Once she'd delivered the hooch, he told her to scram but pushed a Jackson into the front of her only item of clothing so she didn't feel too bad or remember too much of what he looked like. Then he waited for his guests to make their way to the club.

Within fifteen minutes they sat, drank and made plans.

"Do we have any idea where the bums are heading Anthony?"

"Mickey, Frank said he was doing the job to go to California. Told Frankie several times."

"You reckon he's clever enough for a double bluff?"

"No Bobby. Besides when he mentioned it he thought Frankie was on his side and had no reason to lie."

"So you think they ran straight out west?"

"That's not Frank's way. His plan was to head east a while and then double back westwards."

"Should we try to follow his tracks?"

"Worth spending a morning on it. If we get a sniff then fine. If not then we just turn tail and think like a fugitive who's aiming to end up on the other side of the country without getting caught along the way."

"I can do one better than that."

"How Bobby?"

"I know a guy who might know a guy."

"And?"

Mickey sounded impatient, but he was smart enough not to let his annoyance at Bobby show through too much.

"And this dude has a connection in the FBI. They'll have been pounding the pavement today asking the same questions as we just did only they've got a shiny badge and a lot of men on the ground to do the searching. I'll put a call through and see if he can give us a nod."

Although Frankie told him he was only really interested in retrieving his money, Anthony knew the best result would be to walk into the auto repairs with the bags of cash, the two of them tied up and still alive. But if only one of those things happened, he had better have the take.

"So we hit the road to Philly in the morning."

The other two nodded and all three settled in to watch the show. As their conversation ended, two girls—one black, one white—were slowly removing bikini tops on stage while a third sprayed oil over her torso and walked near enough to the edge of the stage so that patrons could seize the opportunity to stuff greenbacks into her hot pants.

An hour later, Anthony spotted Frankie walking across the room and a table set for him near the front of the auditorium. Anthony nudged Mickey with his elbow.

"My boss has just sat down. Time for us to split. He'll want to think we're spending every waking minute searching for his nephew."

Mickey nodded and Bobby shrugged. The hit man didn't really see the point of watching girls not quite take all their clothes off for tips. If he bought a whore, he just paid for a slut and didn't bother pretending otherwise. A man after Frankie's heart.

Under different circumstances, Mickey would have spent a hundred or two on the girls only to see them wrap themselves in circles on stage. He never paid for ass but he was a sucker for a floor show. Anthony occupied so much of his time waiting for Frankie at the Kitkatt, he forgot there was tit on display. He thought of the place as a glorious liquor bar and nothing more—unless he felt like an afternoon fuck.

With the bottle empty, he threw down sufficient notes to cover the cost of another round of scotch and called it a night. He knew they had some long days ahead of them.

"See you outside this joint at seven. We've got a lot of driving to do."

Mickey and Bobby nodded while staring at a bouncing nipple on stage. Anthony shrugged and headed home for a good night's rest.

ANGELO BIANCHI PUT the phone down after Charlie Pentangelo hung up and remained sat down for three minutes. This gave him enough time to conjure up a plan. He considered what he would pack in his overnight case and who he would call to join him on the hunt for a bag of money and two heads on a plate.

He stood up, walked into his bedroom and squatted by his open wardrobe to pull out a soft leather holdall he used on these occasions. Angelo threw in shorts, socks, a spare pair of pants, two shirts and some toiletries. Then he grabbed a box from under the bed to remove a pump-action shotgun and a revolver, along with enough ammo to last a week on a firing range. With the rifle in the holdall, Angelo placed the pistol in a holster he wore under his jacket. He always exited the apartment wearing a black three piece suit and a brown fedora. Today was no exception.

Mulberry Street was a shabby place to live but he called it home. Along the street, left two blocks and right one brought him to a small restaurant where men in suits sat at tables and talked in hush tones. He melted into this tableau and waited.

Soon a sallow complexion of a man appeared opposite and ordered a double espresso. Angelo nodded at him and leaned in, elbows on the white tablecloth. The new arrival mirrored his position.

"Thanks for coming at short notice, Rico."

This nickname hung around his neck since his childhood. Before he'd been a mobster, he had loved gangster movies and Rico was his favorite character. Now he lived the dream.

"Happy to help a friend, Angelo. What seems to be the problem?"

"We have two fugitives carrying money that is not theirs. Our job is to retrieve the cash."

"And the escapees?"

"My associates don't care about them. Alive or dead. It doesn't matter: it's the money. Their bodies breathing or otherwise is of secondary importance."

"But there's benefit to them being conscious?"

"I am sure if we hauled their asses back with us, some appreciation would be shown."

Rico sat in his chair for a minute, pondered and sipped his coffee. After two mouthfuls, he added a small amount of sugar.

"Where's the cash now?"

"Location unknown. The ultimate destination is California according to the Shylock whose problem has been dumped on our laps."

"Where did the money start its journey?"

"Baltimore. The good news is that the FBI is on their tail and my associates have connections there who can give us the inside track."

"Although I have no desire to pry, Angelo, by any chance did the green reside within a bank until recently?"

"That is my understanding."

"Holy Mary. That's a lot of cash to chase down."

"We should assume we are not the only ones with an interest in the recovery of the money. I expect the Shylock has sent after it and if he succeeds, then my associates will be happy but you and I won't receive a dime for our time."

"So we need to be the first to the greens."

Rico nodded again, mulling over the conversation.

"Where to then?"

"If you were running for your life to the Pacific, how would you get there without drawing attention?"

"Car or bus."

"Yep. And if you wanted to clean the dirty money along the way?"

Rico thought for ten seconds.

"Vegas."

"Why?"

"Casinos and enough Shylocks to cut a deal fast."

"I agree. I think they'll be sufficiently desperate to head straight for the biggest concentration of mobsters outside the Big Apple and the Windy City."

"When shall we leave?"

"We fly tonight and hole up until they catch up with us."

"And if we're wrong about Vegas?"

"I'll check in with our associates so we keep abreast of the Feds. Those G-men know how to track a fella down to the ends of the world."

Rico smiled. He enjoyed working with Angelo. The man had a good head on him: looked for the angles but was a stand-up guy when times were tough and bullets were flying. They finished their drinks and headed for LaGuardia.

THURSDAY JUNE 19

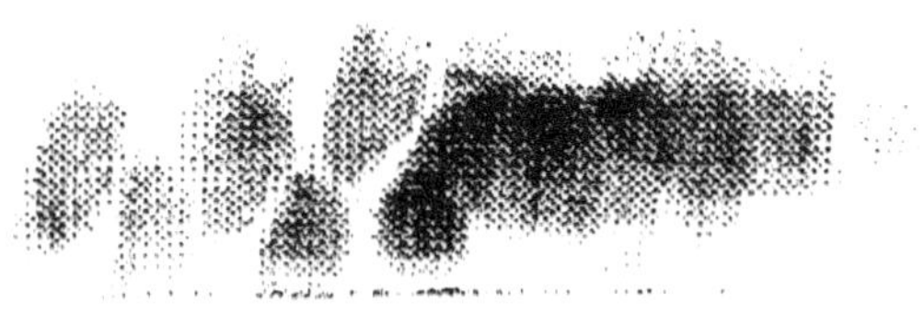

14

MARY LOU SNORED in the passenger seat: her head flopped backward to open her windpipe and maximize the airflow to her brain. Frank gripped the wheel and tapped fingers along to the rock 'n' roll beat. The Falcon went straight through a pothole and bounced violently causing her skull to bob around.

She awoke with a start and glanced into the darkness.

"Where are we?"

"Outskirts of Pittsburgh."

"Did I fall asleep?"

"Judging by the snoring…"

"I don't snore."

"Okay. Judging by the heavy breathing, I'd say you were snoozing."

"Do you think they're still after us?"

"Better believe it."

Mary Lou rubbed the sleep out of the corner of her eyes and glanced at her watch: midnight.

"Are you tired?"

"On the way."

"Wake me next time and I'll take over."

"I wanted you to get some rest. You deserved it. But we'll pull over as soon as we see a motel."

Ten minutes driving landed them outside the reception of the Pittsburg Plaaza, which was nothing more than a string of prefab cabins and a hut with a desk where you wrote any false name you chose and signed next to it. Customer privacy was a priority at the Plaaza.

Frank asked for a quiet cabin away from the main road implying they were a young couple up to you-never-your-mind and didn't want to embarrass any of the other guests. The clerk sneered a lecherous glance at Mary Lou in the car and Frank gave him the space to conjure up pornographic images in his head.

With the key in his hand, he took the Falcon to the far end of the parking lot. Bags in tow, they shut the door on the world and sat on the edge of the bed.

Frank stood up and switched the TV on, loud enough to mask any conversation.

"We've made it to Pittsburgh but what should we do now?"

"I reckon we need to assume that everyone has seen the Falcon, change of plates or not. So we should ditch it first thing tomorrow. Then our next stop should be Cincinnati. If anyone has followed us they'll be searching for a couple. So the obvious move is to split up. We can both slip by any Fed because we will not be what they are looking for."

"I dunno, Frank."

"We'll be fine. One drives and the other goes by train. It'll mean a day apart but make it so much safer by nightfall tomorrow."

"We're a team though?"

"Yes we are, but strong enough to be separated from each other. For a single day only. That's all."

"I don't like it. Remember, when I get stressed I forget to do things. The explosives: I didn't set them. What happens if I screw up when you're not there?"

"Mary Lou: I've complete faith in you. You'll do well. I know it. We take one bag each from the heist just in case anything goes wrong."

"Wrong?"

"If I get caught, then you still hold half the money and can carry on."

"Caught?"

"I'm covering all bases. Nothing more. We shall meet up at Cincinnati and everything will be fine. You'll see."

"Now you're scaring me, Frank."

He put his arms around her and she let his body engulf her. Mary Lou felt safer than she ever had before in her life surrounded by the smell of that man and the comfort of his breathing near her ear.

She hugged him back and they sat holding each other until the stress of their conversation left her shoulders and they both relaxed.

"One day, right?"

"That's all. We'll be miles away from the Feds by then and changed our MO along the way. They'll never catch us then."

"And do you think Uncle Frankie will give up too?"

Frank didn't answer. His silence spoke volumes but Mary Lou waited, hoping the response would be what she wanted to hear and not reality.

"One day at a time, babe. Uncle Frankie'll be harder than a bunch of G-men, but we'll get away from him too. Somehow."

They remained hugging another five minutes, she closed her eyes and soaked in each moment of tranquility in the cabin, although she noticed roach traps all along the walls.

"Ever been to Cincinnati?"

"No."

"Me neither."

He kissed her on the forehead and they allowed themselves a laugh.

"Rob a bank and see the sights of America."

"Yeah, I didn't count on this happening."

"No one did, babe. It's how the cards landed. You only play the hand you're dealt."

"Ain't that the truth."

She pecked him on the cheek twice. Tenderly.

"Once we meet up in Cincinnati, where to then?"

"I was thinking Oklahoma City. It'll be a long drive but then at least it won't be too far to Vegas and we can relax in the anonymity of the bright lights and one-armed bandits."

She distracted him by kissing his cheeks then poking her fingers under his shirt to caress his chest. Frank placed a hand on a breast and squeezed until she felt a tingle running up her spine from her groin to the back of her neck.

Mary Lou undid his buttons while he pulled at her bra until they were both under the blankets and naked. An hour later with him fast asleep, she slipped out from under the covers long enough to switch the television off and remembered the nights soon after his last stretch in the State Penitentiary.

FRANK WOKE FIRST and couldn't remember switching the TV off the night before. He smiled as he recalled what they'd got up to before he'd fallen asleep. He felt calm and a sliver of happiness soaked into him as he looked at Mary Lou—until a roar of lust exited past his throat which she mistook for a belch.

"Good morning to you too."

He laughed and licked her back as it was the nearest part of her body to his mouth at the time. His fingers landed between her thighs.

"Not now dear, there's traveling to do."

Mary Lou took his hand and placed it on his dick. Then she flung the covers off the bed and scampered into the bathroom. Frank let his palm rest where it was and used the moment to consider what they had to do before leaving town.

He got dressed, put the bags back in the Falcon then waited for Mary Lou to be ready. He liked to watch her get undressed and he loved to gaze at her as she took off her clothes, slowly revealing her soft skin and curves to him. There was something deeply satisfying about being the only one privileged to experience those moments.

In the car and out for breakfast and a place to swap vehicles. A mile down the road they found a diner to eat. It was a popular venue and cars crammed until it nearly burst. The Falcon got lost in the sprawl as soon as Frank drove in.

Coffee and pancakes later, Mary Lou stared out the window from their booth and watched the world go by.

"There's a bunch of trees at the end of this lot."

"Yeah?"

"Lots of shrubs too."

"Okay."

"You could hide a car in that undergrowth."

Frank pricked up his ears as he worked out why Mary Lou cared so much about the details of the parking faciities. The pancakes had landed at the pit of his stomach and he was feeling sleepy while he digested them.

"Where should we get our next ride do you reckon?"

"Out there, maybe?"

"Yes but if we boost something here, chances are someone will connect us to the vehicle."

"There's another restaurant half a block down the road. I can make out its neon sign from here."

"Much better idea. You ready to head out?"

Mary Lou swigged back the last mouthful of coffee and Frank paid up. They sauntered over to the nearby lot and took their pick of the saloons. Nothing too fancy, new or old. Just a sensible ride that'd turn no heads.

A black hooded family saloon squatted three spaces from the end. Mary Lou stood in front of it pretending to check her make-up in her handbag mirror while Frank opened the driver's window, popped open the door and slid inside to kick-start the engine. It roared into life within two seconds and she jumped in as he drove off.

"That was fast."

"Sometimes I'm lucky. There's a full tank of gas too so I can make it all the way without stopping."

Back to the other lot where they transferred their possessions into the new vehicle and pushed the Falcon into the copse. They kept going until it got stuck in a rut or ditch. Then they grabbed some branches and threw them on top for camouflage.

Frank remained behind the wheel as they headed for the station. She was quiet, aware they would split up soon and still not happy about the situation—even though it was the safest thing to do.

Twenty minutes later they were in the middle of Cincinnati and the main building was in front of them. Frank and Mary Lou divided their spending money, so she'd enough for the train fare and a bite to eat on board and he could still buy food and more gas.

"Would you like me to come in with you until you're on the platform?"

"Yes I would, but no you shouldn't. If the cops wired a description, it'll be of me, not you, Frank."

"All the more reason for me to ride shotgun until you are safe in a carriage."

Before she could argue the point any further, he pulled in and got out the car. Mary Lou knew she wanted him by her side and stopped any further attempts at protesting. They each carried a money bag and she stuffed her clothes on the top of the notes so she'd have less to carry. There were only two passengers in the line and soon she held a one-way ticket in her hand and the knowledge she was facing a twelve-hour journey ahead of her.

The next train for Oklahoma City was due to depart in fifteen minutes so the couple had enough time to saunter to the platform and for Frank to hug and kiss her before he helped her find the right passenger car and settle into her seat. He put her bag in the rack above her head and passed her a fashion magazine he'd found on a bench.

"I'll be waiting for you in the station when you get off. We'll be lying in bed together tonight."

He kissed her again and walked out the carriage without looking back because he was certain he had seen a tear roll out her eye and that broke his heart.

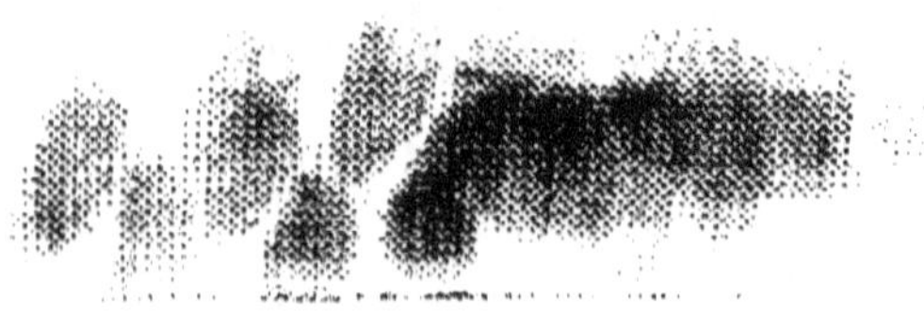

15

FRANK KNEW HE would take less time than Mary Lou because he could go a direct route and she'd have to follow the train tracks as they zigzagged across the country. So he took it easy, never going over five miles an hour under the speed limit and letting folks pass him as they saw fit.

Even though he chose not to use the expressway, he still found straight roads and desolate countryside. The highway was as flat as this morning's pancakes. This gave him the advantage of seeing any impending traffic coming from the rear or head on. And nothing appeared on either horizon.

Frank cranked the music up and opened a window because this would be one long dull journey. The black bag with the cash was back in the trunk and his clothes were strewn on the backseat. He had dumped them there when he returned to the car after leaving Mary Lou. He figured if any prying eyes were to take an interest then levels would subside at the sight of his shorts and a tee.

His plan was to travel parallel to the expressway as that represented the shortest distance between cities but he needed to avoid the freeway itself. There was nothing to see but painted lines on the highway so Frank got to thinking about Mary Lou and her rose.

A man's mind was bound to wander on a journey such as this. The more he thought about the tattoo nestling below her belly button, the more he wanted to savor it there and then. For a second, the car rumbled and Frank found himself in the dirt and dust of the side of the highway heading towards the gulley edging the field. He swerved the steering wheel hard right and the rear of the vehicle swung sideways. The rear passenger tire lost footing and dangled in mid air over the ditch as he tried to cling to earth. Another twist of the wheel and the back end lurched in the opposite direction until all four tires were eating tarmac and he settled the automobile squarely in the middle of the only lane pointing to St Louis.

With the car stable, he pulled over to the side of the road and stopped. A minute later the cold sweats ceased to pour out of his armpits and back and he breathed again. His stomach churned, so he leaped out just in time to spew into the ditch which had tried to kill him less than sixty seconds before.

Frank slumped into the dirt to regain control of his body, which seemed to be trying to escape from him. Mary Lou was right: they should never have split up. He was safer with her by his side. Too late though—and the thought of her rose entered his mind's eye yet again, almost taunting him with the lust of his poor decision.

He found spittle returning to his mouth and he sloshed it around to take the taste of vomit away from his teeth. Frank'd have killed for a glass of water then. His heart rate subsided to a normal level and he considered standing up but waited another minute before doing anything so ambitious.

Four minutes later Frank sat behind the wheel and released the clutch. The vehicle kangarooed forwards and, ten feet further, he regained control and the saloon purred onwards while he accompanied the rock 'n' roll with loud singing. He hit two or three of the right notes but no one was judging, which was just as well given the noise he generated.

The car carried on following the lines of the road all the way to St Louis. Frank drove round the outskirts rather than open himself to the possibility of the city cops somehow having his identity to match with his face but he needn't have worried. No police around here were watching out for him.

His stomach rumbled and he realized he'd been sat in the damn car for three hours without a piss or a bite to eat. The boredom of escape took over and he allowed himself to be consumed with the idea of a cheese burger with fries, onion rings and a coffee.

All the places he passed in the burbs were way too empty, making him far too memorable a patron, or jam packed and he wasn't prepared to wait too long for his food. Thirty minutes more and he was the other side of the urban sprawl heading towards Cincinnati.

A sign appeared announcing the nothing town and Frank parked in the House Springs Deli, which claimed short-order cooking was their speciality. The lot was half filled with cars but there were sufficient spare tables he could get served fast enough for his stomach.

As ever, he brought his bag with him and placed it under his feet beneath the booth. Norma Richardson approached Frank and asked him what he'd like to drink.

"Coffee, please."

As she walked away to grab the pot, he noticed the bottom two buttons on her dress were undone. He watched the flesh of her legs rise above her knees until it vanished in the murky shadows of her clothing.

With those thighs locked in his mind, Frank inspected Norma's face and the rest of her body. Long brown hair with a slight wave. Bright blue eyes with a pointy nose. Average height. Breasts that created a pronounced cleavage because she had big tits or because her blouse was too small. Either way, he liked what he saw. The image of her decolletage and Mary Lou's rose merged as he ordered the food he'd been salivating over for the last hour.

NORMA LAUGHED AT another of Frank's jokes. He knew he wasn't that amusing but the falseness of her reaction didn't stop him continuing to like her. The tension in her blouse caused a gap between the top buttons to emerge and revealed a bright yellow bra beneath the light blue material of her uniform.

He mopped up the juices from his burger with a slice of bread Norma had brought over.

"Is there anything else I can get you?"

"Something sweet would be neat."

She chuckled once more and touched his shoulder.

"I got a mighty fine piece of pie to offer you."

"I'm sure your pie is mighty fine, Norma."

He winked and could not believe he'd said what he did. Norma giggled again and slapped him in jest.

"Now Frank, talk like that is liable to get you in trouble."

He glanced at her left hand and saw no wedding ring.

"You got a fella then?"

"Why Frank, no I ain't. Whatever are you thinking of?"

He knew she knew and this was part of the game they were playing.

"Just wondering when you're off your shift."

Norma leaned down so he could get a good look at the space between her tits and whispered.

"About five minutes time if you play your cards right."

He threw down a bunch of notes to pay for his meal and waited for Norma to return with his change. He was still on a budget.

"Meet you out back."

She then walked up to her boss and he heard her spin some story about women's trouble. The guy shrugged and she hung up her apron and trundled through the kitchen. He took his cue and scuttled round to the rear of the building in time to see her walk out and light a cigarette until he stood next to her.

"You near here?"

"Frank, you are so forward."

A giggle and she led him down three blocks and left onto another until they arrived at a shabby condo. Nothing a lick of paint and replacing all the pipe work wouldn't fix.

Up to the second floor and into Norma's one-bedroom apartment. She dumped her clutch bag on the kitchen table and Frank placed his black holdall next to it.

"You always carry something that large with you?"

"Don't get fresh, Norma Richardson. A man has to look after the tools of his trade."

With that, he cupped her cheek in his hand and they kissed. Within five minutes a trail of clothing formed from the kitchen where a yellow bra lay on top of a woman's blouse and a man's shirt covered them both. At the door a skirt nestled in the folds of a pair of jeans and at the foot of the bed: panties, shorts and socks. Two pairs of feet stuck out from the end of the covers—Norma's pointing upwards, Frank's down. Both were deep-breathing and she had wrapped her legs around his hips, preventing him from getting inside her. This momentary pause caused Frank to think and realize what he was doing. His lust had overpowered him and he was about to make a mistake.

"Where've you gone?"

Norma let the disappointment ooze out her voice. They were having fun and this breeze-through man had all the right moves for her. Then he curled up and vanished.

"What gives?"

She repeated her question wanting to know why Frank had just turned off to her. He remained silent.

"Was it something I did?"

"What? No? No. Sorry. Look, I should never have put us in this situation."

"Is there another woman?"

"That obvious?"

"'Fraid so, mister."

"While you are mighty attractive, I should leave before things go any further. And they almost did."

Frank rolled off Norma and sat on the edge of the bed. She wrapped herself around him so tightly he could feel her hairs against his buttocks.

"It was fun while it lasted. Shame it didn't last a minute or two longer."

She nibbled his ear and he inhaled her vanilla perfume. Later, she made him a coffee while wearing her yellow underwear and they sat together at the kitchen table while he put on his socks.

"Frank, if you're ever passing through…"

"…I know. Keep on going."

She giggled and kissed him on the forehead before he popped on his shoes and left the apartment. A short hustle back to his car and he hit the road—but always five miles an hour below the limit. Even with this layover, he would arrive in Cincinnati six hours before Mary Lou.

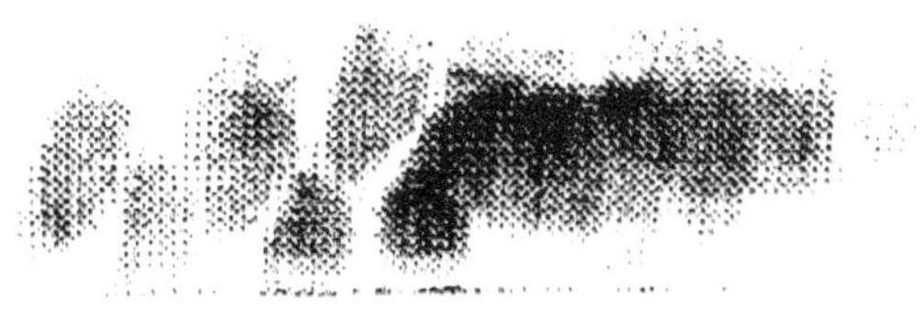

16

GLENDA'S SHIFT AT the Joppa diner ended at five. She sat in the staff room smoking a cigarette and sipping at a coffee to give herself the energy to leave the place and head home. A small portable TV was on and the news anchor showed an artist's impression of three men from the Lansdowne robbery. While not a great likeness, Glenda thought she recognized Pete and placed a call through to the cops.

Four hours later and a knock erupted from the front door of Glenda's apartment. She shared it with her girlfriend, Annie Price but she was out working shift in a local shoe factory. Glenda put on a housecoat and sauntered to the entrance. Two men stood on the doormat, backs straight. One in black jacket and pants, the other in uniform. The suit spoke first.

"Inspector Philip McNamara from the FBI and this is my colleague, Detective Edward Goodwin of the Baltimore Police Department."

"Come on in. We've got enough for a party if you don't tell my super."

The two men eyed each other and entered the premises. Glenda pointed at some seating and the gentlemen made themselves comfortable.

"Coffee?"

"We're good thanks."

The suit crossed his legs and the uniform took out a notepad.

"When you called, you told my colleague you recognized one of the deceased from the Lansdowne bank robbery."

"Yes."

"How did you know him?"

"I hadn't so much been acquainted with him, officer. I'd seen him before."

"Call me, Phil."

"Okay, Phil."

Glenda eased back in her chair and worried less whether the two front pieces of her house coat met in the middle.

"Where had you seen him?"

"In the diner. The Joppa-de-Doopah Diner—where I work."

The uniform scratched away with his pencil and pad, saying nothing but staring right at her.

"Was he a regular?"

"No, I wouldn't say that but he had been two times over the past few months."

"If he only turned up once or twice, how can you be sure it was him?"

"He was a guy you'd never forget. A sharp tongue and never left a tip. I always remember the ones who don't show any gratitude."

"Harsh words?"

"He just thought he was better than everyone else and didn't pretend to hide it. A thin long streak of piss if you'll pardon my language. Can I rustle up a coffee for you fellas?"

"No thanks. We're fine."

"You sure are, Phil."

Ted laughed and covered his mouth to generate a cough while Phil's cheeks turned a shade of red.

"When did you see him?"

"Last week I think. He came in looking for Lucy."

"Another customer?"

"No, we work together. When I told him she wasn't around, he finished up and left. Didn't even order any food."

"Any idea what business he had with this Lucy?"

"He was Lucy's latest ride."

Phil rarely experienced such directness from waitresses.

"Did she often have gentleman callers?"

"Don't get me wrong—she's no whore. Like me, she enjoys the company of men during the dark lonely nights, right?"

He noticed Glenda's knees had separated a few inches. What did they put in the water round here to make these middle-aged women so horny?

"And had this guy been around much?"

"Only a couple of times. From what Lucy told me, he was quite a cold fish to her too. Hardly spoke a word before or after any… intimacy they might have had. But he had smokes and was a warm body; none of us are getting any younger."

She stretched her arms out across a neighboring chair and Ted saw her look down to check she had revealed the curve of one of her tits.

Goodwin took down a description of Pete and then they left Glenda's apartment.

"What you think?"

"Horny old vixen."

"About what she said."

"Sounds like Pete the Wheels liked to dip his dick in the local service industry."

"Good move."

"Not if Lucy looks anything like Glenda."

"Smart move to set yourself up to hide away in this backwater from nowhere."

"Ah yes."

"Sometimes Ted, the trick is to look at their faces and not their tits."

"Yes Phil, but not always."

LUCY GAVE UP waiting for Pete a day before. She wasn't sure when she figured he wasn't coming back. Perhaps when she heard about the bank robbery on the news or that night when he failed to show up. Men were unreliable at the best of times and after the previous night's tequilas, today was not the best of times.

She woke up in her trailer not clear what day it was or quite where she was. Only after ten minutes was she able to open her eyes and let reality seep into her consciousness. Before the morning took hold, she reached out and grabbed a cigarette and a lighter, combining the two deftly.

In a moment of paranoia mixed with amnesia, Lucy flitted her head sideways to make sure she hadn't brought anybody home with her. The bed was empty. She inhaled, leaving the filter to hang from the corner of her mouth. Lucy's next challenge was to remember when her shift started at the Joppa-de-Doopah Diner. The good news was that her trailer was nearby: a six-minute walk. Her blurred memory held onto the idea she had the late shift which ran from five until they shut the place up for the night at midnight.

The fling with Pete had been fun but now all she had left was an itching sensation in her groin and a fat travel bag. Lucy switched on the radio and the news gave an update on the robbery. The description of one of the dead sounded a lot like him. She sighed. He wasn't a talker but they'd had a fabulous ride together.

After she got dressed, she fixed a coffee and cracked an egg into it. Sometimes that made the pounding fists in her head go away. As she tried to swig back the awful concoction, her eyes caught sight of Pete's holdall. She'd thrown it on a chair because the lummox had dropped it on the floor and her trailer didn't enjoy spacious accommodation.

She dragged the bag onto her bed and unzipped it. Nestling on the top of Pete's clothes was a carton of cigarettes and beneath the smokes was a roll of notes. She took both and counted the greenbacks. Five shy of two hundred dollars. Quite a find. She added up a second time to make sure. Under the clothes: a metal object. She didn't need to pull it out to be certain it was a revolver. Pete had left a gun in her trailer. Nice move.

She removed the carton and roll of notes and zipped up the bag. When she felt better, she'd take the contents and scatter them in the trash around the area. Until then, she placed the smokes on the small table near the kitchenette and stuffed the money into a drawer.

The only question left for Lucy was what to do with the cash. She could splash it on a new hairdo and a pretty dress—or take a trip with a girlfriend to Atlantic City or travel even further afield. To help her decisions making, she fried an egg and grilled some toast while in her dressing gown.

Once she'd sat down at the kitchenette table, Lucy's mind whirred as she thought through all the possibilities Pete's cash could buy her. It wasn't enough to quit her job at the diner and take her chances on the open road, but she sure was sick and tired of serving donuts and coffee to the middle-aged men who frequented the place. She might make good tips by thrusting her chest out through that tight blouse and bending down, but there had to be more to life than pouring brown liquid into mugs.

At this point in her reverie, a knock erupted on Lucy's trailer door. She opened it and greeted two men: one in uniform and the other in a suit, both holding badges.

"Can I come in, Miss.?"

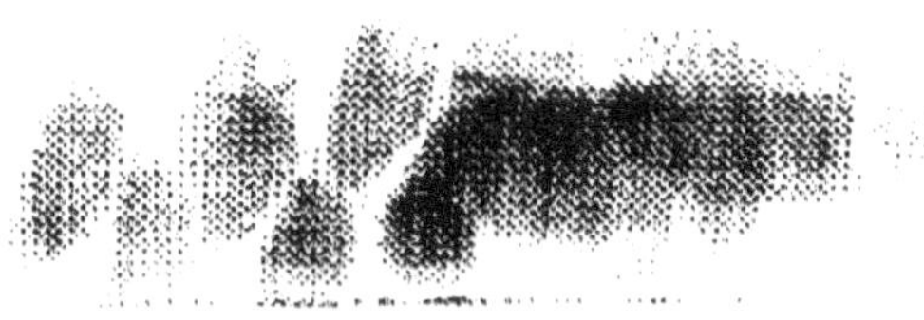

17

MARY LOU WATCHED Frank step off the carriage and she felt alone. Really alone. The bag was in the rack and she didn't feel she should go anywhere in case someone stole it. Their future hung above her head.

The passenger car was composed of row upon row of pairs of seats all facing forwards and Mary Lou sat three rows from the back. Just far enough away from the exit to not catch a draft when the train pulled into stations but not so distant that she couldn't run off.

The head-high baggage compartment was nothing more than a shelf with no attempt made to prevent bags from falling. Mary Lou kept her eyes on the black bag. Not because it was in imminent peril but because it might be in danger during the journey.

The last few days had shaken her. She wasn't that kind of person until then. She'd spent years with Frank in the can staying out of trouble. With the bank job going south, her self-possession was ebbing out of her.

Perhaps this was just her way of coping with the sudden change in their lives. They both waited for the day of the robbery for such a long time—months—and she hadn't given a second's consideration what life would be like after the takedown.

And now she lived that moment for real—and it was nothing how she was expecting. They'd talked about spending three or four weeks together while Uncle Frankie handled the money end of the business and they laid low. In theory, once the dust settled, they would hook up with Frankie, get the laundered cash and split up from the crew forever.

Instead, she was stuck on a train running from the Feds and Uncle Frankie without even Frank to offer reassurance. As she looked around, half the seats contained heads but she had no sense of how many passenger cars there were or where potential danger may lie. She needed to go scouting and prepared to get up from her seat. Her one quandary: to keep the bag with her and stand out as unusual or leave it and risk it getting stolen. A middle-aged woman sat on the other side of the aisle.

"Sorry to bother you, but I need to… freshen up. Would you mind keeping an eye on my luggage up there?"

She pointed at the rack and the harridan nodded.

"Of course, love, don't worry about a thing."

Mary Lou thanked her and stood up. It was a risk but lugging the bag down the aisles would have made her more visible if she was heading toward trouble.

Four sets of doors further on, she reached the dining car where people were ordering a late breakfast. She carried on and six cars down she hit the end of the line. Just a baggage wagon in front and nobody would be getting past that.

On the way back, Mary Lou paid more attention to the individuals as she passed them. Three guys caught her eye. Two wore hats and one sported a crewcut. All reeked of cop. She noted where they sat but did nothing more than that for the moment. They might have just been cops going to Cincinnati or beyond. Being on the train did not mean they were on the lookout for her.

Back at her seat, she thanked the woman again for watching her bag.

"You have a long journey ahead of you?"

"Ten hours. And you?"

"Much longer: all the way out west."

"How exciting. Are you visiting friends?"

"Oh no. My husband died last year so I'm seeing my inlaws. We never got on and this'll be the final time I have to put up with them."

Mary Lou considered this news. The social awkwardness of hearing about the disquiet in her family gave no wiggle room for further conversation. They both lapsed back into their own little worlds.

THE CREWCUT LINGERED in her head until Mary Lou could no longer sit still in her seat. She forced herself to investigate what he was up to. Another excuse to mind her bag and off she went to find him. He had stood up and was talking with the guard: a peaked cap, starched shirt. She carried on walking past to eavesdrop.

"Do you think they'll catch 'em?"

"Not if I've got anything to say about it."

"And what'll you do?"

"I aim to arrest me some bank robbers."

"Is that right?"

"Sure is and why not? I've as good a chance as anyone else. The FBI have said them two are heading west. And so's this train. Who's to know if they ain't even on this train?"

With this statement Mary Lou shuddered. She kept on walking down the aisle and waited for a rest room to become available. When she'd closed the door on the world, she splashed water over her face and leaned on the walls. Why had she and Frank agreed to split up? She was a few feet away from a transit cop who mistook himself for Eliot Ness.

After an indecent time, she left the confines of her sanctuary and walked past the officer to return to her seat.

"Do you have a description?"

"Sure do. They issued one this morning. Man and a woman carrying some heavy duty bags. Let's face it if they are on this train, it won't be that difficult to spot them. They are walking around with a million dollars between them."

The guard whistled at the sound of the size of the haul.

"Tell me," he leaned in. "If you found them, wouldn't you be tempted to take the money for yourself?"

"I am a fine upstanding member of the police force. I'd grab the cash for myself."

They both laughed but only one of them knew if he was joking.

"Have you got any leads?"

"Two Caucasians, one male, other female."

"That narrows it down."

"Yeah, but how many couples do you see walking round with a million bucks in their back pockets?"

"Now that is a great point."

"Say that again, bud."

The guard chuckled.

"And how do you know they haven't split up? I mean, you called them a couple but they might just be two gang members, if you get me?"

"Hadn't considered that. You're right. I should look out for one or both of them."

"I've made your life a lot more complicated."

"Sure have, but I forgive you. If I make the reward, I'll remember you."

"Don't remember me; share the bounty."

"Yeah, like that's going to happen. I'm off for a recce."

Mary Lou scooted back to her seat while the cop headed toward the baggage car to start his search. She stared at the bag above her head and wondered what the hell she should do. There were too many notes to hide them—this was not an option.

Perhaps the holdall needed to go. Mary Lou thought hard and fast. Just because one overzealous cop was on the lookout for a woman—or a man—on her own carrying a stash of cash did not mean he would look at her and know she was worth searching.

And if she didn't hide the notes or the bag, should she hide herself? Make a beeline for the washroom and stay there for the rest of the journey? Mary Lou gave this more serious consideration.

But that middle-aged hag across the aisle had spoken with her and might provide a description of her. She was sat there now and Mary Lou got the feeling she was staring at her this minute. There was one car Mary Lou hadn't explored, which she and Frank had skipped when they boarded the train.

She turned round to get a sense of what was there: a buffet car. Somehow she missed the fact there was food behind her and ahead. She looked up at her bag and tried to imagine seeing it for the first time. Did it say money or undies to her? Even though her chest was tightening and adrenaline was coursing through her veins. The holdall was too dreary to raise any suspicions unless she created a reason for the cop to think ill of her.

She did not want to sit here and wait for him to arrest her. Mary Lou stood up—yet again—and walked behind to the buffet car. There were tables and seats along one side and a bar area where people ordered food and drink. At the far end were a series of windows for passengers to stare out at the passing scenery as it shot past at sixty miles an hour.

Mary Lou headed for a seat near the viewing area so she'd have plenty of warning when the cop burst through the doors. Then she grabbed a menu and held it in front of her to hide behind when the time was right. This was the best plan available to her. It wasn't the greatest idea but a piece of laminated card would protect her from the might of the local law enforcement.

Ten minutes later, the door opened and the cop walked in, checking everyone's expressions who made direct eye contact with him. Mary Lou gulped and gripped her menu tighter.

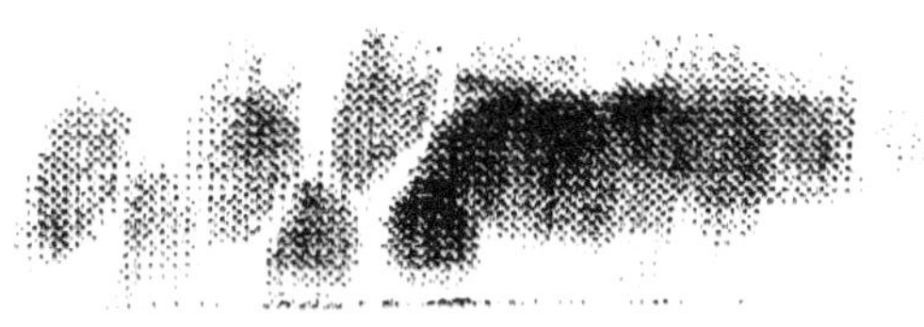

18

MARY LOU RAISED the menu in front of her face as she'd planned to do. This prevented him from taking too close a look but also meant she couldn't see quite where he was in the car.

"Can I get you something?"

She ignored the voice as she was concentrating too much imagining how long he'd take to walk the fifteen steps to reach her.

"Miss?"

"Huh?"

"You want to order anything?"

The buffet barman had a point as the place was filling up and she was taking up valuable counter space. He had left her alone for enough time. An answer was required.

"Java and a slice of cake if you have any."

"We got cake. What you want?"

"Coffee cake?"

"You sure like your coffee?"

Mary Lou had lowered her menu so she could speak with the barman just as the cop sauntered past.

"Huh? Yessir. What girl doesn't love a nice piece of coffee cake?"

"What indeed, honey."

The conversation petered out, much to Mary Lou's relief, and the officer carried on until he reached the end of the car and made his way back. He passed her a second time but on this occasion, he stopped right behind her and she wished she'd kept a gun in her clutch bag.

He leaned past her so she could smell the acrid stench of his aftershave. His hand brushed her shoulder and he took a menu from the counter.

"Excuse me, ma'am."

Her throat was too dry to respond and she half-nodded instead. The menu disappeared beyond her peripheral vision and the cop considered his food and drink options. Blasts of stale breath launched onto the back of her neck and she sensed he was stood there.

"Coffee to go, bud."

"Sure thing, Simon."

Mary Lou noted the cop was a regular on the route else the waiter wouldn't have known his name. Ordinary flatfoot on his usual train journey shooting his mouth off to the guard about his chances of a big break. She relaxed knowing he wasn't here as part of some special detail. He was just a uniform with no imagination trying to put food on his family's table. Deadbeat gumshoe with hopes and dreams and no opportunity to reach them—like every other schnook in the country.

The guy dropped a coffee and cake in front of her. Soon after, another Java landed within an inch of her mug aimed at Simon. He leaned in again and ensured his arm touched hers as he picked up his drink. She did her best not to react. He was a cop and the last thing she needed was to draw attention to herself. That said, she didn't need some dirt ball rubbing himself against her: peaked cap and uniform or not.

Mary Lou unclenched her jaw to chow down on the cake and sip her brown drink without turning her head. She had no desire to catch his gaze or engage him in any conversation. Mooks like him needed only the slightest invitation and she was in no position to deal with him in her usual manner: her hot coffee lingering on his crotch as she walked away.

Instead she threw down some coins on the counter and dismounted from her bar stool. Simon gave her enough room to get past him without moving a single muscle of his body. She considered elbowing him in the balls but the train came to her rescue as the driver took a bend too fast. All the standing passengers in the buffet car lurched to one side including Mary Lou, who reached out with her fist into Simon's stomach. His gut took the entire weight of her blow as she ensured he received the full brunt of the impact.

"I'm so very sorry, officer. I completely lost my balance."

"Don't mention it. The driver needs to stop speeding."

This wheeze of a response created a warmth of happiness inside her and Mary Lou ricocheted back to her seat as the train steadied itself along the tracks.

As she reached the door, she looked behind and saw Simon the cop heading her way. She kept on walking past her possessions and on to where she had found the washroom before. If he was following her, she needed to find out. Besides, she was trapped on this train whatever happened. She felt for the knife she'd stolen in the buffet car and hidden up her sleeve. The blade was far from sharp but it could still do some damage if aimed right.

Inside the washroom, she closed the lid of the toilet and sat down, ear pinned to the door listening out for Simon. Sounded like there was a constant shuffling outside but she wasn't so panicked she couldn't tell the difference between the noise of the train, the sound of her blood pumping in her ears and cop footsteps two feet away.

Someone tried the door and she bit her lip: the desire to yell out was beyond painful but she said nothing, holding her breath trying to hear what was happening inches from her head. The footsteps got quieter and whoever it was—Simon or some other passenger—moved on to find a different place to freshen up.

Back in her allotted seat, she saw a hulk of a man sat next to the middle-aged woman. Mary Lou surveyed him. They were not a couple for sure as the hag was doing her level best to ignore the Neanderthal. After eyeing him up and down the length of his body, Mary Lou felt a severe pang of fear run down her spine and land in her stomach. The slick black hair cut neatly above the ear lobe, crisp suit and what looked like Army-issue shoes. He had a newspaper opened but his eyes were looking above and beyond the paper along the car. He was a Fed.

WHERE HAD THE G-man come from? This stress would be the death of her. Then in a moment of clarity, Mary Lou remembered the train had stopped at least twice since she'd done her first walk up and down the cars so there had been plenty of opportunity for this dude to hop onboard. Didn't make it any better he was here but removed the mystery of his appearance.

She eyed her bag yet again, hoping somehow that she could convince herself it didn't look as though it contained half the proceeds of the robbery at the Lansdowne branch of the First Bank of Baltimore. The black leather appeared sturdy—like it had been purchased from a quality shop. Carter would have been dumb enough to spend good money on bags to rob a bank he'd throw out at the earliest opportunity.

Only there it was hanging above her skull with a Fed camouflaged by the Cincinnati Chronicle only feet away. If the cop was searching for Frank and her, then the Fed must be prowling round sniffing them out.

He turned his head toward her and she pretended to stare out the window, all the while straining her peripheral vision to figure out whether he was still looking at her. After twenty seconds, which felt like a lifetime, Mary Lou turned to look at him.

She smiled at him hoping to disarm his gaze. To prove he was a Hoover boy, he didn't respond at all, preferring to grind his eyes at her, boring a hole into her. He was one mean mother.

Simon the cop arrived and tapped the Fed on the shoulder. He grinned and stood up to shake Simon's hands.

"How goes it in Federal law enforcement?"

"No complaints, Simon. How's life in the sheriff's office?"

"Don't be like that. I'm a city cop not some local yokel."

"Whatever helps you sleep at night."

The G-man play-punched Simon in the upper arm so she knew they were buddies kidding around.

"You in transit or on the hunt for a master criminal mastermind?"

"Out hunting—and keep your voice down: this is serious."

Mary Lou strained her ears yet again as the men leaned into each other to carry on a private conversation in the middle of the train. She heard 'Baltimore' mentioned and 'couple' which was enough for her to know the Feds were on their case.

A bead of sweat dropped off her ear and landed on her neck; she hoped this wasn't visible to anyone but herself. A transit cop was one thing, but the G-men operated in a different league. With all the whispering she couldn't tell if they had her likeness plastered over local news. They might even have Frank in custody already.

Another drop of perspiration on her neck and a sinking feeling in her stomach. The rational part of her brain processed the information which was panicking her. If they knew what she looked like, they'd have grabbed her by now: they were unlikely to have spotted her and were waiting for her to lead them to Frank. That's not how cops operate.

Mary Lou took a deep breath and considered her options. The longer she stayed in the seat the greater the chance one of these lunks would notice that bag and try to do something about it. She checked her watch and saw she had another hour before she reached Cincinnati. Time to hide in the washroom again.

She shuffled past the two cops and hustled down the aisle hoping her movement wouldn't catch their attention. They'd have to check everyone: the amount of talk could not exceed their efforts to find the felons. The question was how she could avoid them. Despite her strongest desires, Mary Lou knew the washroom was not the long-term solution she craved.

Instead, she considered the problem from every angle until she arrived at a conclusion. The train guard was a pushover and not worth consideration. Simon was a local cop: greedy but fundamentally lazy otherwise he'd have got a promotion and moved on in his life. The only dangerous guy among them was the Fed and he was the one she'd need to charm. But how?

Mary Lou left the washroom and carried on until she reached the baggage car—and walked through. There were a series of cages either side of the usual central aisle. Each cage door was on a latch with bags packed in behind them. There were no locks: the entire system kept the luggage from floating around during the journey and to speed up disembarking.

Flipping the lock mechanism enabled the doors to swing open and for suitcases to fall out of their secure lodgings. Mary Lou bent down and unstrapped a couple of cases to make sure a proper mess was made. She dragged a case along the floor until it was right by the carriage door and visible from outside the car.

Back to the washroom to catch her breath and a wait until the guard spotted the chaos she created. Ten minutes later and she caught the stomping of feet and only then did Mary Lou return to her seat. Simon stormed past her making for the baggage and she knew her plan had worked. She banked on the suspicious flatfoot believing someone had caused the mess as they rushed through. He was close but no cigar.

The Fed was slowly walking along the car and stood between Mary Lou and her seat. He was leaning over people, asking them questions and moving onto the next row of seats. She swallowed hard and headed back past him.

"Excuse me, ma'am."

Mary Lou stared at him to give the impression she wasn't in the habit of talking to strange men on trains just because they looked like cops. The train juddered to a halt and she peered out the window.

"Sorry, but this is my stop."

He lifted his hat and stood aside. Mary Lou rushed past and tried to reach the holdall on the shelf but Frank'd pushed it to the back to prevent it falling and now it was too far away to get any purchase. She only had a minute or two before the train would set off again.

An arm stretched up and took the bag, resting it on a seat. She turned her head to thank the stranger and saw it was the Fed.

"Safe onward journey, ma'am."

"Thanks."

Mary Lou picked up the holdall and got off. She remained there desperately wishing to find Frank and, at the same time, not wanting him to be within a thousand miles of this place until the train—and the Fed—had carried on their way.

FRANK STOOD THE other side of the gate for platform two and saw the train pull in. He waited but there was no sign of Mary Lou. Where was she?

Just before the train pulled away, she appeared with a single black bag and headed toward the gate. The station guard had already explained that Frank was not allowed on the platform without a ticket so he remained where he was until she got past by herself. Then he rushed towards her and picked her up and squeezed. He put her down and they hugged and kissed.

She smelled vanilla around his neck but thought nothing of it because she was so relieved to see him again. She didn't want to let go because she had missed him so but eventually their bodies parted.

Frank and Mary Lou held hands as they sauntered out the station while he led her to the car.

"How was the train?"

"Surrounded by cops."

"Kidding me."

"Not at all. There was a city cop and a G-man."

"Jeez. What happened?"

"The Feds know there's two of us and that we're a couple."

"How?"

"No idea. Man and a woman they said."

"Any descriptions?"

"None that I heard."

"But we don't know."

"No clue. We need to get the hell out of Dodge."

Mary Lou put her bag in the trunk and sat in the passenger seat while he got behind the wheel.

"Take me away from this place, Frank."

He squeezed her knee and reversed out the space before joining the road and heading out on the long haul to Oklahoma City. Once they were trundling along in a straight lane, his hand returned to resting on her thigh.

She enjoyed experiencing the warmth of his fingers on her flesh and relaxed for the first time since they'd parted in Cincinnati. The thought remained at the back of her mind of G-men catching them and dragging him off but, for now, this wasn't her primary concern. Instead, she focused her angst on the long car journey ahead and how she needed to get some sleep before she'd have to take over the wheel from him. Three hours on, three off. Repeat for the fifteen hour trek.

SATURDAY JUNE 21

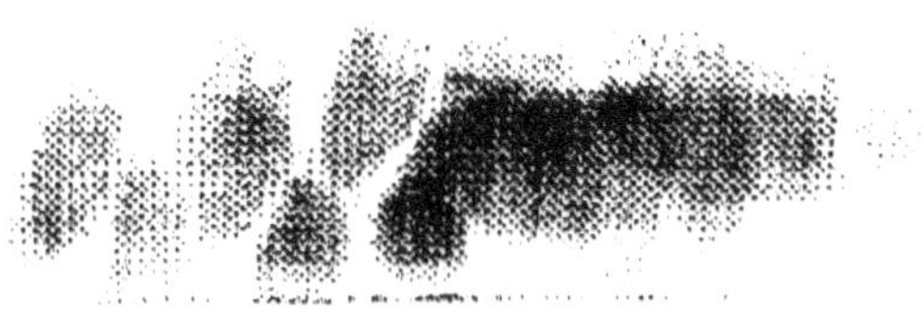

19

IN THE EARLY hours of the morning, Mary Lou woke up with a jolt. Frank had taken the car off the highway and had parked in yet another motel. They all looked the same: he found the ones which were slightly run down with a dark corner in which they could hide. The run-down establishments cared little about their customers provided they paid for their rooms up front.

The other advantages of these low-rent dives was that they were surrounded by equally low-rent bars where characters prop up the counters and deals are available to be done. For this reason, They headed off to grab a bowl of peanuts and a beer.

Food was still being served so Frank grabbed a steak sandwich and Mary Lou took a lamb cutlet. When he made enquiries to the barman where to go if he wanted to buy some weed, the guy carried on wiping the glass in his hand and nodded in Hank's direction at the far end of the bar.

"Hi."

"Hiya."

"I've been told you're the man to see if I'm interested in getting hold of some goods."

"You reckon?"

"That's what I've been told."

"You a cop?"

"Nope. Just a guy with his gal hoping to make a trade."

"Well, I'm going to ask if you are a cop first."

Hank laughed.

"No. What you looking to buy?"

"Are you in the buying and selling business?"

"I can get hold of stuff, for sure."

Frank looked into Hank's eyes. The dude was seventy at least but didn't look like a hippy. If marijuana was his game, he wasn't getting high on his own supply.

"I might have something for you to buy but I need some discretion. Are you up for that or isn't it your bag?"

"I can be cool. What you got?"

"Couple of hundred bucks."

Hank chuckled again.

"You're selling money? Man, you've been at the reefers early buddy."

"I'm serious."

Hank stared at Frank long and hard, sipping at his drink. Eyes checked out every aspect of Frank's appearance.

"The only guy who will be moving cash is sitting on notes they can't take to a financial institution. That money is the cash that's come from a bank —without authorization."

"And?"

"That's outta my league. Love to help a rogue in trouble but I don't get involved in business like that. Not good for my health."

"Thanks for your honesty."

"De nada. If you're feeling the heat, I can offer you a place to hang. Commerce is one thing but helping a rogue is another."

Now it was Frank's turn to stare at Hank. How far could he trust a barfly he'd only just met and whose claim to fame in the local dive bar is that he was the neighborhood drug dealer?

"Got space for me and my lady?"

Frank pointed at Mary Lou with his thumb. She'd stayed by their beers so Hank didn't feel crowded out.

"I have me a plot of land in the woods west of here. I live in one shack and a little way on there's another hut. You and your missus can hole up there for a day or two if you'd like. Nothing fancy but it's dry and no one'll come sniffing around. And if they do, I'll shoot the fucker before they get near you."

Frank raised an eyebrow.

"Don't appreciate trespassers. See?"

"I prefer people who mind their own business too."

The two men shook hands. Frank returned to Mary Lou and explained what he'd agreed.

"Do you trust him?"

"A little. He's smart enough to know we're trouble and sufficiently clever not to ask questions in case he gets answers he doesn't want to hear."

"Will we be safe?"

"Safe enough. Besides, if we don't travel at the speed the Feds expect that'll make it harder for them to pick up our trail. Vanishing for a day or two could be just what we need."

"Or just the opportunity for him to squeal to the Feds."

Frank kissed her on the lips.

"I got a good feeling about him and besides, if he double crosses us I'll put a bullet between his eyes."

HANK HOPPED INTO his car and Mary Lou drove behind him—to give Frank free rein in case matters took a turn for the worse. Instead, they rode for ten minutes until the lane burrowed its way through twists and turns in a wood. Hank slowed and then halted.

"Wait for it."

He ran across the road and opened a gate, hidden by ivy creepers. Lit by the car headlamps, he gave a thumbs-up and used both arms to point at the now-open space. Mary Lou followed him down the dirt track and they both stopped. This time, Frank got out and closed the gate.

Onwards half a mile until they arrived at a clearing inside the wood with two log cabins. Hank drive rightwards and signaled in the opposite direction so Mary Lou drove to the left cabin and parked outside. They were five hundred feet away from Hank and there was nothing but short grass between: nowhere to hide. On the other side of the hut were dense trees as the forest continued to choke the world around it. Frank and Mary Lou took in their bags and Hank appeared a moment later.

"You guys should be fine here. Come and go as you please—just keep the gate shut so's we don't encourage any visitors."

"Thanks Hank."

"Folk like us need to look after each other."

"Like us?"

"Yes missy. People who work outside the conventions of the law."

Mary Lou smiled. Hank was all right.

"One thing I want you to respect though."

"Name it."

"Two hundred feet that-away is a field of vegetation I don't want touched. Reckon you can keep your hands to yourselves?"

"We reckon we can. Is that the weed?"

"Yep. It's my livelihood."

"We respect folks who work hard for what they earn. We won't go messing with the crops."

"Much obliged. Oh, and one other thing, if you want to have any heat in here, you must chop wood out there."

Hank closed the door and was gone.

The cabin comprised a sitting room, a bedroom, a kitchen and a bathroom. All the essentials for life and nothing much more. Mary Lou checked the cupboards and found a tin of condensed milk and some coffee grounds. The living room and bedroom shared a wall with an open fire.

"It is cold in here."

"Yep. I'll get some logs."

Fifteen minutes later, Frank returned with both arms steeped in chopped tree. He threw a match onto the kindling and the flames roared after a moment. They both sat right next to the fire to keep each other company and to gain from the heat of the licking flames. Frank wrapped his arm around her and they relaxed in silence, regaining lost energy from the stress of the day.

"Fancy some Java?"

"For sure, babe."

They went in the kitchen and opened all cupboards until Mary Lou found a small saucepan in one and Frank discovered more matches in another. The faucet produced water and the hob had gas. Within ten minutes two mugs of black coffee sat on the table.

"There'll be bits at the bottom but it should be fine until then."

"Hot and wet. That's all I ask, babe."

"Don't talk dirty. I'm really not in the mood."

Both smiled and they pecked each other on the lips. Then back by the fire, mugs in hand.

"How was your journey?"

"A long road, diner, more driving. The usual. And the train?"

"A lot of stress for one day. A local cop and a Fed sniffing around for bank robbers."

"Trouble?"

"Nearly. I was lucky Cincinnati arrived when it did. I spent way too much time hiding in the john."

"Do you think they made you?"

"Nah. Way too many people on that train with far too much going on for them to notice me in the crowd. But they were planning on doing a more detailed search just as I got off."

"And you reckoned they don't have a description?"

"No, not yet. They've figured out we are a couple. That was the Fed; the locals know nothing—only what the G-men tell them."

"How did they figure out about us?"

"No idea, hon'."

"I mean, who's left alive to snitch?"

20

MARY LOU HAD not wanted to open up these wounds so soon after a sticking plaster had been placed upon them but she had no choice if they were to survive.

"Uncle Frankie. He's alive and we know he's double-crossed you once already this week."

"Makes no sense. Not to me, anyway."

Silence while she stared at him.

"Frankie had more than one heist planned for the same money."

"Huh?"

Frank considered for a minute.

"Carter?"

"Yes."

"That's why he had the bags under his desk."

"Yes."

"How long had you known?"

She felt the tension in his shoulder that was leaning into her body.

"A day. Maybe two. I didn't tell you because I was confused. I wasn't sure what to do. And I was afraid: scared you'd take your anger out on me."

"I see. And was the plan for you and Carter to transport the haul to Frankie and sell the gang down the river?"

"No. This is why my head was all over the place. Carter intended to steal the money from Frankie and leave both of you high and dry. And I did not know what to do. Anyone I told would assume I was lying. I couldn't tell Frankie…"

He put his arm around her and squeezed her shoulders. He understood there was no way she could go near Frankie, given what his uncle had done to her.

"…and I didn't believe I could go to you."

The complex unspoken triangle between Frank, Mary Lou and Uncle Frankie conspired to destroy them all.

"I get it. How did Carter think he could succeed?"

"Well he didn't think you guys would storm into the place first thing. He reckoned he had all day to take the money and run."

"And what about you?"

"Carter's plan was for me to meet him at the back of the bank and drive him out of Dodge."

"And your strategy?"

"Take the money, shoot him and get the hell out of Dodge."

"Nice."

"Heads, Carter escapes with the money and we win. Tails, you leave with the money and we win. I never expected the coin to land on its edge."

"You and me both."

"I'm telling you the truth Frank. I don't want any lies between us but I'm afraid how you'll react now I've told you."

"What's done is done, babe. All we have is each other. We all do things we might regret later on. Stand up people are the ones brave enough to admit the truth out loud."

Mary Lou turned to Frank and they hugged. She nuzzled her head deep against his neck and noticed that vanilla aroma again.

"As we are being honest with each other, I should tell you I missed out a detail about the robbery."

"What was that?"

"I shot Carter in the balls before we left."

Mary Lou pulled away from Frank, recoiling in shock. Tense.

"Wh… why?"

"Because I was jealous of him and because he looked like he was stealing my money. Besides, he was a coward. He let me hurt the bank manager rather than handing the cash over. That was dishonest of him and I didn't appreciate that."

The image of the cashier's slashed breast flashed across Frank's mind but he laid it to rest as soon as it appeared. Another detail he had omitted to mention to Mary Lou.

"So Frankie has informed on us to the FBI?"

"No babe. There's only one thing Frankie'll have done when he worked out we did for Luigi and Paul."

"And that is?"

"He would make phone New York. Give them the bad news early. If the bank was claiming a million dollar loss and it was only half that then you can bet your last nickel that he had over promised and under delivered. So a call was the least that man would need to do."

"Then what?"

"Two things. First Frankie will have sent out other goons after us. And New York will send out some of their guys too."

"Jeez Louise."

"Yep. The New York connection will have influence with the Feds. They always have someone planted in the Bureau. So I'm guessing Uncle Frank told them who was in the gang and they figured out the rest from there."

"So you are saying Frankie's guys and the mob are after us—and the Feds."

"I reckon. To be honest, the Feds are the least of our worries. Frankie won't just need a return of the take: he'll want revenge."

"And the mob?"

"Just the money. For them this will be business and nothing personal—but they are more ruthless than anything Frankie might ever be. And relentless."

"So what are we doing by this fire, Frank? We should run as fast and far go."

"Yes and no. You see, they can calculate how the distance a train, a car and a plane will take us each day and they are able to figure out which cities we are likely to appear in because of that. But if we don't run, then that throws out their calculations. They'll arrive at our destinations too early and we won't show. I'm hoping they will give up and try somewhere else instead."

"And if they stick around and wait to catch us?"

"Wherever we go that will be a problem. Once we obtain some clean money in our wallets, then we can get new identities or leave the country. The ID we are using now? It's fine for now, but Frankie'll figure out who I used to forge them eventually. And the Feds will know soon after."

"What about the mob?"

"Cut them a deal or find out why the take was so low."

"Do you think JH embezzled some of the money?"

"Who?"

"The manager."

"No way. That sniveling lump? Wouldn't steal a dime that wasn't his."

"The rest were too straight too."

"Well if it wasn't someone inside the bank, must be an outside job."

"I always thought it stupid to make that office the one to carry so much cash overnight when the security was hardly there."

"Set up?"

"Yeah. Do you think the branch was dirty? Mob run or owned or something?"

"No idea, babe. Uncle Frank was too low on the totem pole to be anything close to that and the most I saw when I was clambering up it was his ass bearing down on me."

"Might explain a thing or two though."

"For sure. Right now we are in the middle of a wood where only one person knows we are alive. Hank might sell weed instead of earning an honest buck, but I trust that hemp weaver more than I do my family."

"Know what you mean, hon'. He seems a stand-up guy."

"He'll be a local yokel who wants to stick it to the man."

"You know a man who wants to stick it to someone close?"

"Now who's talking dirty?"

Mary Lou cupped her hand around Frank's cheek and they kissed. With the flames still roaring away, they skipped into the bedroom and hurried under the blankets. Clothing flew out from under the covers: pants, blouse, shorts and panties. Before the fire turned into glowing embers, they fell asleep wallowing in their own juices.

FRANK SLEPT FITFULLY despite the pleasure of sharing a bed with Mary Lou. His mind flitted in a thousand directions—from Uncle Frankie to the Feds to the mob and back to the woman sleeping beside him. Every time he thought about one idea another thing pushed to the front of his consciousness. Lying naked and sticky next to Mary Lou, all he could smell was that waitress's vanilla body.

As he drifted off to sleep, Frank thought about the three men who'd died in the last few days: Pete the Wheels, Andrew and Brian. They had all known the risks, for sure, but that didn't mean he was freed from the responsibility for their bullet-riddled corpses.

Pete was a vicious piece of work. Would spit on your shoe soon as look at you. A classic Southern States redneck with grits coursing through his veins, He was a great driver but showed himself to have anger management issues and was intolerant of people who didn't share his white skin color. A streak of sadistic violence ran through him too so you needed to be careful what you said and what you did near him.

His no-nonsense approach to life was in stark contrast with Frank. He might get hot-headed but his nuanced perspective meant he had been able to keep Mary Lou and manage a gang of bank robbers. She grounded him well; spending time in the joint calmed him down and helped him to focus on what was important. First getting out the can and now California—almost a year since he'd vowed to himself that was where he was heading.

Pete's scrawny face hovered in Frank's mind's eye. He was a scary dude when you were in the same room as him but his clinical approach to every heist was the one benefit of having him around. Apart from the fact he could drive a car.

What would Pete do if he were Frank? Simple: run like a crazy mother until he reached Vegas. Then he'd play fast and loose until he had enough scratch to create options for himself. The man would kill to stay free—the same way he had murdered Martin almost a year ago.

Frank lapsed into unconsciousness with the image of Pete the Wheels driving from Vegas to the Canadian border. And just as he got to the customs house, he vanished from his sports car in a puff of gun smoke leaving the vehicle awash with blood pouring out the windows like a burst faucet.

Sunday June 22

21

FRANK WOKE UP before six in a sea of sweat. Although he had slept, he was not refreshed. He rolled over to see Mary Lou's ass, round and perfectly smooth. One of his fingers stroked her to appreciate her beauty and she stirred, flicking his finger away like it was a fly.

He moved his head to lick her and she swatted him in the face. Dang insect. She turned over onto her back and he was close enough to the rose to reach the stem. Mary Lou giggled a sleepy joy.

"Go on then. While you're down there, you might as well do some good."

THEY DOZED FOR an hour and later, Frank awoke feeling more refreshed than before. He rubbed his eyes and found himself alone. Then Mary Lou appeared with a mug of coffee for each of them. She nuzzled next to him and they petted in between slurps of brown liquid.

At nine, she glanced at her watch, rolled off her man and jumped out of bed, leaving Frank without any blankets.

"We've a long drive ahead if we're ever to make Vegas."

"Eighteen hours I reckon."

"Another overnight motel, then?"

"Yep."

By the time they got to Vegas, the mob would be there waiting for them and, as Frank had pointed out, there was no need to rush into their arms. An extra night's sleep would set them up for when they did eventually arrive in town, but the cabin was a little snippet of luxurious safety they hadn't known in a long while—and were unlikely to see again for even longer.

They shuffled round the rooms searching for clothes and anything else which might tie them to this place if the cops ever came calling. Bags packed, money accounted for, they put everything back in their car.

Frank stomped off to the other cabin to speak with Hank but no dice.

"Not there."

"Shall we leave a note?"

"No, nothing but our memories."

Mary Lou pecked him on the cheek.

"Let's meet our destiny."

She scuttled off and got behind the wheel, waiting for Frank to catch up. Once they returned to the tarmac, she hit the gas but never went more than five miles below the speed limit until it was Frank's turn to take over. Mary Lou shifted the passenger seat rearward as far as it would go to give plenty of stretch. His hand landed on her leg and the comfort of his fingers helped her to drift off to sleep.

TUESDAY JUNE 24

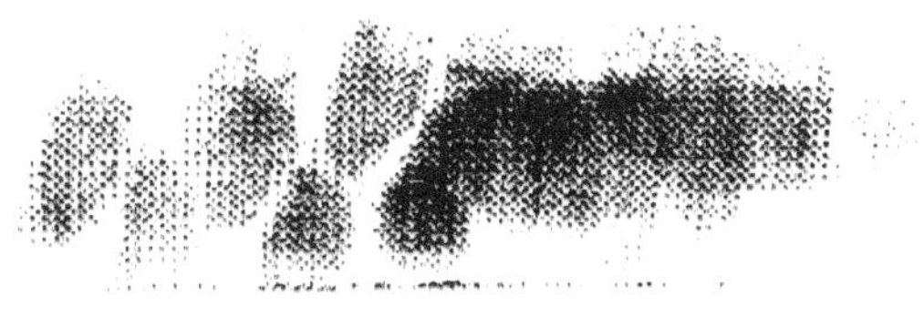

22

MARY LOU DROVE the car into Las Vegas, crossing the city line just before one in the morning. They came in off the Salt Lake Highway and followed the train tracks until she halted outside the Union Pacific Railroad Station.

"You want north or south?"

Frank eyed both options in the neon-lit night.

"It's the same either way. Mint or Queens Hotel: you decide."

She chose North Main Street and stopped the car in the Mint Hotel parking lot.

"Looks like we've arrived."

Frank fished out their fake ID and left Mary Lou while he walked inside to book a room. They'd have a soft mattress and hot running water soon. When he returned with a key, they carried their bags themselves and, for the second time, Frank refused the offer of help from the bellboy. He had the smarts to give the guy a tip, anyway. The last thing they needed in the first hour in Vegas was for some teenager with an attitude to spill his guts to a fella with connections.

Their room faced onto Fremont and looked almost directly at the Queens Hotel and the Golden Nugget. This was a gambling town for sure. The entire city reeked of greenbacks and hard luck. Even though there were famous names packing the theaters with cabaret chic, if you stayed in Las Vegas long, you needed money to burn and a barrel of self belief.

"We can't keep these bags with us the whole time and they can't stay in this room either."

"Trip to the lost luggage at the station?"

"I reckon."

"In the morning, honey."

"We have to assume the mob will be here soon and all they want is the money—and that's all we got."

"Jeez."

"It's getting real, babe. I can taste it too."

"Let me with you."

"No. Stay hear and run us a bath: I'll only be two minutes. It's a swanky hotel: let's take advantage of it."

Mary Lou watched as Frank pulled out a handful of notes and zipped the bag back up. He placed the extra green in his pants pocket and walked out the door with both bags. Down in reception, people were coming and going—unlike any other hotel he had seen. The casinos never sleep.

Over the road, he found the lockers for in-transit folks and opened one at the far end of a row near the floor-to-ceiling window. Nobody could get close to them without being spotted—and they couldn't leave without getting cornered.

Frank stuffed a bag in a locker and found an adjacent one for the second holdall. He popped quarters into both and held the two keys in his fist all the way back to the Mint. Through the busy reception and up the elevator to the fourth floor. Turned left then right and used his hotel key to enter room 409.

He heard Mary Lou singing to herself and the splashing of water. Frank appeared round the bathroom door and saw a bath filled with soapy bubbles and Mary Lou's head bobbing above the surface. He imagined he made out the curves of her body but all he saw was the white froth.

"Come in and get warm."

Frank threw his clothes off and stepped in to join her. She rubbed the grime off his torso as he sat between her thighs and then they lay in the suds stroking and massaging each other. She had thrown a towel near enough for her to dry her hands and light a cigarette which they shared.

Then they wallowed in the tepid liquid as the silence of the night engulfed them—interspersed by the giggling drunk sounds of patrons heading out to the tables or back to their rooms to console themselves over their losses. But Frank and Mary Lou were content in that bathtub sensing each other's hairs without words.

Twice they emptied the water and topped up with more hot. Mary Lou saw her wrinkled fingers and wondered if that was what she'd be like when she was in her eighties. Then she laughed inside, knowing she and Frank were not the sort of people to grow old at all.

They dried each other off with the abundant quantity of towels provided by the Mint and slipped into bed.

"These are crazy days, babe."

"Sure, hon'. We've just got to be ready for whatever comes our way."

"You said it. They're after us and chances are they are already here waiting."

"If we're getting the take laundered, this is the best place to be."

"Yep. Which is why they're here. They know that too because the mob cleans all the money in this town."

"But then we will be free to head for the border."

"Sure will. Get away from this hell hole."

"Together."

Frank looked at her, smiled and touched her cheek.

"Yes, together. We'll make it out of here."

"Or die trying."

He nodded, not wanting to express that thought out loud. Mary Lou didn't mind: the truth never scared her—lies and secrets kept her awake at night and the two of them had their fill of both these past few days and weeks.

"We're in this together. Don't you forget that mister."

"I know. That's what keeps me going: being with you and wanting to spend the rest of my life with you on some beach."

"Steady Frank. Next thing you'll be down on one knee and proposing."

"Would there be anything wrong in us getting hitched?"

Mary Lou thought for a minute and realized this man may not be perfect, but he was the only guy she'd ever met who looked after her without a slap or a punch.

"Nothing at all but I'm too tired to think about it tonight."

Frank fell asleep first and snored straight away while she stayed awake thinking about marriage and the mob. Half an hour later, she was snoring loudly too.

THEY WALKED DOWN South Main until they turned right onto Charleston. This end of the strip contained several bars and financing firms. They catered for a particular segment of visitor: the ones with little money and even lower chance of getting any.

The couple were heading to a loan shark recommended to them by the concierge at the Mint. This was the best option in the absence of any of Frank's own contacts because he'd admitted to Mary Lou he couldn't be sure he could trust them. Inside the building, Frank eyed the pawnbrokers and checked out the loot lining the shelves behind the counter. The usual mix of jewelry, musical instruments and firearms were packed onto every inch of the walls.

"Wonder if you can help?"

"What you got?"

The proprietor sat on a stool, elbows leaning on the glass surface.

"I have some merchandise and I've been told you're the fella to see."

"Oh? A recommendation. Who's been so kind?"

"The concierge at the Mint Hotel."

"Good guy."

"He brought us to you, so yes."

"So what you got?"

"It's tricky."

"Come into the back for a more private conversation."

He nodded and they followed Richard through a door behind his stool. The room contained a desk and three chairs.

"Talk to me about your delicate situation."

Frank looked round and could see nothing to give him a clue whether he could trust this man.

"I have some money."

"Then you don't need me then."

"Well, this cash can't be spent—not retail."

"How dirty and how hot is it?"

"Very hot and exceedingly dirty."

Mary Lou stared at Richard's expression desperate to divine if he was a stand-up guy.

"I see. And the obvious question: how much you got?"

"Right now I'm looking to offload a few hundred dollars."

"But there's more?"

"Don't you worry about that. Let's deal with what's on the table."

"Okay. Nothing personal but how hot is the cash?"

"Hot."

"Hot as in traceable or fresh from a robbery?"

"You need to price up your services. I get it. And yes, this is larceny hot."

"Your East Coast accents make me think you're from somewhere like Baltimore."

"Do they?"

"I reckon. And if you've come from out there then I cannot help you. Nothing personal you understand."

"Why does that put us out of your reach?"

"Word from above. That's why."

"You connected?"

Richard sat back in his chair and strummed his fingers on the armrest.

"If you're in my business, you can't work alone. You always need others in a similar line."

"And?"

"And if I take on a risk, I must offset it somewhere."

"I thought all the junk out front was collateral for secured loans."
Richard laughed.

"The trash is collateral but you know I make more money out of the conversations here. For those kinds of deal I call for backup—and some of that support is Italian."

"Thanks for your honesty."

"No problem. Just telling you how it is."

"And will we get the same response from everyone else we approach?"

"Pretty much. Anyone who can afford frontage here is tied to our Italian cousins. There may be an independent operator in Vegas but you won't find them anywhere near the strip."

"And they'll be small potatoes?"

"Yep. They could work your few hundred but nothing else. You'll need an outfit without East Coast connections for that much action."

Frank and Mary Lou looked at each other.

"And once we leave, are you going to mention this conversation to your associates?"

"Not planning on it. This is a deal that didn't happen."

"Is there no order to report our whereabouts then?"

"But I operate based on trust. How could conduct any transactions if every time someone entered my shop they wound up dead? That'd be bad for business."

"No bounty on our heads then?"

"You're not Bonnie and Clyde."

Mary Lou laughed out loud and the two men turned to her.

"Sorry."

"No harm done."

"I won't lie to you. Tomorrow, I'll make a call and let a person know you came visiting. But I'm in no hurry because the percentage isn't big enough for me to want to rush and rat you out."

"Honor among thieves."

"I'm no thief. I offer cash for clear repayment terms."

"Don't kid yourself. Takes one to know one."

They all shook hands and Richard led them back into the shop. As they headed for the door, Frank stopped to check out some gold jewelry.

"This for sale?"

He pointed at a tray in the display.

"Yes but not with your money. I won't be able to use it."

Frank nodded and walked away.

"What are you interested in?"

He showed him the item and Mary Lou smiled.

"You got any real green on you? The sort you can spend without the cops coming down like flies on shit?"

Frank put his hands in his pants pocket and drew out half the notes from his wallet. Richard took a dollar bill and Frank pocketed the goods.

"Must be your lucky day."

"Much appreciate your generosity."

"I hope you get where you're going before our Italian friends catch up with you."

Out the pawnbrokers and right down Charleston until they went on Las Vegas Boulevard. Two blocks away ran a line of casinos. As they approached, the number of people on the sidewalk increased until they slowed to a crawl by the time they reached the Sahara, the Thunderbird and the Riviera at the end.

"Where's your locker key?"

Mary Lou had one and Frank the other—if they caught either of them, the other still had a quarter of a million to play with.

"In my panties. I figured if I'm stopped nobody's gonna frisk me down there."

"You are a sexy smart cookie. Do you think Richard kept his word?"

"Would you, babe?"

"No, I'd take the money."

"You and me both."

"Better keep an eye out."

"Like never before."

They held hands and judged the expression of every single face that passed them on the street.

23

"WE NEED TO find an independent operator, wouldn't you say?"

"Yes, hon'."

Frank led them left onto Desert Inn Road and right to Paradise Valley. With a golf course on one side and the Convention Center on the other, they both looked out for anything like a pawnbroker without mob connections. Neither had any clue how to recognize one, but they searched anyway.

In the hinterland beyond the back of the Sands lay a row of shops which bled into the desert ahead. There was a market, a gunsmith and a pawnbroker.

"What you reckon?"

"Only way to find out is to go inside."

"Yes, babe."

"But what if it's not safe? Then what?"

"Okay. I'll pop in and browse to check it out."

Mary Lou stood there and lit a cigarette to pass the time until Frank returned two minutes later.

"Well?"

"Can't say. There are no Italian accents if that's what you mean. But I have no idea."

"Better give it a wide berth."

"Yep."

As they carried on walking down the street, Mary Lou kept deciding every man she sauntered past was a gangster. No matter what they looked like, she couldn't shake the memory of that train journey from her head. Greased-back hair and a three piece dark suit: this was the uniform of old-school New York organized crime.

Frank was no better. He saw the same men and asked the same question: is this guy connected? He had no way of telling the answer by looking. Then he considered the possibility the mob weren't heading towards them, but were behind them instead.

He forced Mary Lou to duck into a shop window to give an opportunity to check who was walking a block away. Just a bunch of people minding their own business.

"They know what we look like, don't they babe?"

"Yeah. Is it time for a change of appearance?"

"Fresh hair color for both of us and a cut for you. New clothes and see what happens."

"A hair cut for you too?"

Frank stared at her and ran his fingers through his locks.

"I could shave it all off but there's only one way to brush this mop."

He had a point. His average hair length was about half an inch.

"Turning you bald will make you stand out more than ever. Are you going blond?"

"Dunno. What color do you want to go to?"

"Jet black with a bob. It's all the rage."

Frank nodded like he knew what she was talking about and they carried on until they reached a pharmacy to buy hair dye and a pair of scissors. They continued on their journey to find an elusive Shylock without mob connections.

An hour later, they had traveled to the far edge of town but found nobody to fit the description. Instead they circled around several times to evade potential mobsters although none appeared to be real. The one thing they could be certain was that if the outfit tracked them down, they'd know about it.

Back at the Mint, Mary Lou cut her hair while Frank watched inches of blond fall onto the floor. His Mary Lou was altering before his eyes and, no matter how disappointed he was feeling, she would hurt more. Women hold a different attitude to their looks than men, he noted.

Before she'd finished, he strode into the bathroom and ruined some hotel towels with his hair dye: from brown to a yellow blond in less than an hour. Mary Lou joined him and blacked out what was left of her mane. With the bottles of chemicals spent, she turned to the mirror and stared at herself. She appeared so different, but the bob suited her, even though it looked so jarring right now.

Frank glanced at his reflection as a final check he hadn't missed anywhere but he didn't care either way. What was important to him was surviving their time in Vegas and laundering the take.

"What are we going to do? We're still stuck with the dirty money."
"I've got an idea about that we can try tonight."
"Oh?"
"But first I should check if you did a good job on your hair."
"What do you mean?"
Mary Lou headed straight back to the mirror in the bathroom and could see nothing wrong. Frank followed her in and stood behind her. She watched his arms wrap around her torso and his hands land on her breasts.
"I need to check whether the carpet matches the drapes."
He pushed his fingers under her skirt and panties until a shiver ran up her spine from her crotch to her neck. She pulled out his hand and led him to the bedroom, giggling.

THEY WOKE IN the middle of the afternoon, Mary Lou first by the noise of her stomach rumbling. For a second she wondered what her head was doing at the foot of the bed. She remembered and smiled. Stretched her arms and legs, almost kicking Frank in the face. The covers were on the floor and she grabbed a corner and threw it over them.
He opened an eye and hugged her ankles, then he licked her calves and carried on working his way up her body, stopping near her rose, until his head took over her entire field of vision. She felt the warmth of his crotch on hers and relaxed into the tenderness of the moment.
"Wait one minute."
Frank leaped off her and Mary Lou frowned—she'd been enjoying what he was up to and could see no reason to stop. The day was a washout, but they sure had fun in the evening, a brief respite from the horrors of their situation.
He bounded back and kneeled in between her legs, forcing her knees apart. He placed one hand on a thigh, stroking it occasionally but his other formed a fist, tightly clutching something.
"We've been together a long time, right?"
"Sure, Frank."
Mary Lou couldn't help letting her mind wander as he spoke because of the tingles he was generating with his palm and her thigh.
"Through thick and thin."
"Oh yes."
He realized his fingers were getting too much attention, so he removed them from her, damp as they were.
"No, listen."
"Ow, all right."

She chuckled and placed both her hands on his dick.

"No, stop it, Mary Lou. I've got something serious I want to say."

She relented and lay there, listening. The last time Frank was this focused he had told her about the bank robbery and his plans for California.

"You've been there for me—even when I was inside. And I hope you think I've been there for you too."

"You have, hon'."

Mary Lou remembered how supportive he had been when his uncle had laid hands on her. She gritted her teeth and relaxed them again as Frank's words soothed her.

"And I may not have always done the right thing, but I always tried."

"I know Frank. We work well together—and you fit so brilliantly inside me."

Another giggle.

"There is that. But more to the point, there's one phrase I have never told you: I love you. And I do."

She'd spoken it to him but Frank found a way to not respond in kind. To be fair, when Mary Lou said it she didn't always mean it. But sometimes it's the right thing to say—like when a guy has fucked you so much you can barely breathe. Memories of Miami floated into her head and she smiled inside.

"And I love you, hon'."

"We've never been as close as we are now. Here in a cheap Las Vegas hotel room, I feel we're inseparable, you and me."

She beckoned for him to kiss her and then he sat back up.

"So, if we are indivisible, we should do something about it."

"Like what?"

He unclenched his fist to reveal a gold ring and Mary Lou's eyes widened.

"Mary Lou Belle: will you marry me?"

"Francis Lagotti. Yes I will."

She uttered those words without thinking. He was the only guy ever to consider such a thing. Every other guy wanted to fuck her and walk away. No one else cared about her. Not even Carter. She realized he was just a lonely man swimming in seas he didn't understand.

But married. How crazy was that? If anyone would make her happy, it was the fella sat with his dick dangling in front of her face right here and now.

Frank tried to put the band on her finger but it was too large. Instead, he bent down to kiss her and Mary Lou wrapped her legs around his body. She didn't let go until all the tingles ceased running up and down her spine many minutes later.

FRANK GLANCED AT his watch and placed three fingers on her cheek. She smiled but kept her eyelids shut. He stroked her skin and then stopped.

"Aw. I was enjoying that."

"As much as I'd like my hand to go wandering again, if we haul ass now, there's enough time to get a license before the place shuts."

Mary Lou's eyes opened and she grabbed his fingers and put them in her mouth for a second.

"What're we doing here? Let's go!"

She leaped out of bed and threw on some clothes—the ones left lying on the floor were easiest to find. Frank did the same. They ran down the strip to reach the Marriage License Bureau before five. They had twenty minutes.

One fast walk along Fremont from their hotel and a brisk right three blocks south took them to the Bureau. Two couples were ahead of them and they waited on line.

With moments to go, Frank and Mary Lou sat opposite a Clark County official who read them their legal obligations and duties while they provided various bits of information as requested. While they were heading over, they agreed to use their real names so the marriage wouldn't be some sham affair. By the time the County had filed the paperwork and made it available for public view, they'd be long gone out the state. They completed and signed the forms using the guy's fountain pen. The ink flowed smoothly onto the administrative pieces of paper.

"Congratulations. Now you have a year to get yourselves married anywhere in the state. You can find a chapel or there is always the Office of Civil Marriages."

His eyes narrowed, with disapproval showing across his face. They thanked him for his help and left clutching their license.

"You want a church, babe?"

"Hell no. God turned his back on me when I was fifteen and I've no need to go looking for his approval for anything that I do, sonofabitch."

"Fine by me. God's done nothing for me. And if he has, I'm damned if I noticed."

They kissed and sauntered over to the Mint, all the time keeping an eye out for the mob, the Feds and Frankie's boys.

WEDNESDAY JUNE 25

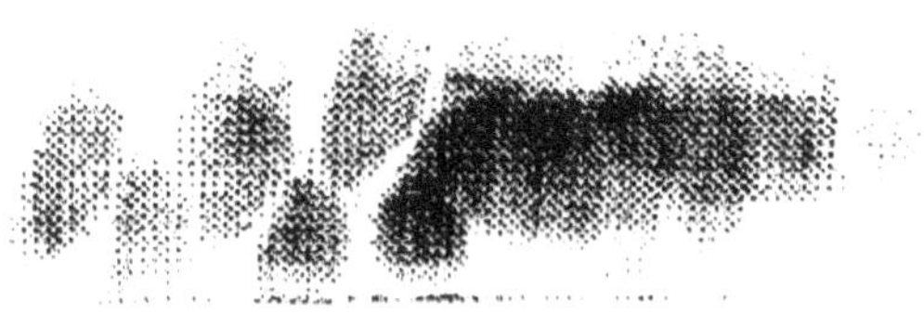

24

THE OFFICE OF Civil Marriages was around the corner from the License Bureau and contained all the charm of a municipal building. High ceilings offered a cathedral quality to the venue but you couldn't mistake the smell of musty paperwork and old files. If someone threw a match in the wrong direction, the whole place would go up in flames.

Mary Lou stood at the entrance and looked up at the vaulted ceiling.

"Hold my hand; I feel tiny."

Frank did as he was bid and they sauntered inside. He couldn't help but notice the security guard at the door and scoped out the reception area for police and other armed government officials but a squeeze from Mary Lou reminded him why they were there.

One brief enquiry with a woman at a counter sent them in the right direction down a corridor. At the far end were a series of benches and several couples sat waiting. Each time a couple returned, everyone shuffled forwards until Frank and Mary Lou were next in line, in front of a never-ending slithering snake.

The betrothed talked to each other about where they'd come from, honeymoons and how they met. They tried not to engage with them because every person they spoke to was another rat. Suddenly Mary Lou turned to the girl sat next to her.

"Will you be our witness? We've been in such a hurry, we forgot to ask one of our friends to come along."

"Sure thing, if you'll return the favor."

"Happy to."

Frank scowled, but Mary Lou leaned in to him and whispered: "You need a witness, hon' otherwise it's not official."

She was so wrapped in her own thoughts, this was the first time she looked around to see what everyone was doing. With disappointment, she noticed she was the only one not wearing a wedding dress.

"Frank. My outfit: all the girls are in their Sunday best. And what have I got?"

Frank saw her eyes redden.

"It's not your clothes that count, but what's in your heart that matters, babe."

He was right and she smiled and wiped the dampness off her left cheek. The door opened and a happy couple appeared. Now it was their turn. Rows of chairs lined the room; a desk stood at the far end, a chair and an official sat upon the latter.

"Come in."

The man behind the table beckoned them nearer and Mary Lou, Frank and their witness scurried toward the distant figure.

"This won't take long—and don't worry. Everything will be fine."

Frank held Mary Lou's hand and the girl stood to one side. Chuck got up and walked round to stand with the two of them.

A marriage ceremony is the verbalization of a contract between willing parties and once you've stripped out all the guff about God and worship, you're left with a simple proposition: do you take—and so on. Once Chuck covered all the legal bases, he pronounced them man and wife.

"You may kiss the bride."

The girl smiled and gave them a brief ripple of applause. Everyone with a writing hand signed paperwork and Chuck ushered them out the room. They turned round immediately to witness Trudy's nuptials. Stood outside the Office of Civil Marriages, Trudy and her new husband William asked them if they'd like to go to a bar to celebrate but they declined.

"We're heading out of town this afternoon. Off on our honeymoon straight away."

"Ooh, where?"

"Hawaii."

"Sounds wonderful. We'll stay in Vegas and then head to San Francisco tomorrow."

Frank shook hands and Mary Lou kissed Trudy. Then they walked in whatever direction was the opposite to their newfound friends.

"Let's hole up at the Mint, babe. The longer we are on the street, the worse it is for us."

As they headed up Las Vegas Boulevard, Mary Lou saw a suit a hundred feet behind them.

"Kiss me."

She twisted round on the sidewalk so she could face what she thought she'd noticed in her peripheral vision and Frank complied because he detected the note of authority in her voice. He remained with his back to the potential threat.

"What you seen?"

"Possible Fed. They all dress the same and he looks as though he is in the same uniform as the G-man on the train."

"Spotted him?"

"Yes, he's stopped to check out a shoe store window. Must like the heels."

"Let's walk half a block and see what happens."

Arm in arm, they strolled along the sidewalk allowing everyone to storm past them. If the guy was a civilian, he'd have to catch up with them soon because of their ridiculous slow pace. One minute later they stopped to kiss again, like the lovebirds they were.

"And now where is he?"

"Still hundred feet behind. Maybe a hundred fifty."

Frank eyed their vicinity and took Mary Lou toward a women's boutique.

"He won't want to follow us in here or stand outside."

She knew he was right: the place was a lingerie store and no Hoover man wanted to hang around lady's panties for long.

They grabbed some items off the hangers and she asked the location of the cubicles. A sales assistant pointed to the back of the retail outlet.

"You don't mind if my husband joins me. We've just got married."

Mary Lou giggled coquettishly and the helper agreed.

"Well, as there's no one else trying anything on."

The changing rooms comprised a series of cubicles with a curtain and a door leading out. Frank tried the handle and it opened without effort. He took a glance outside and came back inside.

"It's an alleyway."

"Can I take the bra and panties set? They're divine."

"You're not a thief, babe. We're hardened criminals on the lam. Come on."

Mary Lou dropped the underwear and followed Frank out the door. Ten minutes later they were at the Mint with no sign of any G-man in their wake.

PHIL MCNAMARA AND Ted Goodwin stepped onto the Union Pacific platform with one carry bag each and headed out the Las Vegas station. Fed sources were certain the couple was in the city but Phil had no idea who were these sources. If he had known the mob was the source of their information, he might not have been so keen to head west.

They stood on the sidewalk and hailed a taxi to their hotel, the Hacienda was near the interstate and opposite the Tropicana, way down Las Vegas Boulevard at the far end of the strip.

After they checked in, McNamara called his local office.

"There've been several potential sightings of our couple but nothing confirmed."

"How many men are on the ground searching?"

McNamara looked down at the floor.

"Just the two but I'm assured they're very good."

"They'd need to be to cover an entire city. What gives, Phil?"

"Upstairs wants to catch the Lansdowne gang and recover the money but you have no idea the rivalry between all the offices. The FBI is a series of mini kingdoms. Hoover plays one against the other. The whole thing is a mess."

Goodwin listened in disbelief.

"I always thought you guys would be different. It's just like in Baltimore only with bigger cases. We are in trouble."

"Yeah. The good news is that the information we've gathered has been mighty accurate. First those waitresses gave an excellent steer on the couple and our New York sources have sent us here."

"How did New York here about this?"

"We have several undercover operations in progress and they pick up all sorts of gen."

Goodwin nodded to show he understood but Phil hadn't answered his question. If well-placed persons in the Five Boroughs knew about the Lansdowne gang, there was far more to this caper than a bank robbery.

Sounded more like something mob-run and that made Ted nervous. He was a small town cop out of his home state chasing down a million dollars in cash. What world was he living in?

"Let's get out there and catch us some bad guys."

"Yep, Phil."

They strolled up and down the strip hoping to see a man and woman matching the description Glenda and Lucy had provided but no joy. Hardly surprising—they didn't even know if the pair were still in town. Needle in a haystack.

"Shall we split up and cover twice the area?"

"Sure. Can't hurt. Let's meet at the hotel in two hours."

"Sounds like a plan."

Goodwin prowled round the strip until he reached the Union Pacific Railroad where he took a right onto Fremont past the Mint Hotel. Then back on Las Vegas Boulevard followed by the left fork of Paradise Valley Road.

The places on this drag were less fancy and would be where criminals might head.

As he sauntered, hands in pockets, he noticed a couple kissing in the middle of the sidewalk. This was not what people did: strange. He halted at a store window to keep an eye on them and realized he was facing shelves of women's shoes. Too late. Looking for his wife, maybe?

The pair continued and Goodwin carried on following from three hundred feet away. They stopped again, so he ducked into another store window. Had they made him? Again, off they trawled twenty feet and then it was their turn to duck into a lady's emporium. He continued walking towards them hoping to get a better look.

By the time he'd caught up, they were inside somewhere. Then his cheeks reddened as he saw the underwear—panties and bras in all shapes, colors and sizes—hanging in the window. There was no way he could stay outside here to wait for them to come out. Goodwin moved on, not even certain if the pair was anything less than a lovey-dovey type. An hour later he met up with McNamara.

"Any luck?"

"Perhaps. There was one couple I saw but I can't be sure. She had a black bob and he was blond."

"That's not the description though."

"No, but their features looked like the artist's impression. And anyone can dye their hair."

"If you thought it was them, why didn't you carry on following them?"

"Because I wasn't sure and because… well… they popped into a lady's apparel boutique."

McNamara laughed. "You were afraid of a pair of panties?" He carried on chuckling so much so that Goodwin got annoyed.

"Keep your wig on. It's not that funny. And besides, a single man walking into a place like that would have let them know they were being followed."

"You crack me up. You fell for the oldest trick in the book: embarrass a cop with lace and fluttering eyelashes."

McNamara broke out into laughter again and Goodwin sat and seethed. Once he'd calmed down, McNamara called the Vegas FBI office and let his people know the description might be wrong about hair color. Later they dined in their hotel. Steak and coffee, then they agreed to hit the casinos hoping to spot their fugitives in the hustle and bustle of life on the nighttime strip.

FRANK AND MARY Lou stood in the lobby, holding hands. The adjusted wedding band still felt strange on her finger, not so much digging into her flesh as just there. Married. It was good if uncomfortable.

"Best if we lie low for a while. The streets aren't safe for us, babe."

"You said it. Where shall we go?"

"I owe you a honeymoon."

"We owe each other a honeymoon, Frank. Where were you thinking?"

"I know a little place not too far from here."

Mary Lou's expression scrunched up quizzically. He dragged her toward the elevators and hit a button. Perhaps they were off to the top floor. Two seconds after they'd started their ascent, the elevator stopped and the doors opened. Frank took them out. No rooftop bar, then. They padded along the carpeted corridor until they arrived at their room. He looked at her and smiled.

Inside he helped her take off all her clothes and then she reciprocated. They stood naked opposite each other soaking in the sight of the other. Then he stroked her fingers—ever so gently—and their fingertips touched. He ran a finger over her palm, up her arm and around the front of her neck. Then it followed a downward trajectory and cascaded over her left breast, over her heart, and toward her belly button. Then it reached the top most petal of her rose and downwards, heading to the base of the tattoo's stem.

Tingles ran up and down her spine but she stood there, soaking in the rapture of the moment. Motionless.

Frank stepped closer and kissed her on the lips, his other hand caressing the back of her neck. She raised one leg and wrapped it around his calf—and then as high past his knee as she could manage. He held her so she didn't lose her balance. They carried on kissing and the tingles increased.

Within a few minutes they were lying on the bed, Mary Lou licking Frank's chest and stomach. She looked up, along his torso to his head. His eyes were closed and she sensed the strength of the muscles in his body. This was the man she was married to. With his brown-dyed hair and half a million bucks. Mrs. Mary Lou Belle Lagotti. She carried on kissing him until his moaning began. Then she giggled and stopped.

Frank opened his eyes, questioning, as she made her way back up his torso to kiss him on the lips. As she did so, the intensity of Frank's kissing meant he'd figured out her plan too. Ten minutes later, Mary Lou slithered off and lay next to him. He stared at the ceiling and moved an arm so Mary Lou's head could use it as a pillow. She stroked his chest with a hand.

"Happy honeymoon."

"Straight back at you, babe."

"That was lovely."

"Straight back at you, babe."

"Is that all you can say?"

"Pretty much, yes. You've a mighty powerful rose down there."

A flashback to the tingles which screamed through her brain in intense pulses only a few moments before.

"I love honeymoons!"

"Me too, babe."

Given the physical exertion, they dozed until the late afternoon merged with the early evening and her stomach rumbled loud enough to wake Frank and stir herself.

"Should we call room service?"

"It is our honeymoon after all."

Half an hour after they ordered food came a knock on the door. Mary Lou scuttled into the bathroom, still naked, and Frank put on a robe and held a gun behind his back.

The bellboy walked in with a tray and Frank hid the weapon before pulling a note out of his wallet, passing it to the boy in a handshake—the time-honored method of delivering a tip.

Once they'd eaten, Mary Lou flopped onto the bed to rest and digest. Frank cleaned his firearm and then he checked the revolver he'd given to her. Never can be too careful.

"What we gonna do now, hon'?"

"We need to get ourselves some clean money, babe."

"Any ideas?"

"Yep. We should play the wheels."

"Huh?"

"By the time we come back tonight, we'll have two hundred bucks in good notes. But you must put some clothes on before we can start."

Mary Lou used one finger to beckon him toward her.

"In that case, you'd better finish your marital duties before we do anything else, Mr. Lagotti."

She opened her legs and Frank lay in between them. Forty-five minutes later, they left the room hunting for a roulette wheel. In any other town, that would have been a tall order, but this was Las Vegas, the gambling capital of the world.

25

CHARLIE PENTANGELO SENT word to his Las Vegas colleagues that he needed some help. The promise of a finder's fee also focused minds. The Jewish community arrived early in the city when Bugsy Siegel saw the potential for an oasis in the sand and, in liaison with some Italian New York friends, several casinos sprung up as vehicles for the East Coast gangs to make a thundering amount of money.

Charlie's interest in Frank and Mary Lou reached Paulie who oversaw the mob operations throughout the Flamingo casino and hotel. What Charlie asked, you wanted to deliver—especially when greenbacks were involved.

Paulie greeted Angelo and Rico from the Five Boroughs and they hit the streets to find the man and woman who'd stolen Charlie's cash. There's nobody worse than a thief who steals. Paulie felt nothing but contempt for Frank and Mary Lou.

The three men walked all day and found nada. Lots of couples but none fitting the description provided by their source in the FBI. They also had the inside track from the Baltimore Shylock.

Rico reckoned the smart thing to do was not to walk round town trying to find two people in tens of thousands. The way he saw it, neither Paulie nor Angelo cared whether they found the man and the woman—what they wanted was the money. So instead of asking about the couple, Rico thought he should ask himself where he had hide a million dollars in cash if he was new to the city.

His answer was telling: bury it somewhere or shove it in a safe. Vegas was surrounded by a desert, so if he buried the take, there was no way anyone would ever find it. If he'd stored it with a hotel, he had a chance. A trip around town revealed only one new couple who had asked reception to put aside sufficiently large bags to fit that much cash. Trouble was they were thirty years too old to be Lagotti and his moll.

This left Rico with a final idea: there were only two other places with locked boxes he could think of: the lockers at either the railroad terminal or the airport. The other guys were obsessed with stalking the wide streets of Las Vegas to catch the couple but Rico was convinced.

He popped over to the airstrip to scout the joint but the lockers were too small. That left the station. So he hunkered down and waited for his prey to come to him.

After five hours sitting in the corner of the depot, nothing had happened, no one had appeared and Rico was in desperate need to visit the head. The only thing that stopped him was the fear that if he left his post for even a minute, that would be the time they grabbed the cash and exited the city. And Paulie did not want to be the guy to give them a free pass out of town.

Meantime the three others had given up on the streets and looked inside the casinos. What else do people do when they come to Vegas? Without the gambling there is literally nothing to occupy a person in a city stuck in the middle of the desert.

It's too damn hot to stay outside for more than thirty minutes and the only places open are hotels and casinos. So stood to reason the two thieves were playing poker, blackjack or trying their hand at the roulettes or slots.

Their problem was that they were outnumbered. Three of them and countless gaming dens to search but they had something no law enforcement officer could call on: the influence of the mob.

Each casino was awash with guys behind the scenes watching. Watching for card cheats on the tables and checking the staff weren't taking a sneaky dip in the house winnings. There was an army of eyes staring at the inside of the casinos and once they received descriptions of the Lansdowne robbers, all those eyeballs were in the pay of Paulie's men. It would only be a matter of time before someone spotted the two and they'd be done for.

Having passed the description to every casino they could find, the three guys headed to the bar at the Sands and waited for the word.

"Like taking candy from a baby."

"Or a million from a pair of douches."

Meantime, Charlie Pentangelo sat in his loft apartment in New York and wondered why everyone was spending so long recovering his money. Two small-time crooks shouldn't be that hard to find—not in a city where there were so many hoods hanging around.

THE NEON LIGHTS of Vegas were shining when Frank and Mary Lou appeared in the Mint reception after their honeymoon.

"Where do you feel lucky?"

"Caesar's Palace."

"Let's do it."

They walked down the strip passing the Riviera, the Stardust and the Desert Inn until Caesar's loomed on the right-hand side. Into the lobby, past reception and off into the casino.

They left the neon lights behind and passed the fruit machines to reach the cards. First thing, Frank stopped near a blackjack table and watched, draping his arm around Mary Lou's shoulders.

"We need chips."

Off to the side, between the card tables and the roulette wheels stood a glass-fronted cashier counter. He pulled out two hundred dollars in dirty notes and handed them to the cashier who swapped them for a series of colored chips: ten blue and twenty red.

He split the chips fifty-fifty between them and they headed to a table with three others already playing.

"Just bet the opposite color to me, okay?"

"Sure thing. This will work, right?"

"Should do. You go first and I'll be over in a minute."

Mary Lou approached a table and sat down, watching the bets land and the wheel turn. She kept the chips tightly in her hand although the others left theirs lying in front on them. After a lifetime of waiting, Frank appeared on the other side of the table.

He placed a red chip—five dollars—on red so she did the same on black. They were almost certain of one of them winning—there were two green zero and double-zero options too. The small white ball stopped bouncing around the wheel and settled on black. She couldn't remember the number— it didn't matter. She had won and Frank had lost so she received a ten-dollar blue chip. Ten bucks bet and ten dollars returned but with some different chips. They carried on like this for a while, churning through their chips. For the first minute, Mary Lou was up and then for the next two, Frank won.

She was down to her last two chips: one red, one blue. He winked at her and placed two chips over four numbers each. She didn't know what to do because she couldn't cover his bet. His two chips were on both black and red numbers: he was gambling for real now. He'd thrown their scheme out the window. The past three balls had come up red-black-black so Mary Lou went for broke with a fifteen dollar ride on red.

The Getaway

The ball hurtled along the edge of the wheel and settled down into a slot. Red. She'd up their ante by fifteen dollars. Then she looked up at Frank who was grinning from ear to ear. The croupier pushed four green chips over toward him—that was one hundred dollars off that single spin, along with the two hundred they'd already moved around the table.

Frank winked and stood up, followed by Mary Lou a moment later. They headed off to a poker game and perched with several spectators watching a round with over a thousand in the pot. A man with a beard won and they all applauded.

"Let's wait awhile and do that again."

"You confused me at the end."

"Yeah? I had a good vibe about the number two and fourteen. No idea why, but it worked."

"The important thing isn't the winning though, is it?"

"No, but it sure feels great, babe."

There was no answer to that because Frank was right. There was nothing in this world like knowing you've beaten someone. And beating the house on a roulette wheel is a mighty difficult task. They both knew the only way to succeed was to play for a short while—and stop if you ever look as though you're sitting on a losing streak. Not following those simple rules makes you a terminal loser.

He placed all the green chips into his pocket.

"That's what we walked in with so it's safe. This time let's play to win."

"Just don't bet against each other."

"We can have some fun if you like. Don't place any even bets."

"No black-red or odd-evens?"

"Nope. If we lose what's in our hands it won't matter, so we can earn ourselves a little scratch."

Two minutes later they sat at a different wheel and placed a small bet. Frank covered four numbers each time and Mary Lou saw what he chose and picked other sets of a similar value. She reckoned that would maximize their chances of winning something.

The first time, the croupier took all their red chips but the second and third attempts, chips headed first to him and then to her. For the next set of three, first she won then they both lost with he chalking up a win at the end.

She looked down at her chips: one hundred dollars minimum without counting and he appeared to hold about the same. She stared at him as he considered placing more chips onto the green baize. He glanced up and saw her expression and nodded.

They both stood up, took their chips and strolled away from the table.

"I've got around one hundred fifty dollars. You?"

"Hundred forty plus the two hundred in my pocket."

"Let's cash out."

"Shame we can't do this with the whole half a million."

"They'll notice if we did and besides, shifting two hundred an hour would mean we'd be stuck in Vegas until a man landed on the moon."

Frank and Mary Lou headed towards a different cashier counter and handed over their chips. The cashier counted them twice and fished out a bunch of notes.

"Small denominations please."

The woman nodded and swapped out twenties for tens instead. She checked the money and passed them over to Frank, who thanked her and walked away.

He looked around the casino and leaned into Mary Lou's ear.

"Looks like we've got trouble."

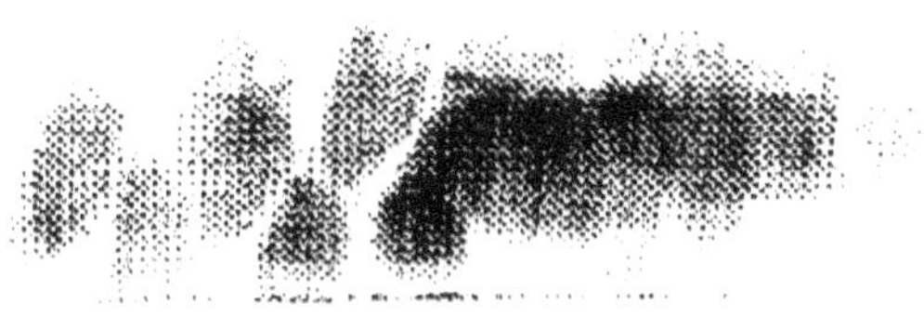

26

FRANK LOOKED LEFT then right, grabbed Mary Lou's hand and they headed straight ahead down the only aisle without a heavy stood in their way. Past the first table, he picked up the pace ever so slightly but not so much to make the casino staff figure they were about to bolt.

Two thickset guys in uniform walked along their own aisles in the same direction as Frank and Mary Lou.

"What we gonna do?"

"Gimme a minute, babe."

She fell silent and kept looking all around her to spot a clear line of escape but nothing was visible. Frank was doing the same and reached the same conclusion. They carried on one step at a time, brushing past blackjack players as they walked. On each occasion, a head turned and someone else expressed their displeasure at being interrupted.

The two continued stomping down the aisle annoying patrons. The heavies were no nearer—but no further away—than when they'd collected the clean money from the counter. At the end of the blackjack tables were a set of roulette wheels. A lightbulb pinged on above Frank's head.

The little white ball had just been thrown into a wheel on the left, so he leaned into another table, picked up a handful of chips and threw them up in the air. The players screamed—one of them tried to punch him but Frank sidestepped and dodged that bullet.

More usefully, everyone leaped to the floor to grab as many pieces of plastic as they could. Bedlam. A pile of people appeared from behind them.

The casino guys had nowhere to go. As much as they wanted to carry on pursuing the pair, their more immediate problem was to stop the fight breaking out right in front of their faces. Punches rained down on a young man and a middle aged woman. Every gambler grabbed at the free money lying on the carpet.

Frank led Mary Lou past the rest of the roulette wheels until he caught sight of an exit. They hightailed toward the sign and out into the night. She looked back over her shoulder: no one appeared for at least two seconds.

"Keep running."

They did so until they vanished in the crowds marching along the strip and that was when they stopped, dusted themselves down and walked at the same pace as everyone else on the sidewalk. Sometimes the best way to hide is to melt into the crowd.

"Did they make us somehow?"

"Could have been the money we deposited, babe."

"Or the mob tipped them off?"

"We were in one of their casinos but that's true of almost every place in the city."

"But they were after us, weren't they?"

"Definitely. They were trying to corner us, for sure."

"But was it the mob or the Feds?"

"No fucking clue, babe."

Mary Lou nodded and fell silent to figure out quite who it was they'd escaped from.

"How much longer can we stay in Vegas, you reckon?"

"If we survive until tomorrow morning, we'll be doing well."

"Think we'll make it?"

"Yeah. The crowds work in our favor and at most they've seen our hair color. Don't mean they know who we are."

"Could it have been the funny money?"

"The First Bank of Baltimore would have issued a list of the notes we stole and they'd have wired the serial numbers to anyone who wanted them."

Mary Lou hoped he was right otherwise they were as good as dead.

"We shouldn't go back to the hotel."

"Is there anything we need from there? Where d'you put your locker key?"

"It's still by my rose, Frank. Where's yours?"

"Heel of my shoe?"

"Doesn't that hurt?"

"Once you've been in the joint, you learn to take the pain of hiding objects in places you hope nobody dares to search."

Those words soaked into Mary Lou and she stopped thinking about it because it created unpleasant ripples in the night. And things were bad enough without images of keys hidden in Frank's crevices popping into her head.

"We need to get off the streets. If they're a few hundred feet behind us, we're sitting ducks out in the open."

"Yep. Where to?"

"Another casino?"

"I wonder if there's a movie house anywhere in this town."

"For the locals maybe. Why?"

"Who'd be stupid enough to catch a film if you're on the lam?"

"Dillinger and no one else."

For reasons that escaped her understanding, Frank's argument made sense. In a warped way that defied logic, but in the absence of any other idea, this became the best plan they had.

At the far end of the strip, they turned left and walked up to the Rialto box office and bought two tickets for whatever had started most recently. They were in luck as *The Thomas Crown Affair* was about to begin. What better movie for them to watch than a tale of robberies, deceit and love.

They sat near the emergency exit in case of trouble but none came calling. They were right: no one expected them to be in a cinema. All eyes were searching for a couple in a casino or in a restaurant.

By the time the end credits rolled, Frank and Mary Lou were tired and needed somewhere to sleep that wasn't the Mint. They took the car out of town and turned off into the desert. When they couldn't see the highway any more, he hit the brake.

"It'll get cold later but no one'll find us here."

Until the sun rose, they both slept fitfully but at least they got some rest. Only problem was they'd have to go back for the take before they could kiss goodbye to Sin City.

OVER THE LAST few days, Anthony had spent all his time with Bobby and Mickey. As entertaining as the guys were, Anthony would have been happy never to live another moment in their company ever again.

Anthony realized Bobby was okay: the fella whacked people for a living, so he wouldn't be the most fun guy to hang around. At least he kept his trap shut most of the time; the same could not be said of Mickey. He'd run off his mouth at a moment's notice and keep going until no one was listening. Then carry on for another minute at a bare minimum in case someone regained consciousness and needed an update on his views on life.

When this happened, Anthony would glance at Bobby who looked like he was planning to ax murder Mickey. With anybody else, this might have been a metaphor but Bobby's expression showed he was giving the idea serious consideration.

As soon as Frank Senior received word from the Feds that Mary Lou and Frank were off to Vegas, Anthony and his merry men took the first plane over and holed up in the Sahara, next to the Thunderbird and on the edge of casino land. Two days in a row they'd toured the station and the airport to find zip. Then they walked around the casinos hoping to spot the pair but nada.

Now they were bored and tetchy. The only thing keeping Anthony together was catching them and dragging their sorry asses over to Frank Senior. If he was lucky, he'd get to torture them before he killed them. If not, the finder's fee would keep him in clover for a while—long enough to buy two girls from the KitKatt Club for an entire night of debauched fun before he came home and bought a necklace for his girlfriend. He might take her to Atlantic City for a weekend too and he could win back the cash he spent on the dancers. Everyone'd be a winner.

First, he had to get the pair of them—and the money. Bobby and Mickey needed to be separated for several hours as there was a limit for any human being to be in the same space as Mickey. Anthony made a mental note never to call on the guy again. A big mistake not to be repeated under any circumstances.

"Mickey, you walk the strip and see if you can find our pair there. Bobby, do you want to check out some casinos? Me, I'll take a stroll toward the airport and then off to the railroad station. Let's meet back at our hotel in three hours."

"Why me?"

"Because I say so and I'm paying your wages. Don't turn everything into a major case."

"I'll cover the Sahara, Thunderbird, Riviera and right on through to the Tropicana. Mickey, which end of the strip will you work first?"

"Dunno."

"Decide."

"Huh? Okay, the Hacienda."

"Fine. As you'll be at one end, I'll start at the Sahara on the other side. That way we'll have more eyes on more places. Right Anthony?"

"You said it, Bobby. For the same reason I'll hit the station and hop over to the North Las Vegas Air Terminal. After that, McCarran Airport."

"Jeez. You guys will be warm and comfortable indoors while I'm pounding the streets."

"Let it go, Mickey. Now is not the time for belly aching."

Bobby and Anthony stared down Mickey until even he understood to shut his mouth and headed out onto the street.

"Thank you for doing that."

"No problem, Bobby. Wish I'd come up with it sooner. I didn't think Mickey would behave this way. Every other occasion I've used him, he might not be the sharpest tool in the box, but he's always been effective."

"I understand. We've all had dealings with his kind before."

"But you get parole after a year."

They both laughed and Bobby tipped his hat before heading out the door himself, followed by Anthony who headed for the station.

When he arrived, there was nothing to see. He stayed for an hour and two trains came and left. Four passengers in total made their way along the concourse. The only unusual activity was a solitary guy hanging around the platform gates.

He wore a normal suit—three piece with a tie—but he was noticeable by being there at all. Anthony was loitering in the station at a dumb time of the night, but no one else spends an hour there for kicks. If you're meeting someone you don't turn up that early when fifty feet away is a hotel bar and casino. Made no sense.

Also, for a man stood by the gates, he showed no interest in any train on any platform. Instead, he spent his entire time facing the left luggage area. As much as he was leaning casually on a wall, Anthony gained the distinct impression those eagle eyes of his were trained on one location and no other.

He considered the suit some more along with the obsession over the lockers. Something clicked inside Anthony's head. Frank Senior was right: they were not the only ones seeking the First Bank of Baltimore robbers. The New York mob must have dispatched their people too and he was staring at one of them as he stood and waited.

This sent Anthony into a flurry. Until this point he had assumed all they had to do was be in the right city at the right time and he'd make Frank Senior a happy man. But seeing the dude in the suit: Anthony knew they'd have to up their game and fight hard to be the ones to catch Frank and Mary Lou. Mickey was a eunuch in a harem so Anthony needed to invest in Bobby if they were to go back home with their heads held high.

THURSDAY JUNE 26

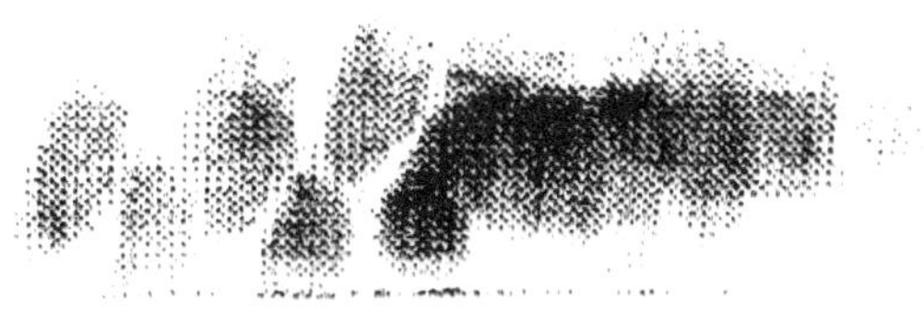

27

MARY LOU'S TEETH chattered her awake in perfect synchrony with Frank's. The sun shone into the driver's side of the car casting a Frank-shaped silhouette on her. He switched on the engine and waited before pushing warm air into the cabin. Ten minutes later, Mary Lou felt the tips of her fingers again, having placed them between her legs next to her crotch all that time.

"Can we get a coffee somewhere?"

"Sure thing, babe. It was Alaska in here last night."

"You're telling me."

Frank drove back onto the highway and they headed further away from Vegas until they hit a diner and gas station, all isolated in the middle of the desert. Four trucks were parked outside and nothing else for miles.

Coffees, scrambled eggs, toast for two. They sat in silence for the start of their meal, thawing out. Frank gobbled down his breakfast faster than Mary Lou could blink. She took longer, not wanting to choke on each mouthful.

The heat from the warm food sunk down her gullet and landed with a splat in her stomach. Then she washed the mixture down with the mug of coffee. The waitress topped up their drinks twice before they declared themselves full.

"Needed that."

"Me too. Warmer now?"

"And some. I'll have to shift the button on my skirt."

Frank grinned and thought about Mary Lou's belly and the rose beneath it. He smiled some more.

"We can rest here a while before we make our next move."

"And what should that be?"

"Well, we need to collect our bags so first we're going back to Vegas."

"They're on to us, aren't they?"

"Yep. For those casino guys to pick up on the money so fast means the mob knows where we are."

"And if they have it figured, then the Feds will know."

"Along with Uncle Frankie."

"Last night you thought the casino had matched the serial numbers on our notes."

"I did but I've been thinking about it. If it was just that, I can't see how they'd have spotted us so quickly by the tables. They had more information than that."

"Jeez. And you want us to go back into the city?"

"We have no option if we're to get our money. I don't want to but we have no choice. Else all we've got is a few hundred dollars in our pockets. And we didn't come all this way to live off chump change until the end of time."

"I don't like it."

"Who does?"

He reached out his hand and placed it on Mary Lou's. They stared at each other for a moment, not needing to express the thoughts their eyes conveyed instead.

"And if we get in, out and survive. Where next?"

"What do you mean?"

"We've always said we're heading to California, but that means Frankie knows too..."

"...and if he knows it then so do the Feds and the mob."

"Right."

"So they'll be waiting for us again."

"California's a mighty big state."

"Yes, but there's only a handful of places to launder half a million. And they know them faster than we can find 'em."

"Where should we go instead?"

Frank's intonation implied a decision had been made but Mary Lou wasn't sure she agreed with it herself: she was only voicing a concern.

"North or south—take your pick."

"Canada or Mexico. You know any Spanish?"

"Enough to order a burrito."

"More than me then."

"That makes Canada our number one destination of choice."

"Perhaps. What would we do there? You got any connections?"

"None that'd give us a line on a wholesale money laundering operation."

"Say that louder, not all the waitresses heard you."

Mary Lou blushed and her eyes darted every which way as her entire body tensed.

"Relax, I was teasing."

She slapped his hand, playfully without spite.

"Don't. That wasn't nice."

"Sorry but this is quite an intense conversation, wouldn't you say?"

If Mary Lou had worn glasses, she'd have looked at Frank over the rims —with disdain. They sat in silence again, ruminating on the possibilities before them.

"Canada might be a good place to hide."

"But not a great location for us to launder the take."

"No. Sounds like we're off to the West Coast, anyway."

"Do you have any connections in Seattle instead?"

"None. You?"

"Nope."

"Done. We'll stick to the original plan and head to California. Once we've cleaned the cash, we decide at that point whether we're Canada bound."

"We are though, right?"

"With what we have now, yes. But we worry about it later. Our only real hope is the mob doesn't know our car so we can move around the city without too getting spotted."

Mary Lou sipped her coffee and thought for a spell.

"How much ammo you sitting on?"

"Enough to get out of trouble but not enough for an all-out gun battle in the streets of Las Vegas. What you planning?"

"Nothing. Just wondered if we were heading into a death trap."

"The Feds will want to capture us alive. It's their job. If we don't produce any heat, they'll keep their end of the bargain."

"Sure, Frank."

"The mob is only interested in the cash. They will only take a pop if we stand between them and the notes."

"Makes sense. What about good old Uncle Frankie?"

"He'll want the money first and foremost."

Mary Lou smiled.

"And then he'll want us dead."

He squeezed her hand and she squeezed back.

"We'll deal with that cocksucker before all this is over."

"Sure will, babe. But right now we gotta focus on getting into Vegas and grabbing our earnings."

They paid up, returned to the car and gunned the vehicle toward the entertainment capital of the world.

FRANK DROVE IN utter silence. Neither he nor Mary Lou wanted to say a word, both wrapped in their thoughts: these might be the last few minutes of their lives.

Along the Salt Lake Highway and into Vegas, the car passed by the Silver Nugget and reached the fork that split North Main from Las Vegas Boulevard. He turned left onto the Boulevard and then right on Fremont. The railroad station loomed straight at them and Mary Lou peered into the distance hoping to catch sight of the mob, the Feds and who knows what.

"Drop into the parking lot, hon'."

He pulled into a space pointing at the exit in case they needed a fast getaway.

"Ready?"

"Let's do it."

They both left the car at the same time and closed their doors in tandem. They took the long route to the building, around the edge of the lot, so they stayed in the shadows as much as possible.

A steady trickle of people came and went: it was still early enough for rush hour. When they reached the main entrance, men and women jostled them as they stood staring into the large open space that made up the station foyer. To the left, ticket counters and to the right, lockers. Straight ahead were the gates leading to the platforms.

They headed off to wait in line for a ticket. He stared at the lockers and she kept her eye on the passengers as they scurried around the concourse.

"See anything?"

"Dunno. Maybe."

"Where?"

"By the entrance to platform one."

She followed the platform signs counting down: three, two, one. Ten feet from the gate stood a guy who spent his entire time staring at the lockers. He remained stationary, leaning against the wall with his full concentration on the left luggage area.

"Three-piece suit in Summer?"

"A mob guy…"

"…or a Fed."

"Not with those shoes."

Frank was right. No Hoover man would wear brown brogues: not regulation footwear. Either he was an honest Joe citizen, or he was in the mob. Mary Lou wasn't certain, but she doubted he was one of Frankie's boys. Over the years, she'd seen almost all of them.

"Let's not waste any money on a train ticket."

They left the line and sauntered, arm in arm, off to a newsstand fifteen feet further away from the main entrance. Frank bought a paper and Mary Lou grabbed some gum. The couple stood next to each other, pretending to read the front page together while staring at Paulie, the guy in the three-piece. He never moved.

"What we gonna do?"

"Have to assume he's not kosher."

"If someone looks like a rat and smells like a rat…"

"…chances are he is a rat."

"And he is gnawing on a scrap of cheese right now."

Mary Lou giggled and dug an elbow into Frank's side.

"That's a mouse, silly. Rats eat anything. They don't care."

"If he's got a description of us, we're toast."

"Where are the bags?"

"Second column at the far end by the window."

"So there's no way to sneak around the lockers, grab them and leave without him spotting us?"

"No chance. He is perched there for a reason."

The two carried on looking, desperate to find some leverage.

"We could always plain shoot him."

"Not from this range, babe. Besides, do you not think people might notice? We need time to reach the lockers and get the hell out of Dodge."

"Okay, shooting him isn't the way but as far as I can tell, we've got to convince him to leave his post. Killing him is one method."

"What do you have in mind?"

"I suck him off in the bathroom and we kill him there."

"Sure, but mobsters tend not to let themselves get lured off the job even by a siren such as beautiful you."

"Charmer."

"You're right. If he was an average Joe it'd work, but this suit is a professional."

"So we must figure out how to whack him if we can't fuck him off his perch."

"Yep, hon'."

"And shooting him is out of the question."

"I've no silencer. A single shot will ring out in this building and bring a ton of shit raining down on us."

"We don't need that, for sure. You got a knife?"

"Um, no. You seen me with a knife these past few days?"

"No but I thought it might be worth asking."

"Let's focus on what we can do rather than making up kit we don't have."

He turned the page to continue the charade of news reading. Meanwhile, they both looked, pondered and peered again.

"Stay here for a minute."

Mary Lou walked off to the other side of the main entrance, leaving Frank to wonder what was going on. When she returned, he noticed the sparkle in her eyes and the upturned corners of her mouth.

"I've got it."

"Spill."

"There's a door in the wall he's leaning on. It leads somehow from platform one to the lockers. Must be a service room in between."

"Go on."

"One of us goes onto the platform, through the service room and sneaks up behind him while the other walks across to the lockers. He'll be staring ahead at the bags and the other can break the fucker's neck."

Frank nodded.

"Like it. Who'll snap the guy's spine and who will risk being shot by the dude as we open a locker?"

28

FRANK BOUGHT A ticket to New York from the kiosk as that was the next train to leave platform one. Mary Lou stood some way off so they wouldn't appear to be a couple. He showed his rectangular piece of card to the station guard, who let him proceed.

That was her cue to head towards the lockers—not too fast but with enough speed so Joe would recognize her and stay glued to his spot. As she walked across the railroad foyer, a man approached her. She gripped the strap of her handbag: he didn't alter his trajectory.

"Excuse me, miss."

She looked at him and carried on walking.

"Sorry, miss. Can I have one second, please?"

He wore a blue suit with a white shirt and no tie and no hat. She remained silent and tried to ignore him.

"Just a moment of your time."

The john wasn't going away soon. If she didn't stop, there'd be a commotion and she couldn't afford that to happen right now. Not at this precise minute.

"What?"

"Did you drop these?"

She glanced down at his hand, which proffered a pair of white silk gloves.

"No. Sorry. Not mine."

Mary Lou started walking again having disposed of the guy nice and easy.

"Well, can I help you with wherever you're going?"

"No thanks. I'm good."

"I'm sure you are but can I help you?"

"Now why do you want to do that?"

"You are an incredibly attractive girl. I can't think of a better way to spend a single second more in your company."

"Get out of here, bud, before I call the cops. I'm a married woman and don't need your sort soiling my day."

"Only saying…"

The guy wandered off to find another person to schmooze. She turned her head to the left to discover whether Frank had got through the service corridor yet but no sign of him. She was almost at the lockers and she must already be within Joe's field of vision by now.

Mary Lou walked down the first line of metal boxes, pretending to check on their numbers. Her key was still hidden and she had no intention of taking it out until they were ready. Having arrived at the end, she worked her way back via the second row passing their own lockers. Then she did the same with the third and final aisle. Then she sauntered nearer the platforms and spotted Joe continuing to lean against the wall. Bad news: he should be dead by now.

FRANK SHOWED HIS ticket to the guard who clipped it and let him through. On the left-hand side was the New York train and on the right was a wall. A hundred feet along Frank made out a door marked for staff only.

He marched for about seventy feet then stopped and leaned against the brickwork and pretended to read the contents of his paper. Once he was sure the guard was busy with another passenger, he moved down the platform and tried the handle. Locked, Goddamn it.

Two deep breaths and he tried the door knob again. This time he twisted it in the other direction and the wood pinged open. A quick dart inside and he entered a darkened room. He'd been so fast at closing the door, he had no light to find the switch. He felt along the wall either side of the entrance until he arrived at a large enough square under his fingertips. In the middle was a flipper which he pulled upwards.

A solitary bulb sprang into life in the center of the ceiling and an array of filing cabinets and a desk appeared before him. On the far side of the room was another door. This is the one he assumed would lead him to Joe. He padded over and tried its handle. This time it was actually locked shut.

A trip to the table revealed nothing but the acid taste of disappointment and none of the cabinets contained anything but papers, files and more sheets. He bent down to examine the lock and breathed a sigh of relief. He pulled a hair pin from his wallet—kept for just such occasions—and twiddled it around the opening while he listened to the sounds inside. He heard a clunk and he knew he'd picked the mechanism.

Aware of the noise he'd generated on the other side, Frank opened it a crack to check what was happening and scanned the reception foyer and Joe leaning against the wall not twenty feet away. The only reason the guy hadn't noticed the door open was because of the hubbub in the station and that his attention was taken up by some activity at the lockers.

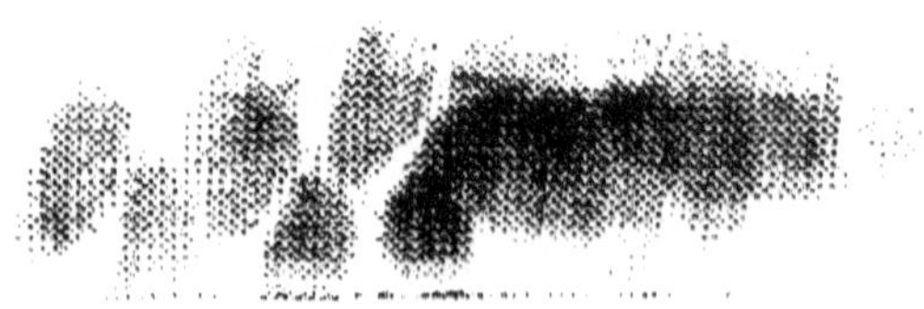

29

RICO WAS BORED rigid. He had been waiting for a lifetime and had achieved nothing apart from a stiff back and aching legs. But that didn't stop him: he was certain he was in the right place if only the thieves would show up and prove him correct. Each time someone walked close to the lockers, Rico watched their every move but there had only been two people so far who'd even gone near that part of the station.

Now a woman had surfaced who kinda looked like the description in his pocket—only she had black hair, not blond. That could have come out of a bottle. The behavior which piqued Rico's interest was that she walked up and down each line of lockers but did nothing more than that. Strange. People know which locker they need to return to. When she got to the end of the last row, the dame hurried back to his side of and stared straight at him. He was sure of that.

Rico stood upright, no longer leaning against the wall. He put his hand in his pants pocket to remind himself he was packing heat. Then he took a step forward—and halted. The dame was acting weird, although that didn't mean she had a million in bank notes in her panties. Yes she looked cute and had caught his attention, but did that make her one of the robbers? He hung there and waited to see what she did next.

Without warning, a hand covered his mouth and an arm engulfed his throat. He choked, but no sound came out because of the vice-like grip of the palm over his lips. Tried to scream but nothing. Four seconds later, Rico ceased to feel anything as Frank twisted his head and snapped his neck. He slumped to the ground and Frank dragged him back into the staff room. All they had to do now was get the money and leave the station.

AS SOON AS Frank returned to the foyer, Mary Lou slipped to the end of the lockers and fumbled inside her skirt and panties to grab the key.

"You okay?"

"Sure thing, babe."

He took the warm metal proffered to him and headed straight to a locker and pulled out one of the black bags. Then he bent down to tie his shoe and flashed the other key in the palm of his hand. Twenty seconds later, he was carrying a bag too and they both walked, fingers entwined, out the main entrance and into the parking lot.

At that point, they heard an enormous bellow ring out around the foyer. Joe had been found and the word 'murder' was carrying in the air. A whistle blew and they had only a few seconds before the cops cordoned off the station and swarmed round the place.

He picked up the pace until they reached the car and threw both bags into the back.

"You drive."

"Are you sure, hon'?"

"Not a discussion. Let's do it."

Mary Lou left the parking space and headed out the lot. A Vegas cop was already standing at the entrance looking in on every vehicle. When Mary Lou's turn came to pass him, Officer Sanchez stopped them in their tracks.

"Steady, babe."

She wound down her window and opened her mouth to speak.

"Hello, ma'am."

"Hi, officer. Anything the matter?"

"There's been an incident inside the station and we're just checking everyone at the moment."

"Oh, how unpleasant."

"Yes, ma'am. Who's in the car with you?"

"My husband."

"Morning, sir."

"Morning, officer."

"Not driving, sir?"

"A long journey to get here and I'm tired. Thought I'd let the little lady take the strain."

"Where you traveled from?"

"Seattle. Been stuck in a tin can for a lifetime."

"I bet. There's no direct route from Seattle to Vegas, is there?"

"Nope. Had to change in Chicago."

"Okay, move along now then."

Sanchez waved them forwards and stopped the car behind them instead.

"Nice and steady, babe."

"Five miles under the speed limit, hon'."

"Let's take a trip to the Convention Center."

Mary Lou did as instructed and rode down the strip, turned left and left again. The convention parking lot was huge.

"Time for a fresh ride."

They drove round a while, like they were in a store choosing a dress. Every so often, she would slow down for Frank to take a better look at a vehicle but either it was too new or too old, too clean or too dirty.

"How about that pickup?"

"Bit big for our needs isn't it?"

"Maybe but it'd be the kind of car to get stolen in this lot wouldn't you say?"

"Good point, but it doesn't feel right somehow."

"We must steal something soon or we'll run out of gas, Frank."

"I know, but I don't want to mess this up."

More slow-mo driving until Mary Lou reckoned they'd covered every aisle in the lot—and still no decision made. She was getting impatient. Each minute they remained in Vegas was another opportunity for the Feds, the mob, Frankie's boys or the local cops to catch them. She ground her molars.

"Let me find one, hon' 'cause we gotta get outta here."

Frank nodded and squeezed her knee. He was paralyzed by indecision but didn't want to admit it to himself or Mary Lou.

She drove round some more until she stopped next to a green saloon.

"Here we are."

"Why?"

"The passenger window is ajar so they're asking for us to steal it. And should be easier to get inside."

"Done."

Less than a minute later, Frank sat in the driver's seat fiddling with wires below the dashboard. Ten seconds more, the engine roared into life.

"You follow me out of town and we'll ditch the old ride in the desert. Pass me one bag: just in case."

Steady as a rock, the two cars spluttered away from Vegas and Mary Lou kept three vehicles behind the green car. She always had a clear line of sight on Frank but, at a glance, they didn't look like they were a convoy.

Four miles out the city, he pulled off the highway and headed inland for six or seven hundred feet. Then he stopped by a dune.

"We can't burn this one—even if we had the gasoline."

"It's a hell of a dramatic signature though."

Instead they searched through every inch of the car making sure there was not one personal item left inside to connect them to that lump of metal. Trunk, rear seat, glove compartment. They both went over the whole thing so nothing could be missed. Frank got behind the wheel and Mary Lou sat beside him. The engine had been running all the time. He was about to move off when she put a hand on his.

"Are we sure we should go to LA?"

"It's still the easiest place to launder the take. I know one or two people there. Anywhere else will be the same as Vegas."

"Won't they be waiting for us again though?"

"The City of Angels is sprawling and spread out. Nothing like compact old Sin City. You could spend a hundred years in LA and never come across someone who lived on the other side of the metropolis to you."

The edges of Mary Lou's eyes were reddening up and a tear was welling in one corner.

"We'll be okay. When we hit town, I'll make some calls, do the business and then we're out of there living the high life where Uncle Frankie and the lot of them can't touch us."

Mary Lou smiled nervously. He kissed her full on the lips.

"Trust me. It'll work out just fine."

He hit the gas pedal and the tires turned but no motion occurred. Frank sighed.

"Damn sand."

He put the shift stick into second gear and tried again. This time they lurched forward until he regained control and the wheels found solid highway.

"Next stop: Tinseltown."

Frank tuned in a rock 'n' roll station and they headed south west. Mary Lou stared out the window and thought about the ending to The Thomas Crown Affair.

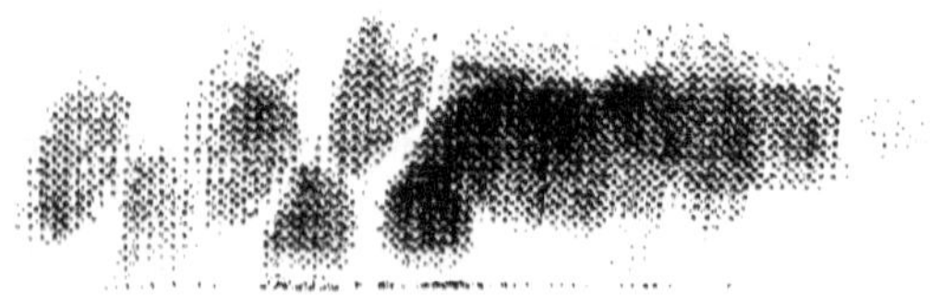

30

WHAT FELT A short time later, they crossed the state line and watched as the highway forced itself through woods and forests: like the trees would take over the road and were chasing them down the tarmac.

"Before we reach LA, we need to get a game plan. We were lucky in Vegas. And we might kid ourselves but it'll be worse on the coast. I know it's a big bad city but we must operate carefully if we're to survive laundering half a million dollars under the radar, babe."

"Well, the least we should do before we arrive is to find some clothes to put on our backs. We've been wearing this lot since before I can remember."

"Sure thing, babe."

"And a toothbrush."

They passed a handful of cabins at five miles below the speed limit. A store broke the monotony of their journey and he pulled into one of the four spaces provided at the side of the road.

They could have been forgiven for thinking it was another log cabin but its neon sign attached to the front flashed that it was a general store. When Frank and Mary Lou walked in, they saw almost any item they could think of available for sale. In one aisle were two piles of red plaid shirts and jeans. They rifled through until they found the correct sizes and picked toiletries, along with some other essentials.

"We're gonna look like quite a pair."

"Yeah, not what I had in mind."

"Let's see if we can find something a little less…"

"…Hicksville?"

"Yep."

A scout round the store revealed a variety of garden tools, digging implements and many cans of food, but no other clothes. Frank took a shovel.

"We'll get more things to wear somewhere else but at least we've got something different for now."

"Sure, hon'. But we'll dress like we're cousins."

"That's normal round here."

They chuckled and proceeded to the front to pay using some of their clean casino cash. Once they'd returned to the car, they changed into their new belongings and Mary Lou took over the driving.

"What do you think we should do?"

"We need to get the Feds, the mob and Frankie off our backs."

"Any ideas?"

"The G-men are looking for the money but what they love is to arrest people. So we should give them some bodies to find."

"Bodies?"

"Yes. We must get ourselves a pair of corpses."

"You're kidding me."

"Nope. Two burnt bodies all crisped and singed. That'd be ideal."

"Frank. Are you saying…"

"We don't have to go murdering anyone, only if we have to."

Frank's expression was more serious than she could remember. He was right though: if the Feds thought they were dead they'd have to give up the chase.

"To the morgue?"

"I reckon—unless we want to become the honeymoon killers."

"Not if we can help it."

"I agree."

Mary Lou set off and headed to the nearest town once she'd spotted a road sign: where there were people, there were deaths. And when folk died, they went to the funeral home.

Fifteen miles down the highway, she stopped the car two hundred feet from the Kingston Range mortuary. The building stood on the edge of a forested area next to a surgery. The doctor must have been out on call because no lights were on—nor in the morgue. In small-town America, the doc was the mortician too so there was little chance of a flurry of concerned citizens arriving to open up for the day's business.

They hopped round the back in their matching jeans and shirts. he jimmied the door free using the newly acquired shovel and they hurried inside.

"Should have bought a flashlight."

"Yes, babe."

Frank improvised by switching the light on and they scurried to a side room to hunt out some bodies. There was a row of small chrome doors on a shelf, as they'd expected. Each door, four feet square, housed a gurney big enough to fit a corpse. One by one, they opened the doors to find what they needed. The first two were empty and the third held a woman, the fourth and fifth contained an old man and a younger guy.

"Frank?"

"Yes, babe?"

"If we take two of these corpses and burn them, even the Feds will work out what we've done and will carry on chasing us."

Frank leaned back on a wall and thought for a spell.

"What if we steal more bodies than we need?"

"Make it look like there's a body snatcher loose?"

"Why not?"

"Won't that bring a ton of G-men down in the area?"

Frank considered the idea some more.

"How about taking the bodies from here and razing it to the ground?"

"We burn this joint down to hide that we're burning two bodies somewhere else. Hon', this won't work."

More silent thinking from Frank as he mulled over various scenarios.

"We need to get outta here, don't we?"

They shut the gurneys, closed the doors and switched off the light. There was no way to hide the smashed door jamb, so he broke open a glass cabinet and took some meds out to make the break-in appear to be kids stealing drugs.

Back in the car and down the road some more.

"We gotta kill ourselves a man and a woman."

"Not a couple though."

"No. Too hard to do and too obvious for the cops."

THEY WERE SILENT as they came to terms with the reality of what they were contemplating. Mary Lou understood why they had to murder two people but she wasn't happy about the situation. Frank saw matters differently: the deaths of strangers would give him his freedom and secure his life with her.

After twenty minutes they reached a town called Baker. There were at least three streets with stores and behind the residential area lay a small airfield. Planes arrived occasionally but there were enough coming and going to create a flow of people through what would otherwise be a tiny gathering of country folk.

The Getaway

Frank and Mary Lou waited in the airstrip lot because someone flying out of town would not be missed for a while. The wait lasted only ten minutes as a car pulled in at the edge of the parking area away from the terminal. They followed it and parked nearby.

A man in his early thirties got out of the vehicle and took out a case from the trunk. The guy was around Frank's height and build.

Mary Lou stood back as he walked a few paces behind him and looked both ways. He saw no one, raised the shovel and slammed it into the guy's head. He stumbled forwards and collapsed. She caught up and helped drag the traveler to his automobile and dump him in their trunk. He returned to grab his bag so it could join its erstwhile owner.

"And now we have a replacement car equipped with keys and free baggage filled with clothes for me, I hope."

They drove round the lot twice in case a woman turned up to make their job easier, but no luck. Instead, Mary Lou motored out with the body in the back and let the vehicle purr around the Baker residences. An hour later she was still driving up and down but no single females were on the streets that day.

"Let's make some house calls. This is getting ridiculous."

"Sure, babe."

She pulled in and parked next to a huddle of suburban bungalows. Mary Lou got out and headed towards one property while Frank walked round the back and vanished from her sight.

The first residence she tried gave no reply, but the second produced more success. A man appeared and she asked directions to the airstrip. She thanked him and hunkered two houses down before trying again. This time a woman opened the door.

"Hi, before you start, I'm not interested."

"Oh, I'm not selling anything. I'm new in town—just moved in across the street—and I was hoping I might borrow a cup of sugar. It'd be most neighborly of you."

"Sorry, we get so many sales reps round here. It's a defense mechanism."

"I understand. I'll end up doing the same in a few months time, I'm sure."

Those were the last words the woman heard because Frank's hands clamped around her throat and he dragged her backwards and snapped her neck in a single twist. Mary Lou ran inside and closed the door. She scampered into the bedroom and took some clothes out of wardrobes until she had a reasonable sized pile on the bed. She rifled through the woman's toiletries too, grabbing a perfume and a hairbrush. When she returned to the hallway, he had thrown a wallet on the floor and was stuffing notes into his pocket.

"This can look like she cut and run away. We'll leave the cops to figure the reason."

There was no evidence of anybody else living in the bungalow—something Frank had checked before he'd scratched the life out of Emily. That was the name on her ID.

He and Mary Lou rolled the woman into a blanket, careful to tuck in both ends. They carried her over to the car and dropped her into the trunk too. With the guy's body already there, he pushed down hard to get them both to fit. But all was good.

Next Frank sat behind the wheel and returned to the airport lot so she could follow him in the new car back toward the general store.

Half a mile short of that destination, they stopped and Mary Lou turned the vehicle round to face in the opposite direction. She parked on the verge, ten feet away from the highway. There were few cars on the road that afternoon which gave them the opportunity to wrestle the bodies into the front seats.

Frank siphoned gas from the tank and spread it inside the vehicle. He placed some bank notes in a valise he'd stolen from Emily. Not much: three hundred dollars.

Mary Lou lit a match and threw it through the window. Orange sparks licked the upholstery and traveled across the rear interior. With the windows open, the small lights grew into yellow flickering wisps and leaped onto the driver's seat until the whole inside filled with heat, darting flames and acrid smoke.

They hopped into the guy's car and motored towards Baker—still in silence.

"That should get the Feds off our tail."

"And if it doesn't?"

"We'll figure out something else—but it should. They'll have two bodies and some bank notes. Even they should be able to work out that equation."

Mary Lou nodded, knowing Frank was right and that once you've murdered one person, you might as well make it three because you can only fry in the mercy seat once in your life.

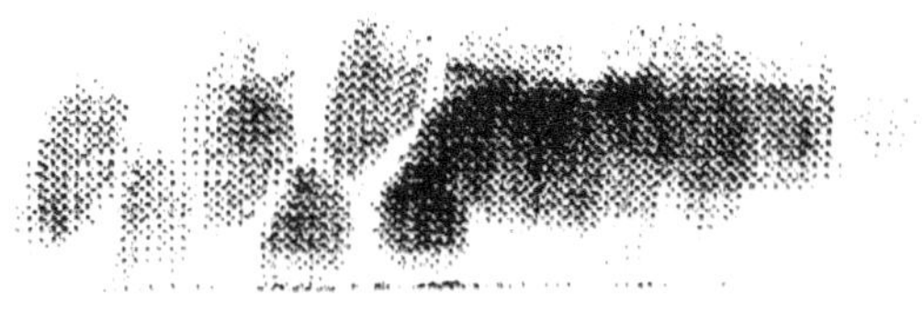

31

DRIVING DOWN THE road, Frank kept a hand on Mary Lou's thigh and left the other hanging on the wheel, five miles below the limit. They remained without talking for an age until she punctured the silence.

"That's not the end of our problems."

"No, babe."

"There's the mob to deal with and then Frankie."

She spat out the last word like a ball of mucus had landed on her tongue.

"Once we've laundered the cash, we should be able to negotiate with New York. If we give them their tithe, we might survive if we stay in this country."

"So if they don't catch up with us that'll leave Uncle Frankie."

"Yeah."

"He'll want the money."

"There'll be guys on the road after us by now. Who knows who it was watching those Vegas lockers."

"Do you think we did for one of Frankie's men?"

"Or the mob's. Neither is good."

"No, murder isn't good."

"Not quite what I meant. If it was Frankie's goon or an East Coast goon. We've killed one of theirs. Spilled blood gets paid with spilled blood—not an apology and a payoff."

Mary Lou pondered for a minute, eyes darting left and right as though she should now be hyper-aware of any sudden movement in case it is a goon seeking revenge with a gun.

"What are we going to do? We can't live like this for the rest of our days."

"We must make peace with everyone. It's the only way."

"Even if we leave the country?"

"They can cross the border as easily as you and I."

"What'll we do about Frankie?"

"Reason with him and convince him to give up the chase."

"We have gunned down his men, hon'."

"And he was expecting to get his hands on a large amount of money we have in our trunk."

Mary Lou giggled.

"There is that."

"He's not laughing though."

"Do I look like I care?"

"Probably not, but he does and we must focus on that."

"We're in the middle of nowhere but when we find a phone, we should talk and try to get him to agree to call off the hounds."

"Do you think he will?"

"We've got a better chance if we ask than if we carry on running."

"That's not what I asked."

"I know. Truth is I have no idea at all. But if we do nothing, he'll keep on coming until he takes all the money off us."

FRANK LAGOTTI SENIOR liked the Kitkatt Club—not because it made him an amazing amount of cash each week, which it did, but because it gave him wonderful access to pussy. These two items were the most important things in his life—passions he could not quell.

While he counted his marriage to Fran Lagotti in decades and not years, they remained together for a simple, irrefutable reason: they were Catholic and a divorce was impossible. And anyway, she was a good cook and ensured his clothes were cleaned and pressed.

When you are a Shylock, you don't always get paid back. On these occasions you can break bones or take advantage. Frankie became the majority owner of the Kitkatt Club because its founder was a terrible gambler and handing over the stock was the only way for him not to be thrown off the top of a tall building. Fair trade.

The Getaway

The reason the club made so much money was that it had two revenue streams. First was the bar where men came to drink overpriced hooch away from their wives and girlfriends. Second, there were the girls: the place was a strip joint and an occasional cathouse depending on the clientele.

Frankie sat near the back so he could keep an eye on his investment and enjoy the show. With all the troubles with his step nephew, Frank and the skirt Mary Lou, he needed to relax a little. The last few days had been stressful. He never wanted to deliver bad news to New York and his conversations with Pentangelo had been tense at best.

To relieve this tension, he had taken the girl known as June into one of the private rooms and fucked her from behind. After, he threw her out because she'd been stealing notes from patrons' wallets. That was not good for business. Now he sat and watched April and May on stage. April wore red panties and May sported green. They had both already got out their tits and he enjoyed the scene. June's titties had been too small for his taste but he wouldn't have to see them again.

There were only a handful of customers in the room but it was early yet, only seven. These guys were on their way home and would leave in the next thirty minutes or they were from out of town and were here until dawn.

August came over and replaced his cocktail.

"Thank you, but no. Get me a coffee."

Too many drinks this early in the night would not help Frankie's head the following morning. And clarity was king. As the girl walked away with his drink returned to her tray, he stared at her powder blue hot pants and the way her ass cheeks moved in a wonderful rhythm and bounce.

Two minutes later, she came back with his coffee which appeared with milk, sugar and three biscuits on a small plate.

"Thanks for the meal."

"You're welcome."

"When does your shift finish?"

"I've another six hours, Frankie."

"Anyone else working the tables right now?"

"Only me. It's quiet, but March starts at eight."

"See me once she's arrived and we can have a private conversation."

"You got it, Frankie."

He took another opportunity to stare at her body but this time watched her back and her hair. Then returned to her best feature: that ass.

After ten minutes, he was bored by the floorshow. There was nothing wrong with April and May's performance but with little energy in the room, everything was dull. And he didn't like the shape of their tits either.

He wandered into the office to look at the books. If semi-naked girls weren't working for him, counting cash would. The Kitkatt Club represented a mountain of money because nobody paid for the girls' services with a credit card. When Frankie took over the joint, one of his first acts was to improve security: dancers, bartenders, everyone were taking from the till and nobody had a clue. That stopped within a week. A barman lost a finger and a girl was thrown out after her face was slashed. No one dipped their beaks in his register anymore.

The Kitkatt was a regular depositor of large quantities of cash and Frankie also withdrew huge amounts too. This was a simple and easy way to launder bills for the mob. Dirty money goes into a bank and clean comes out. It was a useful method for laundering drug receipts but not great for the proceeds of robberies because those notes had known serial numbers.

Frankie checked that cash was flowing and went back to his table at the rear and sipped some water. September and November were on stage now but had done nothing more than a few dance steps. The warm-up would soon be over.

August padded over with a coffee and some liquor on her tray.

"Which would you prefer, Frankie?"

"I'll pass, dear, and stick to my water."

"Okay. March has arrived."

"Let's go."

He stood up and headed to the side of the auditorium leaving the girl to carry his tumbler. She followed him into a private room and watched him slump into the red leather couch with his legs apart—wide enough for her to fit in between his knees.

She shut the door and placed his drink on a small table, kneeled down and unzipped his pants. August was only too aware how rough he would be but she had no choice. Besides, if she handled him right, there'd be a Benjamin for her though she wouldn't be able to take a piss for three or four days without it hurting.

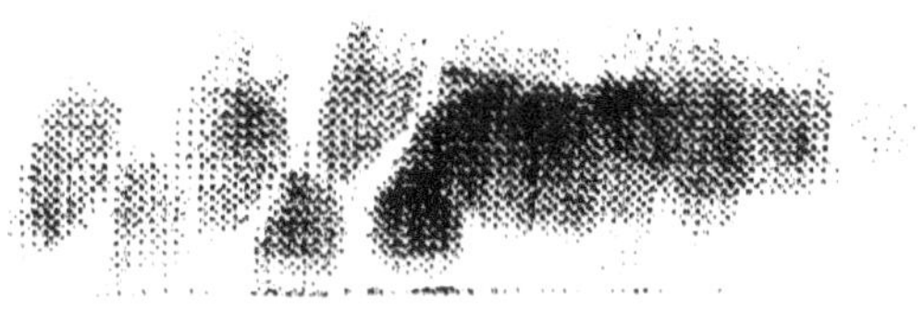

32

FRANKIE LEFT A Jackson on the small table after he'd finished with August, who lay on the couch tired and in pain. He collected his water on his way out and reminded her to get back serving tables in a minute.

He was bored. The sex had been all right but not as enjoyable as he had hoped. Frankie returned to his table and watched the girls on stage for five minutes but got restless. He nodded at his driver who stepped out of the auditorium. Soon after, he stood up and left: the car pulled up outside the entrance as he walked into the night air. Perfect timing. Although it caused him no pleasure to think this, new Luigi was so much smarter than old Luigi.

"Take me to the auto shop."

Frankie never liked talking in the vehicle, instead preferring to melt into the silence in the back seat and watch life unfurl around him. This was his only opportunity to see the normal world—he spent all the rest of his time huddled with crooks, poor gamblers or failed businessmen.

In his office, Frankie grabbed a magazine from his desk drawer, swung his feet up and sat back to enjoy the contents of his latest journal. For fifteen solid minutes, he considered each of the pictures before him with great intensity although none particularly aroused him that evening. Then the phone rang next door.

Luigi popped his head round and waited, knowing Frankie never responded immediately to anyone appearing to get his attention.

"Yes?"

"Call for you."

"Who is it?"

"Says he's Frank."

"Put it through for fuck's sake."

"Hi, Uncle Frankie."

"Hello Frank."

"How are you?"

"All the better for hearing from you. It's late here and you're lucky to catch me still in the office."

"I'd forgotten the time difference."

So the boy had been in the same location for a day or two.

"Four hours?"

"Just the three."

Useful to know.

"And why are you calling me now? It's been a while."

"A lot has happened since we saw each other last."

"Sure has. And how's what's-her-name?"

"Mary Lou is fine."

"Pleased to hear it, dear boy."

"I wanted to speak with you."

"Otherwise you'd have sent a telegram."

"Seriously, Uncle Frank. We need to talk."

"I am being serious, dear boy. You have something which does not belong to you. You are a thief."

"Under the circumstances, I don't think there's any point in name calling—else I've got a few choice ones to throw at you. What you made Luigi and Paul do was not right for an uncle."

"Step uncle."

"It wasn't right, Uncle Frank."

"And what do you propose we do about all this?"

"I was hoping we could come to some form of arrangement."

"What were you thinking?"

"Well, we have merchandise you want."

"You do."

"And we must get away from all this."

"So?"

"If we give you back most of the merchandise, we've had to incur various expenses along the way, can we agree to go our separate ways?"

"What constitutes 'most'?"

"All but a hundred grand. The rest is yours. If you believe the radio, we took more than we were expecting."

"That's full of shit: we gave them the insured amount. The take was around half a million. Right?"

"How well informed for a man who hasn't seen a single red cent of the cash since it left the vault ten days ago."

"Let's say I have friends whose business interests include using a small-town bank for laundering."

Frank whistled.

"Nice. Funny because Mary Lou and I picked that branch as the easiest to steal from in the whole of Baltimore."

"Your whimsical nostalgia is noted but irrelevant. I want it all because it is mine and you have my belongings. This is not a negotiation."

"Uncle Frank, you seem to forget that if I put the phone down now, you will see none of your money again."

"The Feds and our friends in New York might have something to say about that."

"They might. Or they might not. Truth is they've been after us for quite some time but have not got close to catching us. And that means you're no closer to getting your money back. We are your best chance of that."

Frankie knew his step nephew was right. Despite Pentangelo's men and the FBI following them, the nearest they got was in Vegas and that had gone horribly wrong.

"I can be satisfied with ninety per cent of the merchandise."

"Eighty. That'll leave us with enough to keep going for the rest of our lives. We'll never need bother you again—or the guys from New York either."

"Accepted. Eighty per cent of something is better than a hundred per cent of nothing. Where shall we meet?"

"Los Angeles. Sunday. I'll call again to arrange the drop."

"I hope you understand this is purely business."

"Sure is, Uncle Frankie. On Sunday, you'll have the cash I'm promising you, and the mob will not need to find us. That's the deal."

"I promise on the souls of my grandchildren, if I get the money I shall call off my men."

"Speak Sunday. Bye."

"Goodbye dear boy."

The phone purred in Frankie's ear until he replaced the receiver. He laughed. Frank wasn't very bright or not a good listener. Lagotti Senior had only promised to step down his crew; nothing about the mob.

Frankie threw his magazine back into the drawer and called for a mug of coffee. When it arrived, he told Luigi he could go home. Then Frankie dialed New York.

CHARLIE PENTANGELO HAD managed the affairs of his Family for many years. While he was not the man in charge, he held a significant role in the organization. Frank Senior had promised him delivery of half a million dollars from the First Bank of Baltimore—and it hadn't arrived.

This state of affairs fell far short of ideal. More vexing was Lagotti's constant barrage of calls. There had been two in less than a week and each time, there was only bad news. Failure was not something Charlie wanted to be associated with—if matters carried on as they did, he might take action against Lagotti. For now, the man had three or four more days before Charlie would need to make a phone call. As if to reflect how often he was being harangued by the man, Frankie Lagotti chose this moment to put another call through.

"I have news."

"Talk."

"Frank Lagotti has approached me to return the money he has stolen from us."

"And?"

"I've arranged for a collection in Los Angeles in a few days' time."

"You know he killed one of my men. In Vegas."

"No, I did not."

"Well, you should bear this in mind when dealing with your nephew."

"He's my step nephew but we cannot allow him to live."

"You cannot. Robbing from us and murdering our members is unacceptable and you must send a clear message to everyone about the consequences of such decisions."

"I shall."

"Do you think you will recover all the money?"

"I intend to get every red cent they haven't spent."

"That is all I ask. And you will make up the shortfall. It was your project and I've lost a man along the way so that's the least you can do."

"Understood."

"I hope you do, Frank. We are not pleased with the situation you have placed us in and we expect you to resolve this matter."

"I will, Charlie."

A whir and a click in Frank Senior's ear and the phone went dead. Pentangelo rarely behaved that way. When he'd been angry in the past, Charlie explained the reason for his anger and what Frank needed to do to sort out the problem. But he never slammed the phone down on him before. He must be real pissed about losing one of his goons.

His step nephew was more resourceful than Frank Senior had thought him capable of. But now he knew where the fool was heading and would play that hand out to the full as he had a crooked deck.

He wanted his money back—no one likes a thief, but he also felt cheated. Frank Senior had set himself up with the perfect playbook: either the step nephew grabbed the cash or Carter the bank employee hustled out with the take. A win-win for Frank but it didn't pan out that way. And Frank resented that Mary Lou had screwed everything up for him. She had Carter in the clutch of her hand and her talons were into the boy Frank too. They would both need to pay—and not with greenbacks.

The Shylock put a call through to Anthony and told him to get his sorry ass over to City of Angels. He pulled out a magazine and checked out the pictures again in case he'd missed any details earlier on.

FRIDAY JUNE 27

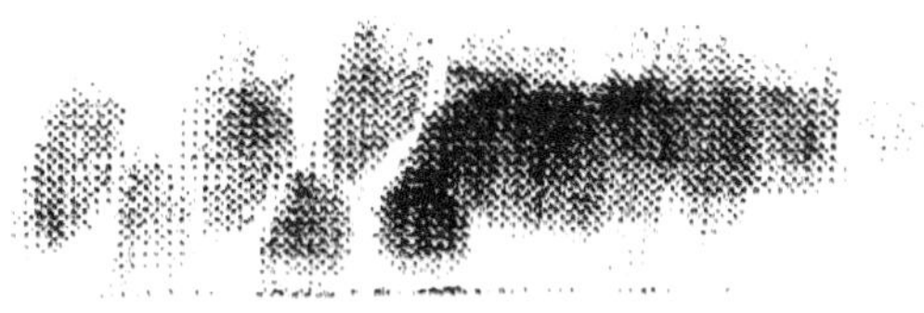

33

THEY WOKE AND hit the road early, not wanting to stay in one place any longer than they had to. Mary Lou took the first turn behind the wheel and they hoped they'd get to LA and strike a deal with Frankie.

"Do you think we'll make it?"

"Yes, babe, but not with all the money."

"He's got to let us keep some of it. That was the arrangement before he double-crossed us. That's at least the deal on the table now."

"And if Frankie disagrees?"

"We must help him change his mind."

Mary Lou turned briefly at Frank to judge his mood beyond his deadpan intonation but she had to turn back as she carried on staring at the road ahead.

"Any idea how we'll do that?"

"Not right now but we've got time: first we hit the city and contact a guy I know. Afterwards, we deal with Frankie."

"He'd kill us if he had the chance."

"Sure would. Our job is to make certain we don't give him the opportunity."

Mary Lou fixed her attention on the four hundred feet in front of the car and stayed in lane, five miles below the speed limit. She had faith in Frank but his uncle would do anything in his power to keep the money and end their lives. She swallowed hard to rekindle the saliva in her throat.

Frank's hand maintained its position on her thigh and his touch put her at ease—the stress in her stomach abating. They'd been through all sorts over the years and had come through fine. But this time Mary Lou was less certain about the future than she had ever been in her entire life.

The car hurtled onwards until the needle on the fuel dial pointed to the empty position. Ten miles later, a gas station beckoned them onto its forecourt. They both got out to stretch their legs and Frank instructed the attendant to fill her up.

Mary Lou walked away and to the side of the small convenience store with its cash register, newspapers and snacks for the hungry motorist. Behind the cash till was a miniature black-and-white TV with a local news channel. She wandered inside in search of chocolate and grabbed some chips for Frank. As she looked outside, the attendant finished dribbling the last drops of gas into the fuel tank. He pointed at her to tell the guy to take payment from her.

Carl walked behind his counter and waited for Mary Lou to complete her purchases. As she idled along the aisles, nothing tempted her. Down one aisle away from Carl and back up the other. As she sauntered toward him, she caught sight of the TV above his head. There were two photos on display: a mugshot of Frank and the other was hers. The only good news was the sound was off, but she stopped short of the register and let her jaw drop.

She twisted around and grabbed some gum to hide her unusual behavior. Mary Lou dropped the items for purchase and put on her sunglasses to cover her face. Money swapped for goods, she smiled a thank you and left the store.

She got into the passenger seat and slammed the door shut.

"Drive, Frank."

"What?"

"No questions. Drive!"

He did as he was told and sped out the gas station.

"Keep it steady, Frank. Five miles remember."

"Sure thing, babe. What happened?"

"We're on TV."

"Huh?"

"Our faces are all over the local news."

"What the…"

"Exactly."

Frank kept at a constant pace and the car lurched along the highway.

The Getaway

ANGELO SPENT AN entire day trying to find Rico, only to discover the guy had his neck snapped at the railroad station by person or persons unknown —according to the local news. Angelo realized as soon as he saw the broadcast: Frank Lagotti.

With that information and another call from the East Coast, Angelo's instructions were clear: it was time to head west and grab Frank and his wife when they reached LA. Dead or alive—but bring back the money. A short conversation with Paulie and they agreed to go together—with Charlie's blessing—but the dude took half a day to get the Flamingo's count room sorted with a trustworthy overseer.

They had one of Paulie's men to drive while he and Rico sat in the back of the black sedan and stared out the window. In their line of work, small talk was unnecessary and led to people knowing more than they should about the other guy. So there was no false tension in the vehicle. Three guys on an afternoon spree to the west coast to chase down two bank robbers.

As the journey would take five hours, they agreed to stop off along the way to grab a bite to eat. The sedan pulled into a hick town with one main drag with nothing of note apart from a cinema and a row of storefronts. Paulie and Rico walked the half-block to a diner and sat in a window booth.

"You reckon they stopped here too?"

"Might well have done. Who's to say, Angelo?"

The tumbleweed of their conversation span out the door, leaving the men with nothing to talk about. With so many hours spent together since they left New York, Paulie and Rico felt little need to supplement their food with idle gossip. Two professionals sat at a table with burgers and fries for company. Rico punctured the silence once their plates contained only crumbs.

"Where are we going to go when we get to LA?"

"What you reckon?"

"They like stations."

"But are they likely to repeat the same game?"

"Maybe not."

Rico stared at his mug of coffee, hoping for inspiration from the brown liquid and white crockery.

"Airport lockers?"

"Possibly. They've got to put the take somewhere."

"Yep. But they also need to launder the money."

"Lagotti has contacted the Shylock to arrange a meet. We should save our legs and turn up to the rendezvous to grab the cash."

"And if the moneylender's people get in the way?"

"Our orders are to retrieve the money. No instructions about anything else."

The corner of Paulie's mouth curled up and Rico understood the situation. His shoulders sagged and he relaxed into the conversation.

"When do we hear about the meet?"

"It's scheduled for Sunday some time. We need to be patient and to get there prompt."

"Hire a car and lie by a pool?"

"Like the plan."

"It has a simplicity even I can remember."

"Works for me."

"Throw the net into the sea and wait to catch a fish."

Rico nodded and they lulled back into silence. Then he looked up.

"Not a fish: a shark."

"Two sharks."

"We'll need a big net."

They both smiled and continued to stare into their mugs. Neither had anything to say to the other by now.

"Let's get going. The sooner we're in LA, the sooner we're soaking in the rays."

"You said it."

Paulie threw a few notes down onto the table and the two besuited men left the diner and headed back to their vehicle.

"Need some smokes first."

Rico nodded and leaned against the car while Paulie sauntered down Main Street to get to the nearest convenience store. Before heading to the counter, he walked up and down the aisles in search of something he couldn't quite put a name to. He noticed the clothing at the back of the store and wondered whether the Lagottis had been here earlier. He tried to memorize the patterns for future use but doubted he had done a fantastic job.

At the counter, he took a carton so if they holed up somewhere, he'd be fine for cigarettes until this escapade was over. Nothing worse than being stuck without nicotine. Back at the car, Rico nodded at him and before he opened the door, he posed a simple question:

"Will the West Coast syndicates leave us alone?"

Paulie left the key in the lock and stared at his colleague and blinked once.

"No. No, we won't. We'll need to be circumspect—they won't appreciate our trampling over their turf."

"Is there anything your connections can do to ease our passage?"

"Let's say there's some bad blood between the families."

Rico stared back at Paulie and took in this new information.

"So we're going into alien territory for the sake of some money two robbers stole?"

"That sounds about right."

"With no backup?"

"None."

"Are you not bothered?"

"Concerned: yes. Worried: no."

"And the difference is…?"

"All we have to do is get to the meet with the Shylock and shoot every dumb fucker who's breathing. After, we walk over, collect the money and leave town before any of Nicolo Licata's men find out we're there. By the time they're checking for fingerprints, we'll be back in Vegas shacked up at the Flamingo with pussy coming out of our wazoo."

Rico's expression glazed over as he imagined what he would do to the women covering his naked flesh with their tongues and other body parts. He smiled.

"I thought you'd see it my way. That's why I'm not worried. We have to keep our wits about us and be handy with our firearms."

"A pistol each and a few rounds?"

"Nah."

Paulie pointed to the rear of the car and popped the trunk. At the back of the space, behind their overnight bags, was a wooden box with a metal latch. He hauled it nearer for him and Rico to see its contents. When Paulie opened it, Rico let out a whistle.

"Semi-automatics: respect."

"Received with thanks. I like to go on a job when I am fully prepared and not a second before."

"That improves the odds in our favor. You kept that stash under your hat."

"A carpenter doesn't brag about his saw."

"Those are serious fucking saws, man."

Paulie closed the box and pushed it to its earlier resting place.

"Shall we go?"

"You bet. We have a date with destiny."

"Close enough."

PAULIE DROVE THEM the rest of the way to LA and they managed about twenty words across the hours in proximity to each other. Rico allowed himself to get lost in the radio station Paulie put on and time passed by.

Once they reached the outskirts of the city with no discernible center, Paulie decided where to head. The West Coast mob was a threat only in as far as it held nominal control of Los Angeles and the surrounding areas. There were only a few dozen men left in LA ever since Old Man Nick took over the family the year before. Even though Nick was under-exploiting his territory—much to the annoyance of Charlie Pentangelo—didn't mean he was without power in his home town. They'd need to fly below the radar for their time by the sea.

They headed to Huntington Beach south of Santa Ana. It was about as far away from the center of Californian life while still being in LA. Once arrived, they checked into a nondescript hotel overlooking the sandy front and waited.

Rico suggested trawling through local fences but Paulie pointed out this would only increase their profile with the West Coast syndicate and do nothing to help them track down the Lagottis. Much to Rico's annoyance, Paulie was right. So making up for their inability to do anything constructive, the pair headed to the rooftop of their hotel, sank some martinis and sat in the sun until Frank and Mary Lou Lagotti appeared in LA.

34

WITH THEIR FACES all over the local news, there was no chance to stop anywhere within the forests of the East Mojave National Scenic Area. A silence descended in the automobile with Frank's hand still resting on Mary Lou's thigh—the only comfort in the cabin apart from the slow warm breeze emitting from the air conditioning.

"Let's ditch the car, Frank."

"But we need to be careful where we're seen."

"Sure thing, but I'm scared."

"We'll get through this."

"They know what we look like and where we are."

"We'll dye our hair again and change our clothes. And they got a handle on where we were—not where we are heading."

"Frankie knows it's LA and so the mob will too."

"But we have the advantage. We set the meet and pick the location. We control the situation. They'll have no choice: we will get through this."

"I want to believe. I don't want to die and I don't want to go to prison either."

"You and me both."

Husband and wife smiled together.

"How well do you know LA?"

"Never been there in my life."

"You're kidding me."

"No. Why?"

"You said you met some people there so I…"

"I have connections but that doesn't mean I've visited the place."

"Oh. But your connections…"

"…are real. This guy was with me in the joint. We got on well—we looked after each other. Mark was from LA and returned there after his release."

"Do you trust him?"

"With my life."

"That's good enough for me."

Mary Lou watched as the car sped past the line of trees at the side of the highway. Nothing but foliage as far as she could see. A small window of light up ahead like a tunnel etched out of the trunks as they looked over them. Always five below the limit.

Fifteen miles later and he barked an order.

"Buckle up!"

Mary Lou didn't need to be told twice: not with that tone of voice. Frank removed his hand from her upper thigh and placed it on the wheel. He maintained their speed at a constant rate and she saw the blur of a state trooper vehicle as it scooted past. Chances were it was out to fill up on a daily quota of speeding tickets but they weren't sure.

Frank kept most of his attention on the rearview mirror for the next minute. Mary Lou tried to use the side mirror to check on progress—she didn't turn around as only the guilty look back.

Another sixty seconds and Frank's hand returned to stroke her thigh. She felt like breathing once more and, despite the lightness of his touch, a small tingle spread from her crotch up her spine. Ten miles more and the trees thinned out until the openness of the country was visible from the highway. Twenty further and they entered Barstow.

On the outskirts was a picture house. Five hundred feet later, they passed a convenience store, restaurant, clothes outlet, a place to pick up a rifle—the usual contents of a hick town with nothing to offer but the dream of departure.

Frank pulled in around the corner from this main drag.

"Time for a change, babe."

"I'll go. You stay here."

He looked at her and thought for a second.

"Sure. Safer than both of us on the street."

"Clothes. Hair color. Something to eat."

"And a coffee if you can find one."

"Will do, hon'. If I'm not back in thirty, get the fuck out of Dodge."

"I'll wait for you for an eternity. Take as long as you need."

Mary Lou kissed him on the lips like she would never see him again. She got out and walked over to the main parade. There was almost no one about. She checked her watch: lunch time. Why was the place so empty? She felt her stomach tighten as her nerves kicked in and the adrenaline flowed around her bloodstream.

First she hit the convenience store, careful to put on her sunglasses to hide her face. She grabbed all she could find and paid, not saying a word to anyone. The storekeeper wanted to chat—not enough customers today—but Mary Lou was having none of it.

In the clothes outlet, their lumberjack look would make them stick out in LA so she sought some city things at the back. Two miniskirts for herself, a pair of slacks and some pants for Frank. Black and white tee shirts for both of them, a pretty blouse and a plain shirt in Frank's colors. And a jacket each to hide any hardware they'd need to carry.

Shoot. She'd forgotten hair dye and had to go back to the convenience store and the talkative owner. She took advantage of her return to buy more pairs of sunglasses and two hats—a beret for herself and Fedora for Frank. He wouldn't be happy about it but it'd help to make his face harder to see.

A glance at her watch again: thirty-five minutes since she left the car. Why had everything taken so long? She scurried back to where he had parked but he wasn't there. She spun round but nothing. He had promised her an eternity and given her less than an hour. Her breathing kicked into overdrive and she leaned against the wall of a building.

In the periphery of her vision, despite the blurring in her eyes, she noticed a vehicle had pulled up in front of her. She ignored it for a second and tried to regain her composure. Then she looked up.

"Frank!"

"Used the time to get us a fresh ride."

She threw her purchases onto the backseat and jumped in.

"I thought you'd gone."

She squeezed his thigh briefly as he drove off.

"Mary Lou, I said I'd wait for you for an eternity—and I meant it."

She smeared away the tear falling down her left cheek.

"Let's go a few miles so we can bury what we're wearing."

Their new dark brown saloon traveled at five below the speed limit out of Barstow and headed toward Victorville on the way to LA.

ANTHONY PUT THE phone down and thought about Frank Senior's instructions: head to LA, meet up with the Lagotti couple, secure the money and torture the pair of them. If they die, bury them in the sand. If they survive, bring them to Baltimore.

"The Lagottis' time in Vegas is over, my friends. They are off to Los Angeles."

Bobby nodded and Mickey stared at Anthony awaiting further information. Anthony looked straight back at Mickey, not understanding what the man was waiting for.

"And?"

"So we will follow them to Los Angeles."

Each word was spat out so Mickey could understand the line of argument with no further repetition.

"Mickey. Let's pack up."

Bobby savored the moment because Anthony's eyes were misting over into rage—and there was no need for any of them to get hot and bothered. Mickey would come into his own very soon. What he lacked in brains, he gained in muscle. The guy handled himself in a tight corner: with a gun, a knife or with his fists. On those occasions he was handy to have hanging around.

Ten minutes later and the three men walked out the lobby with a bag each. Into their car with Anthony behind the wheel and the other two in the back.

"To the City of Angels."

Bobby issued the command after Anthony had pulled away and was on the highway. Anthony scowled at him in the rearview mirror but the corner of his mouth revealed he got the joke. The complacent smile on Mickey's face showed he very much had missed the point.

"Do we wait for instructions from Frank Senior when we arrive?"

"Yep. As far as I know, Frank and Mary Lou are due to arrive in town soon and will arrange a meetup with Frank Senior for Sunday. We go there, we grab the cash and we are done."

"And we can torture them if we want?"

"Once we have the money safe and secure, Mickey. Yes. Only once we have the money."

"Got it, boss."

Bobby's expression showed Anthony he too was finding Mickey difficult—they had been cooped up with the fella for far too long. In the past, Anthony gave the guy a call and, two minutes later, Mickey had sufficient information to whack some dude.

These past few days had tested everyone's patience. Anthony tried his best not to snap at Mickey but, as every day passed, this was getting harder. The guy meant well, but he had only a few brain cells to call his own. Anthony heard a story that Mickey used to be a boxer but had to quit because he got punch drunk. He found the tale difficult to believe: the man was slow on the uptake but possessed a clarity of thought and precision in the art of maiming and killing. He was no Jake la Motta.

The car sped out of Vegas and hit the highway to Barstow, Victorville and beyond. Mickey stared out the window at the wonders of the forestry that surrounded them for much of the first leg of their journey. Bobby tapped his hand on his knee in time to the music Anthony played on the radio.

Like everyone on the Vegas to LA run, Anthony pulled the car over at Barstow and they ate a burger and stretched their legs. The town existed only as a place for drivers to stop and get a breath of fresh air. Inhalations paid for every brick in town.

One diner, three men and two burgers and a steak then back to the road and an uneventful journey to LA. Once they arrived, Anthony took them to a hotel in Long Beach. It was a location he'd heard of before as he had no clue where the meetup with the Lagottis would take place. So Long Beach sounded as good a locale to wait as any other.

Compton Plaza was a small family-run establishment whose income relied on the kindness of strangers passing through town on their way to somewhere else. Anthony reckoned this meant the three men would be left well enough alone and, if anyone came sniffing by, the proprietor knew better than to provide any real information. Discretion in fleapits is quite common.

Anthony and Bobby nested in the hotel room and Mickey talked about planning a tourist trip the following day. Anthony explained how they should stick together and wait for Frank Senior's call but Mickey was having none of it.

"If they ain't showin' until Sunday that means we got tomorrow off."

His logic was sharp and, because he could handle himself so well, he didn't consider the possibility he should lie low until he was needed. From Mickey's perspective, he was in LA for the first—and only—time in his life and he should make the most of the opportunity.

Pizza boxes mounted in the room and the wait for Frank and Mary Lou continued. Anthony would return to Baltimore with a heap of cash and two warm bodies, only slightly mutilated.

SATURDAY JUNE 28

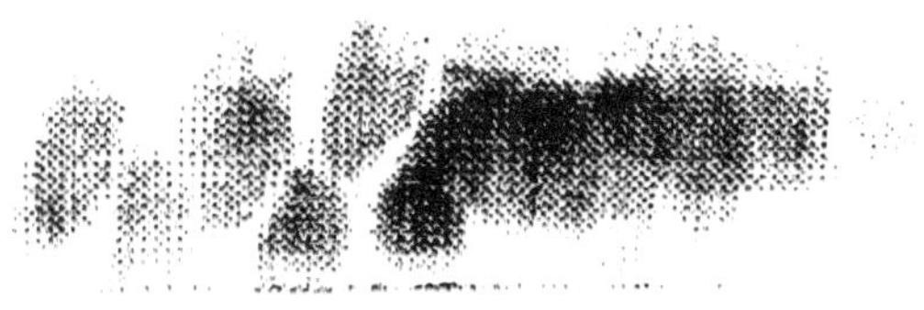

35

FRANK DROVE TOWARD Burbank as it sounded as good a place to aim as any other in Los Angeles. They circled round several times passing three motels and one hotel. He pulled over on the other side of the road to the Clement Fitzrovia Hotel. Then they watched the entrance for twenty minutes.

"Quiet spot."

"Yes, babe."

"Big enough for us to get lost among the other guests."

"That's what I'm thinking too."

Mary Lou continued to gaze at the frontage with its stucco designs alluding to a 1920s heritage. The entrance comprised faded bronze swing doors set in an oak frame. A patio area separated the hotel from the main drag and lent the place an air of refined dignity. Closer inspection of the lobby revealed crumbling wallpaper, botched paint jobs and an overwhelming need for basic maintenance.

If they had been holidaymakers, Frank and Mary Lou would have turned around and found somewhere with more pleasant surroundings. But this was the venue they needed: some place where few people showed up and the staff cared little for the patrons who bothered to show.

"How long will you be staying?"

"At least two nights, but maybe a week."

"Well, if you could be here that long, let's put you in a junior suite."

"No need for special treatment."

"Not at all. We like to give the rooms an airing."

He liked the implication their room would be isolated from the rest of the clientele. The front desk clerk summoned a bellboy to help them with their bags but, despite his best efforts, Mary Lou refused to allow him to take the black holdall out of her hand. To placate the teenager, Frank handed him the bag with their clothes: like every other bellhop before and since, he needed to make his tip.

They followed Tom into the lift and up to the seventh floor, below the penthouse level. Through the hallway and into an area with a couch, an armchair and a TV on a stand by one wall. Opposite the entrance to the room was a wall of glass with a balcony the other side. To the right, and close to where they were standing, was another door to the bedroom and an en suite shower. Along the corridor between the living space and their bedroom was a separate bathroom for guests.

The boy showed them all the rooms and opened the curtains wide to reveal the balcony in all its glory. Then he ceased his talking and stood, almost to attention.

"Is there anything you need?"

"No thanks."

"Then I'll be going."

Despite his words, Tom didn't move a muscle until Frank pulled a greenback or two out of his pocket and placed them in the boy's palm. He looked down and beamed.

"Thanks, mister."

Frank smiled back, knowing he had made a friend he could rely on. Love a town where a stranger can buy loyalty with five one-dollar bills. Financial transaction ended, the boy shuffled out and closed the door behind himself.

The couple placed their black bags on the coffee table by the couch. Frank went into the bedroom and Mary Lou checked out the furniture in the living room. There was a sideboard with sliding doors. If she removed the shelf, both holdalls would fit in fine. As she bent down to her task, Frank came back.

"Let's hide the bags under the bed."

"Isn't that a bit obvious?"

"No more than stashing the take in the first piece of furniture you see when you walk into the room."

She tilted her head, thought for a moment and nodded.

"No better, no worse."

"Let's split the difference."

Mary Lou took one bag and shoved it into the sideboard, sliding the door shut while Frank hid the other in the bedroom. Then they both sat down on the couch to take stock.

"Do you have the number of your LA guy?"

"Mark? Yes. I'll call him soon. We also need to decide how to handle Frankie."

"You told Frankie we'd meet up tomorrow."

"Yes, I know, but I've been thinking…"

"Do you not think we should get him off our back?"

"Of course, but if we clean the money, we could go to ground and reappear somewhere different. And not deal with Frankie or anything."

"I reckon you're right, besides we won't need to worry about him for very much longer."

"Huh?"

"Nothing, just mumbling. If we focus on the money, Frankie will take care of himself."

"That leaves us only having to handle the FBI and the East Coast."

Silence descended as they both thought about the seriousness of what Frank had said. Mary Lou nuzzled into him and they hugged while they sifted through ideas about what to do until the dying embers of Sunday. One step at a time: there was no point planning too far ahead.

Frank placed a call to Mark but the voice at the other end said he was out and wasn't expected back for a few hours. Mary Lou suggested they order delivery pizza—a luxury for the pair of them as they'd been on the road forever.

They told the concierge to get Tom bring the food up to them and handed him another fat tip.

"Tom. You going to be around for the rest of the weekend?"

"Sure am."

"Good. If you hear of anyone asking about us, let us know, right?"

"Sure will, mister. You expecting trouble?"

"Nope but we've eloped see and we don't my wife's family come storming in here giving her hell. They don't like me, okay?"

"Oh, I understand. I'll listen out good."

"Thanks, Tom."

She had opened the box by the time Frank sat back down on the couch and, within ten minutes, they had devoured the large pizza. Mary Lou took the carton and walked round the living room until she spotted the trash bin. She bent the card in two and squished it in. Then she turned to return to her seat.

Frank watched her all the while.

"What're we going to do now?"

In response, Mary Lou slipped out of her skirt, pulled down her panties and unbuttoned her shirt, letting her bra fall to the ground to join the rest of her clothes. He stared just below her tattooed rose. She smiled and looked at his face while she soaked in the desire of his gaze.

"I can probably think of something, hon'."

Mary Lou walked into the bedroom, followed by Frank, who had already removed his jeans before her bra had hit the floor.

PHIL MCNAMARA AND Ted Goodwin took a plane from Las Vegas—one advantage of being on a government salary. Phil had received a report that the Lagotti pair were heading for LA and he saw no reason to prolong their stay in the casino capital of the world. The place seethed with organized crime and this G-man did not like the smell.

They landed at Los Angeles International Airport and grabbed a taxi to the local FBI headquarters on Wilshire Boulevard. McNamara showed his badge and the receptionist let them through—Goodwin signed in as his guest. The Fed hightailed it to the bureau chief: politics are the same wherever you go in the world.

"Just checking in, boss. We're hunting the First Bank of Baltimore robbers and have word they've hit town."

"Thanks for the heads up. Make yourselves comfortable if you can find a desk."

"Much appreciated. If our source is correct, we'll be out of your hair by Wednesday latest."

"Take all the time you need—and if there's a warm body spare, feel free to ask for some help."

"Will do—and thanks again."

"Quick heads up: two burned bodies were found with some cash fluttering around them out in the wilds north east of the city. Serial numbers match the Baltimore heist but the corpses have yet to be identified."

"Mob hit on the Lagottis?"

"Possibly."

They left the suit's office and walked round the floors until they reached the basement where two empty desks stood opposite each other.

"Time to pitch tent."

Ted nodded and flopped down on his chair. McNamara settled in and filled the desk drawers with files he'd been lugging from his case.

"What now? And you never told me the identity of your source."

"That's because it's not on the up and up."

"Oh?"

"You see my agency is hopelessly conflicted as far as I can tell. We spend our time trying to capture the biggest, most-organized criminals the country has ever produced."

"Okay—and your problem is…?"

"But sometimes you need the help of a thief to catch a thief."

"So you have an informant out east who's feeding you their whereabouts?"

"Close enough."

"Not exactly right either though?"

"No. The relationship is closer than that."

Ted's quizzical expression stared back at Phil, who felt no need to expand on anything he'd said.

"Does it go into the mob?"

Ted whispered the question for fear he might hear the answer. McNamara looked left and right but there was no one within earshot. He nodded and Goodwin whistled in a mix of disbelief and the utmost respect.

"While I'll be…"

"So the best information has come from the East Coast, if you get my meaning."

"And what do they expect us to do if we recover the money?"

"Ted, if you have to ask, I'm sure as hell not going to dignify it with an answer."

"You're kidding me?"

"No. If we get the money off Frank Lagotti, we will make damn certain the cash gets lost in the evidence room."

"And the Lagottis?"

"Rumors of their deaths may have been greatly exaggerated. We'll have them in custody and they'll be safe with us. It's not like Lagotti is Lee Harvey Oswald."

Ted stared at him in abject horror.

"You tellin' me…"

McNamara laughed.

"Joke. I was joking with you."

Goodwin tried to guffaw but couldn't bring himself to do so.

"Focus, Ted. Just because we know they are in the same city as us doesn't mean we have any idea where they are. Follow me."

He stood up and Goodwin tailed him as McNamara strode to the stairwell and headed up. He knew his way around the building because he reached the computer room without asking anyone for directions.

"Why do you think they traveled across the country to get to LA?"

"My early investigations told me it was the place Frank Lagotti always wanted to go."

"Sure but why still head here after the bodies piled up?"

Ted shrugged.

"There must be someone or something here to draw them all this way."

McNamara turned to a technician and explained they were looking for any connection with Lagotti who might reside in the city. He was fed some background by Goodwin and the computer scientist sat down at his console and typed away.

"Let's get a coffee. This could take some time."

Ted nodded and they left the building and walked along three blocks until they reached a restaurant. McNamara ordered two coffees and a slice of cake each. And then they waited. An hour later they returned to the computer room where Harry the technician greeted them.

"Some good news, gents."

"Oh?"

"I've got some matches for you. One is a man who shared a cell with Lagotti in Baltimore. Mark Tucker, now in Glendale."

He passed a piece of paper to McNamara with the address and other personal details.

"And the other match is much warmer. Local news has been running mugshots of both your felons the last two days in Nevada and California and they were spotted this morning in Burbank."

Ted nodded and McNamara shook Harry's hand, followed by Goodwin.

"Time to wear out some shoe leather."

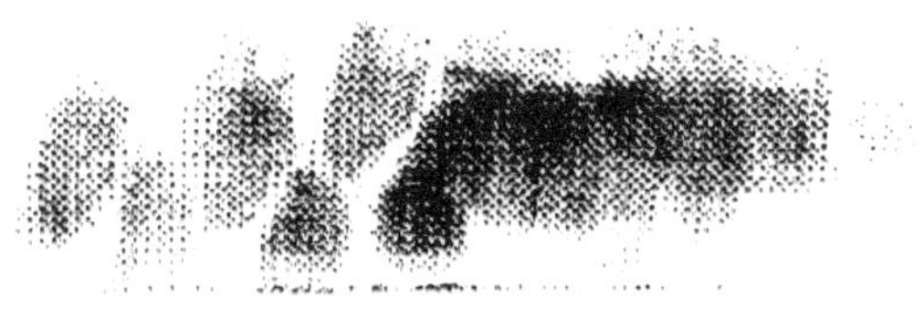

36

FRANK LOOKED IN between Mary Lou's legs to see the time on the bedside table clock. Almost two. He kissed her on the nearest cheek and pecked at her rose with his tongue until he remembered he shouldn't get distracted so easily.

Mary Lou watched as he left the bed and headed for the living room to grab a notebook from his bag and place a local call.

"Is Mark there?... I'll hold."

He turned to check out the rustling sound as she sat beside him on the couch. Both were naked.

"Mark? Yes, it's Frank L. How's it going?"

The first minute was catchup chatter with nothing worth Mary Lou listening to but she leaned into Frank's side in case hearing Mark's words later became important. He let his free hand slide down onto her thigh and played near her groin, which she found distracting but tingles mounted up and down her spine.

"Listen, bud. I've a favor to ask you."

"What's that, my man?"

"Are you still in the same game as when we last met?"

"Well, I'm a lot more free nowadays, but the play is the same."

They chuckled and then got down to business.

"Do you have any goods you want to pass my way then?"

"Sure do. Only these goods need a fantastic clean first."

Mark let out a whistle of approval.

"Glad to hear you've been moving up in the world, Frank. All the time you spent going on and on about your failed coup must have paid off for you. Respect."

"Thanks. We are in a much better position than last we spoke."

"We? You riding with someone else?"

"Sure am. She's my business partner."

"She? How open-minded of you. Good job you're in California—it's mighty used to hep cats like you."

"Can we meet up and talk some more? Phones attract the wrong people, you know."

"Understand, Frank. Best place for our kind of conversation are some flat, wide spaces. You play golf?"

"Huh? No. Have you joined a club or something?"

Another chuckle.

"No way, José. But there's a course right next to the airport and I like to meet associates there. Could you get near the tee off for the fourth hole tomorrow morning? Say ten?"

"Sure thing."

"I'll be easy to spot: I'm the dude in the golf cart who looks exactly as you remember him—only now I shave once a week."

Another chuckle and Mark hung up. Frank put the receiver back onto its perch and returned the phone to its side table.

"You hear all of that, babe?"

"Yes. Sounds like we got the rest of the day to ourselves, hon'."

"We should stay in the suite."

"Are you sure? I wanna be a tourist."

"It's not safe for us out there."

"What if we go in disguise? This could be our one chance to enjoy California. You've spent too much time dreaming of getting here to spend it stuck in a hotel room in fear of your life. Come on, Frank. Let's do it."

He sat back thinking through Mary Lou's argument. She was right: there's no point living like a coward: face the unknown. Of course, he wasn't stupid. He waited a few minutes before starting his trip so that she could finish her slobbering around his groin. The man liked the mystery of California and all it represented to him, but he loved having Mary Lou go down on him even more.

More hair dye, a shower for both and they were ready to take on the world wearing dark sunglasses and hats, turned-up collars and long coats. In case of trouble, they carried a piece each. When they hit the lobby, Tom the bellboy was standing to attention waiting for his next mission.

"Any news for me?"

"Nothing yet."

"Keep your ears open and your mouth shut."

"Will do, mister."

The Getaway

Tom pocketed the dollar without raising an eyebrow. They hopped into a taxi and headed to Grauman's Chinese Theatre on Hollywood Boulevard.

THE CAB DROPPED them off next to the Chinese Theater and they joined the throng staring at the ground, looking at the footprints and signatures of the famous from yesteryear. When Mary Lou looked down, Frank kept watch glancing left then right. After she'd had her fill, he would look at the concrete floor and she would be the guard.

With no conversation between the two, both maintained their hands on their guns throughout the entire experience. Panhandlers filled the area: Marilyn Monroe lookalikes, Bogart buffs and Cary Grant impersonators. If you had a camera around your neck, you were fair game to pay them to stand near you and have a photo taken.

One Marilyn made the mistake of approaching Frank but he used a direct approach to sending her off without fuss:

"Beat it, cutie. This john isn't for sale."

"Suit yourself. This girl's only trying to earn herself a living."

"Then do something honest like turning a trick, you blond whore."

"Take it easy, Frank."

"Sorry, babe. She got on my nerves. Hard to trust people nowadays."

"I know, but a hooker's still only a hooker. Her hot pants don't make her a member of the mob."

He slung a glance at the teenager as she slunk off looking for someone else to punch her card. Mary Lou was right though. He needed to stay calm to survive until the end of the weekend.

As he double-checked the sidewalk for the millionth time, he noticed a heavy-set dude who stood out from the crowd. Not only was he the only guy in a black three-piece suit within ten miles of the place, but he was heading in their direction at a fast pace. No way was the man a tourist—unless he'd just left a meeting and was a stranger in town.

The hat was the final item that set Frank on edge. Despite all the wannabe lookalikes who'd surrounded them the previous ten minutes, this fella looked as though he was trying to be Humphrey Bogart. Only too hard for his own good. Something was wrong in the state of California.

Frank tapped Mary Lou on the shoulder and she stood up as he pointed in Three-Piece's general direction.

"What you reckon?"

"Give me a minute and I'll tell you."

They stepped back from the crowd and inched to a nearby wall. She opened her bag as though searching for some long-lost family heirloom. He positioned himself opposite her looking in all directions but squarely staring at Three-Piece, who kept pounding toward them.

"Well?"

"Not good."

"Yep."

Three-Piece was twenty feet away and they could make out the contours of his face. Frank pulled out his gun and held it lowered. Fifteen.

Mary Lou tried to sink into the wall having pretended to find the mystery object from her clutch bag. She saw the revolver, saw Three-Piece and looked at the gun again. Ten feet.

"Frank…"

Five…

"Quiet!" snapped Frank.

Three-Piece had brown eyes entirely focused on the ground, like he was hurrying to get to his destination with no interest in his surroundings. Given he was marching past one of the most famous sidewalks on the planet, this was unusual behavior. Neither Frank nor Mary Lou liked it.

The suit continued walking as Frank swiveled to continue to face him in case he was about to turn around and act. When he got twenty feet away, he stopped right outside the Chinese Theater entrance. She stepped forward to mask Frank's gun from the passersby.

The guy bent down and appeared to tie his shoelace but she couldn't quite tell what he was doing for real. He stood up and twisted to face the theater. Frank's arm remained poised to extend, aim and fire.

She strode to the kerb and put her hand out to hail a taxi. Whatever happened in the next five seconds, she didn't want to stick around much after. A yellow cab pulled up and she grabbed open the door as Frank stood his ground, waiting.

Three-Piece continued to stare at the theater and turned his head down at the sidewalk. Then he shifted his weight and Mary Lou felt he was staring right through Frank, whose arm stiffened and she braced herself for the crack of the gun barrel. He dug his heels into the paving stones as he too noticed the change in Three-Piece's stance. Mary Lou gripped the door handle.

She blinked and, in that instant, Three-Piece shrugged his shoulders and walked away from the pair, continuing on his way along Hollywood Boulevard. Mickey never knew how close he got to receiving a bullet in his skull, but Frank did and Mary Lou had a good idea too.

Frank slid his gun back into his pocket and hopped into the taxi, followed by Mary Lou.

"Let's hightail it to Riverside Drive and the Warner Brothers studios in Burbank."

The driver nodded and hustled them over as quickly as his cab would take them.

"Why there?"

"We might spot us some movie stars, babe."

She smiled and pecked Frank on the cheek. That was what she wanted: to soak in the glitz of Tinseltown. They stood outside the studio gates along with all the other nobodies waiting to catch a silhouette they recognized in the rear of a stretch limo. But none appeared.

After an hour, they'd both had enough. The surrounding conversations dragged them down—ordinary people leading normal lives.

"Can we go back to the hotel?"

"I'm right with you, babe."

"We could grab a bite to eat on the way."

"Pizza for lunch. Shall we find Chinese for this evening?"

Mary Lou nodded and Frank walked fifteen feet away from the huddled masses to hail a taxi to separate them from the edge of the magic factory.

Sunday June 29

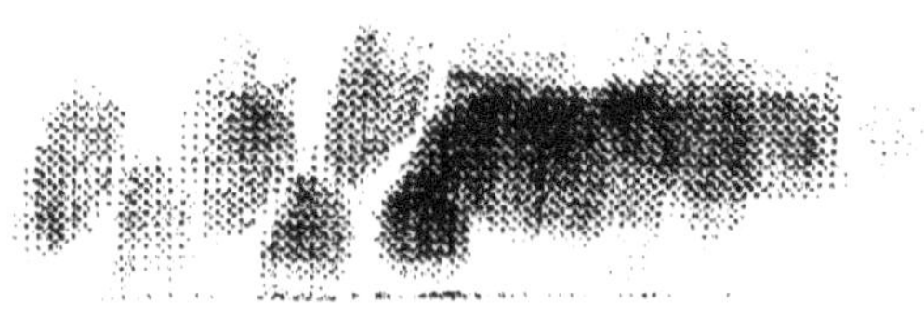

37

THEY TOOK TWO cabs to get to the Wilshire Golf Club: the first was to a random destination made up by the concierge. Then they walked three blocks and caught a different car to where they stood now. The course itself perched on the edge of Los Angeles International Airport. Planes flew over their heads but the site was vast and the noise of the engines didn't drown out conversation.

Frank and Mary Lou crouched behind some bushes next to the tee until Mark sauntered up to them. Frank smiled in recognition and they hugged, patting each other on the back they way men do.

"Damn good to see you again, Frankie L!"

"Mighty fine to catch sight of your face, Mark T!"

"And this must be your accomplice."

"Mary Lou, meet Mark Tucker. We were cell buddies in the day."

"Not that long ago, Frankie L."

"Plain old Frank nowadays, Mark."

"Gotcha."

Mary Lou shook Mark's hand for a greeting.

"Any buddy of Frank's is a friend of mine."

"I'm sure we'll get along just fine, Mark T."

He eyed up the pair, watching how they stood and the relaxed way Frank leaned in towards her body. His eyebrows rose and he whistled.

"Frank, you've got more than an accomplice with you, I'd say."

"You may well be right there, Mark, but we are here for business. We can catch up on old times later in the day."

"You betcha."

Mark walked away from the tee, making sure they stayed behind the bushes and wandered into a clump of eight to ten trees. Smack in the middle was a clearing with some stumps left flat, like they were Nature's own seats.

"Make yourselves comfortable. No one can see us from the fairways and unless we scream at each other, they won't hear anything either."

The three sat on a stump each but only Mark appeared the least bit relaxed on the makeshift wooden stools.

"Let's get down to business, Frank. First off. Are you a cop?"

"No. Are you?"

"No, I am not."

Although law enforcement officers were not the brightest sparks in the firmament, the judiciary had put in place a requirement that undercover cops didn't lie when entrapping felons. This meant the opening to criminal discussions begun with a standard mantra.

"So what do you want to send my way?"

"We've got a large amount of cash needs cleaning yesterday."

"How much money and how fast?"

"About five hundred and fifty thousand. And as soon as you can turn it around."

"First Bank of Baltimore was your hit? Don't answer that. What I don't know can't hurt me."

"It is a sizeable sum."

Frank looked over at Mary Lou who responded in kind. Then they both returned to stare at Mark.

"I thought that haul was twice as big."

"Can't believe everything you hear on the news."

Mark smiled and pondered.

"You got the FBI on your tail? They don't take kindly to people who rob banks."

"I didn't say we robbed a bank but Hoover has taken an interest in our journey across country."

"Is he the only one who's after you?"

"There are other parties involved."

"Baltimore cops?"

"Yep."

"That all?"

"Nope."

"Anyone I should worry about?"

"There are some guys with East Coast connections, Mark. Only fair to let you know. And some Baltimore locals who are less of an issue—for you at any rate."

"Risky business, your line of work."

"And yours. You get stuck with the notes."

"Only for a few hours. With a haul like yours, it's out of my hands before the end of the day. I'm old-fashioned enough to not let incriminating evidence languish at the bottom of a drawer."

"Good policy, my friend. So can you help us?"

"Frank, the question isn't if we'll do some business, but how much it'll cost you."

"If the cash is only with you for a few hours then your risk is minimal, wouldn't you say?"

"You're kidding me, man. It's all mine. You walk away with the clean bills and I'm left holding the baby and the bath water. Your notes can get traced back to me. The only thing stopping the cops knocking on your door is what I tell them. And that's a price worth paying."

"Mark, you know me well enough to be certain of this: if anyone crosses me, I'll kill them. Simple."

"You'd better watch out for him, love. Frank's business partners have a nasty habit of getting buried."

"Don't you worry about me. I know his past. From way before his arrival at the Baltimore Penitentiary."

Mark looked at her with cold eyes, deciding how much to believe this woman. Truth was Mary Lou and Frank got together soon after she arrived in Baltimore, some six years before he did time for the store heist.

She stared back at Mark, letting him make his judgements but not wishing to give him a moment to think she was some pushover. The fact they'd only just met meant Mark did not understand about her and Frank. He might not have mentioned a word about the man since he got out of the can, but Mary Lou could tell there was some special bond between the men.

THE BALTIMORE STATE Penitentiary had never been the most luxurious of penal institutions but it followed a series of protocols designed to keep the prison population as placated and secure as it could be. Two guys per cage was the rule and when Frank's cell mate finally got parole in '66, a new arrival was inevitable within a few days.

Mark waltzed into his life by throwing himself into the top bunk, declaring his possession. As Frank was lying on the lower bed, he didn't care as he wasn't planning on budging from his perch.

The first two weeks passed without incident, both men engulfed by the tedium of their position. Mark kept his mind alive by doing what came natural: buying and selling anything he could lay his hands on and sometimes that included property owned by the prison staff.

Nooks and crannies stuffed with contraband filled their cage. Frank didn't care as he got the occasional perk and nobody would believe he was the perp. Mark's import-export business was thriving, but it relied on him getting goods of interest to the inmates. He operated a barter system which meant other convicts were invited to offer items they'd found to swap for objects in his cell.

The big problem was that it encouraged criminals, many of whom were habitual thieves, to rob from each other. The more desperate prisoners would take the biggest risks, leading to Mark rubbing shoulders with the more dangerous elements of the prison population.

In the third week, Donald "The Hatchet" O'Reilly came into the cell. His nickname said it all: never cross him unless you wanted to be wearing an ax embedded in your skull. Frank was on his own, polishing his shoes.

"Where's Tucker?"

"Dunno, O'Reilly."

"Not good enough. Where is he?"

"I don't know. He's been out the cell most of the morning."

"Tell him he needs to find me."

"Sure thing, O'Reilly."

The lumbering giant, bedecked in tattoos of every conceivable pattern and image over every visible inch of his skin, lurched toward Frank, grabbed him by the throat and yanked him upwards.

"Listen closely, Lagotti. You don't appear to be taking this matter seriously enough. When Tucker gets back from fucking whoever he's fucking, send him over before he nestles down between your great hairy, white ass cheeks. Get me?"

Frank nodded as best he could, blinking acknowledgement to the bearded behemoth who ran the block. O'Reilly's hand relaxed around Frank's larynx but maintained a basic grip.

"The slug has my property and I want it back."

"Okay. Understood. What is it?"

"Are you his agent?"

Frank thought for a minute and realized O'Reilly was right. The last thing he wanted was to get involved but here he was with a hand around his throat and a question out his mouth.

"Smokes. Ten cartons."

"I'll let him know. That's a lot of smokes."

"Better believe it. If I don't receive restitution by four this afternoon, he's a dead man walking."

O'Reilly growled and exited the cell, leaving him alone knowing Mark was due to die. Just before five, Mark entered the cage, torn overalls, bruises around his cheeks, mouth and forehead. One eye was closed up; Frank couldn't work out how the man could see.

"Jeez, Louise."

"Shoulda seen the other guy."

He attempted a smile but the pain of moving the muscles in his face was too much for him.

"O'Reilly found you then."

A nod.

"He set you a four deadline."

Another nod. Mark sat down on Frank's bed.

"I tried to find you but you vanished. Thought you might have had the good fortune to have escaped."

Further attempts to chuckle by Mark but winced with the pain.

"It's not over yet."

"Still wants his smokes. You got them?"

Mark shook his head.

"Sold them on?"

A nod again.

"Anything worth ten cartons to trade?"

Another shake.

"Huh? You always have stuff coming and going."

Amid the spit and drops of blood:

"O'Reilly owns all my stash now. I owe him twenty cartons on top of it all. I got zip."

Frank stood and thought. Mark made this problem for himself but he guessed the guy didn't realize he was trading in O'Reilly's cigarettes.

"How long to pay the debt?"

"Two days."

"Jeez."

Mark looked up at him with plaintive eyes. The men shared a cell, but that was about all.

"I might be able to help."

He gave a quizzical expression in between the cuts and bleeding. Frank kneeled next to the head and pulled a small plastic bag out of a cubby hole. Without letting him see the entire contents, he took out a roll of notes and replaced the pouch.

"First, I must find a new hidey place. Second, you can pay O'Reilly off with the green here. It's at least the price of twenty cartons, but you have to understand that was my bribe money. Without it, I can't keep the guards away—and I haven't been too friendly with some of them in the past, see. So if I hand over this cash, you must look after me instead. Got it?"

If Mark had been able, he would have smiled, but a ghoulish set of teeth showed across his expression.

That night, Frank went to bed first and Mark slipped in under the covers beside him. He did nothing to push him out and Mark looked after Frank's interests from that moment until he got parole three months before Frank himself stepped out into the bright Baltimore sunshine.

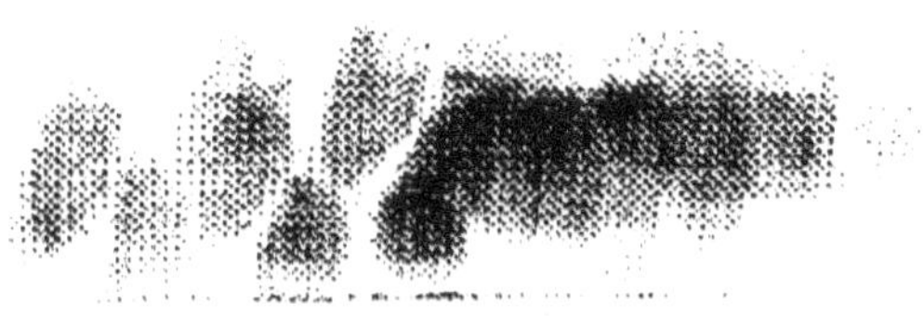

38

MARK AND FRANK stared at each other, the memories of the penitentiary flickering across their expressions.

"You guys will be off out the state while I'm stuck with a bunch of questions from the Feds or a bullet from the mob. So be serious, my man."

"Mark, let's not get ahead of ourselves. Yes, I want us to do business but we need to remember what is what and what has passed."

"The past is gone and all we have is our future."

"Past but not forgotten."

"Sure, Frank. But gone."

He fell silent as he didn't think it wise to push the guy too far because he so needed him, but he thought Mark and he had some connection the boy wanted to ignore. Maybe it was just negotiation.

"What of the future then?"

"You've got racks and you want me to swap them for greenbacks. Untraceable and with no consecutive serial numbers unless I miss my guess."

Frank nodded, knowing his old friend had the upper hand—but that had been the case before he'd picked up the phone and contacted the only person from California in his address book.

"What can you give us?"

Now Mark was silent as he mulled over his opening offer.

"Your uncle: what deal did he throw at you?"

"Forty cents on the dollar."

Mark smiled.

"That was the offer. In reality he planned on taking it all and leaving you with nothing, so anything I put forward will be better than the only offer you currently have on the table."

Frank ground his molars because Mark was squeezing him. There was no need to behave like this. Why play a power trip on him?

Mary Lou watched the proceedings and wondered why Frank was trying to do business with this guy. Better for the two of them to torture him until he spilled where he stashes his clean cash. Must be somewhere and not that far from here either. But that's not how Frank wanted to play it—and she respected him too much to take action now.

"Me and Mary Lou can slice your throat open right here and take all the money you've got stored around the city. But you and I have a history and I'm hoping you remember that as we carry on our conversation."

"Stay chilled, Frank. Just jerking your chain. Nothing more. How about twenty cents on the dollar?"

"That won't give us much. We'll have to leave the country—at least until everything dies down and that could take years, not weeks or months."

"I hear you, but you understand I have overheads and I'm trying to do the best I can for you under the circumstances. If you flee the heat, chances are it'll descend on me and we must factor that into the price."

"You and I appreciate there's plenty of fat in the eighty cents you're talking about keeping. All I'm asking is for you to share a little—like I shared my stash with you when we were inside."

Mark gazed down at the earth, eyes unfocused. Mary Lou couldn't tell if he was having an attack or had fallen under some hypnotic spell. After fifteen seconds, he blinked and looked up.

"Twenty five cents. And that takes account of everything that happened in Baltimore."

"Appreciate that, Mark. Is that the best you can do for us?"

"Better believe it. How much are you sitting on again?"

"Five hundred and fifty thousand."

Mark's eyes widened until he got them under control and let out a quiet whistle.

"Total respect man. And to you, lady."

Mary Lou nodded. She was seeing a different side to Frank than he'd shown these last few days. Almost like she'd forgotten how he spent a year planning the heist and leading the gang all that time.

"Tell you what. Round the total up to one hundred and forty thousand and we'll call it quits."

"Frank, as it's you, I'll show a splash of generosity. You and your missus have yourselves a deal."

He had managed to squeeze an extra two and a half grand out of Mark. All three stood up and shook hands to seal their fates.

"Unless you've got the racks stuffed in your pockets, you'll need to collect the goods."

"Yeah, we decided not to bring it with us. Nothing personal, but it's a dangerous game we're playing."

"No explanation necessary. You didn't know if you could trust me. No worries. I'd have done the same."

Frank seized Mark by the cheeks and planted a kiss square on his lips.

"I knew you were the right man to come to."

A long hug as they relived their shared past. Mary Lou stood by, wanting to join in but knowing there was a private experience connecting the two felons. Once they'd separated, she gave Mark a peck on the cheek.

"Thanks for everything. For helping us now and being there for my Frank through his prison time. He's always refused to talk about it, but I can see you too had something special."

She squeezed Frank's hand and he placed an arm around her shoulders. Everyone was square.

"How long will it take you to get the money together?"

"It's ready now."

"Seriously?"

"Yep. I've been doing well since you last saw me."

"Good for you."

"The stash is in some lockers, nice and secure. I need to go back to my pad to pick up the keys."

"Shall we meet in sixty minutes? Will that give you enough time?"

"Sure thing. We're off to Burbank Airport."

"That still going?"

"Yeah, for cargo now, which is why I like it. No screaming kids but plenty of traffic."

"An hour then."

"You get outta here first. I'll go five minutes later once you're safely away."

Frank and Mary Lou crunched to the edge of the tree line and waited until two men had sent their golf balls flying down the fairway. Then they boosted a car in the parking lot and headed straight back to the Clements.

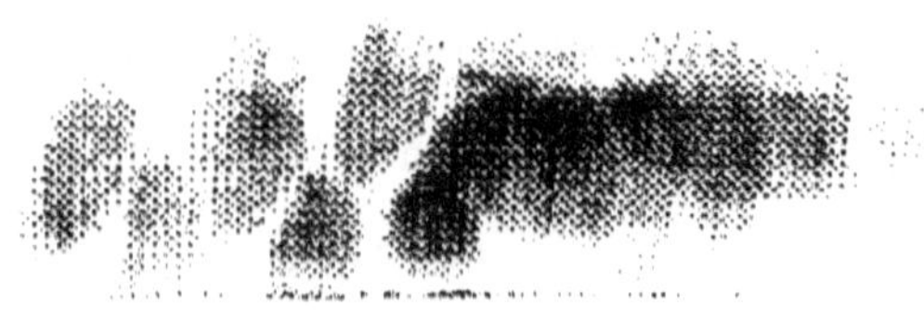

39

FRANK PARKED FOUR blocks away from the Clements and they walked back to the hotel. Through the lobby and up to their room. He pulled out their fake ID from their nightstand drawer while Mary Lou grabbed the two black bags from their hiding places and dropped them onto the coffee table. She went into the bedroom to find out what was taking him so long.

She found him sat on the bed, head in his hands, fake driving license and passports lying next to him. Mary Lou kneeled in front of him, her body between his knees.

"What's the matter, hon'?"

She wiped a tear off his cheek. He'd never behaved like this before and a fear was gripping the middle of her stomach.

"Nothing, babe. After all this time, I can't believe this is coming together. That's all."

Mary Lou's shoulders relaxed and she kissed him, holding the sides of his face in her hands.

"We'll be okay. The only thing to think about is getting the money today. Nothing else matters."

"I know. We'll figure everything out later on. It's Mark we need to focus on now."

"You bet. In a year or two we can come back to California."

"To be honest, babe, for me it's never been about California. It wasn't where we went that counted: it was about leaving. Baltimore was killing me and it would have killed the pair of us if it had the chance."

"That's thousands of miles away."

"Good, isn't it?"

Frank kissed Mary Lou again and let one palm slide down her spine and reach her ass. She put a hand on his groin and separated their lips. In a whisper: "We can fuck ourselves to oblivion later. Now is the time for money."

He squeezed her cheek and sneaked a finger in between her thighs making a single tingle race up her back and reach the nape of her neck. She kissed his hand and placed it on his lap.

"Let's go, hon'."

"You bet."

As ever, they took one bag each, holding hands while they waited for the elevator. In the lobby, Tom stood near the concierge. He walked toward them as soon as he noticed their arrival.

"Mister, I got news for you."

"What's happening?"

"There's been men asking after you and I thought you should know."

"How many?"

"Two pairs. All in suits."

"Four in total?"

"Yessir. I heard them ask the receptionist about you. The first turned up an hour past. You almost bumped into the second set. They were here ten minutes ago."

"They in the lobby now?"

Tom searched round but shook his head.

"You done good."

Frank planted another five spot on the bellboy.

"We're off out again but keep your eyes peeled and your ears open. We'll be back later and you can give us an update. Okay?"

Mary Lou and Frank scurried out the lobby. Before they left the confines of the building, he checked up and down the road but nothing appeared suspicious. At a brisk pace, they hurried along the four blocks to their boosted ride.

Bags on the back seat, he sat behind the wheel. They both pulled out their guns and each counted six slugs in the chamber. Mary Lou looked up and down the sidewalks trying to find the two sets of men. One pair must be Uncle Frankie's goons and the other from the East Coast, she reckoned. The knot of fear in her stomach returned but for a different reason than before. She was more confident because she'd handled dangerous fellas all her life but she couldn't handle things if he could not cope.

"See anything?"

"No."

"Me neither, babe."

"We better get to Mark then."

Frank played with the wiring under the steering block until the engine fired up. He looked over to her and winked. She smiled back: there was something magical in starting a car without the use of a key. And the magic rubbed off on the conjuror who performed the feat.

AS THEY ARRIVED at Hollywood-Burbank Airport, Mary Lou studied the L-shaped building that straddled two sides of the rectangular parking area. The short side was at the far end by the arrivals, whereas the long edge ran the full length of the lot and was designated for departures.

Frank parked the car near the arrivals. They had driven for five minutes before they found any space at all, but the place only coped with two hundred vehicles, so they shouldn't have been that surprised. The advantage of driving round in circles was that it gave them a chance to spot anyone who'd previously visited the Clements Fitzrovia but there were no obvious candidates.

"Keep one hand on your gun, okay?"

"Got it, hon'."

They walked through the parked vehicles until they reached the far end of the departures. With most planes picking and dropping cargo, there were only two gates for passengers left open nowadays. In the previous five years, several major airlines had moved to LAX and Burbank was heading for a decline. A perfect rendezvous location and a great place to hide money in plain sight. Mark was a clever cookie.

Once inside, Mary Lou's and Frank's eyes followed the long corridor that made up the main building. There was a fair buzz of people despite the lack of passenger flights. Mark had failed to mention the number of private jets that still called Burbank home. A series of concession stands broke up their line of sight.

"It's going to be hard to walk down this building without getting spotted."

Mary Lou nodded as she was thinking the selfsame thing. Then she froze, legs unable to move from their position.

"Three hundred feet ahead. By the coffee concession. Two guys. You see them?"

"Got 'em."

"Recognize them?"

"No."

"Might have seen one of them before. On the strip in Vegas. When we hid in the lingerie store."

They both watched Ted Goodwin talking with Phil McNamara, each holding a mug with steam pouring out. Conversation and sips for five, ten minutes while Mary Lou and Frank remained where they were.

"They're not moving any time soon. Has he recognized us?"

"If he's any kind of cop, he should make both of us."

"Let's go."

Mary Lou followed Frank out the building. They stood by the entrance in case of trouble but nothing came. So they padded down the sidewalk until they reached the next door. The wall of the terminal was pure glass, which meant they could see they'd passed by Goodwin and McNamara. If Goodwin made either of them, then he saw where they were standing too.

When they walked inside, they were still amid the gates and concessions, only this time the nearest ones were sealed up, unused. The airport authorities had established a clear separation between the departure area past Goodwin and McNamara and the arrivals section, which Mary Lou and Frank had yet to reach.

They strode away from Goodwin, following the overhead signs for lost luggage. As they walked, both sets of eyes were flitting from one group of people to another. Mary Lou figured that if the FBI were here, then the mob or Frankie's men couldn't be far behind. What she couldn't understand is how they knew to be at this airport at all. An hour ago, she and Frank had zero clue they would end up here before lunchtime, so how could the Feds know? Either they're covering all airports and train stations or Mark dropped a dime on them after he left the golf course. Frank nudged her side as he stared straight ahead.

"Looks like we have more company. Anthony and the guy from the Chinese Theater."

Mary Lou scanned the end of the cavernous room which Frank was facing until she spotted Three-Piece. She gulped.

"What now, hon'?"

"Time to find Mark and get outta Dodge."

"Okay."

They skipped back outside and carried on further along the sidewalk. Anthony and Three-Piece were so busy checking out everyone in the building, they didn't bother to keep an eye on anyone on the other side of the glass wall. Frankie only ever hired the cheapest; never the brightest.

Mary Lou and Frank reached a door with an enormous Arrivals sign above the entrance. Inside there was an arrow for lost luggage.

They walked past the two carousels for baggage collection and sauntered, as casually as possible, round the corner to reach three rows of lockers. In the middle of the second row stood Mark whistling to himself as he leaned against the metal containers. When they approached him, he half-saluted and took his hands out his pockets.

"The place is crawling with fellas. Let's make this quick."

MARK NODDED AND wasted no time as he hurried to the far end of the row and pulled out a bunch of keys from his jacket. Mary Lou and Frank sidled up next to him, both facing away from his activities to keep an eagle eye on anyone who might be intent on getting their money. She heard various clunks, slams and twists of metal. Brown holdalls appeared at Mark's feet.

"Do those bags hold the loot?"

Frank nodded and passed his over to Mark who threw it into a locker and slammed it shut. She did the same.

"I trust you not to have to count it."

"If when you open it there's just cut-up bits of newspaper, find me and shoot me where I stand."

"I will, my friend. And your missus too."

"I wouldn't have it any other way," Mary Lou added.

Mark smiled and picked up the two holdalls he'd retrieved.

"One has a hundred grand, the other forty. Count it if you need to."

"We don't. If it's shreds of newspaper, you know where to find us."

"Standing over my cold, dark grave."

"You said it, muchachos."

Then from the far end of the row of lockers:

"Put the bags down, place your hands over your heads and no one will get hurt."

Goodwin and McNamara trained guns on the three of them and Mary Lou's stomach clenched in knotty fear.

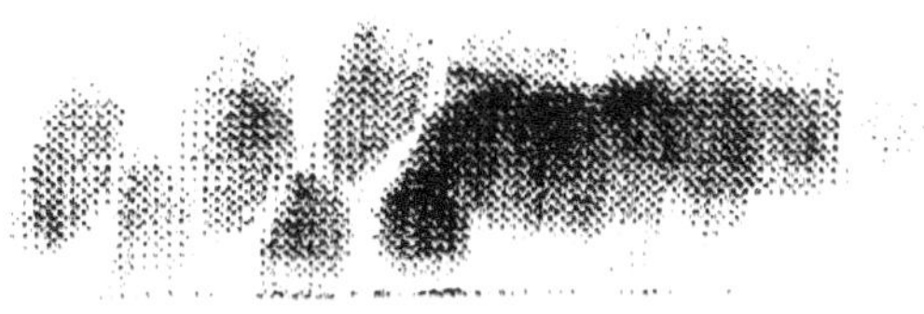

40

MARY LOU AND Frank looked at each other and stared at McNamara. He was the older of the two and had been the one to issue the warning. They clung to the holdalls, gripping tighter than before.

"I said to put the bags down."

"Hands on your heads!"

McNamara's voice contained authority and he was attempting to sound reasonable. Goodwin barked an order at them. Mary Lou watched as McNamara winced at Goodwin's instruction.

The two men edged along the row of the hundred-foot lockers until they were only seventy feet away; McNamara's gun remained pointing at Frank all that time. Goodwin's barrel flitted from Mary Lou to Mark and back again. Behind the three was the glass wall of the terminal building so they had to get out of this metal alley. Whichever other aisle they chose—even if they split up—the cops could pick them off from the other end. The only place to go was nowhere.

A single shot rang out and the they dropped to the ground. Mary Lou and Frank pulled their guns out and Mark fumbled in his pants trying to yank out his piece. She looked around to see red gushing from Goodwin's chest. McNamara had his back to them and was firing off into the distance. Anthony and Three-Piece had made their move—but too early.

Frank, Mark and Mary Lou scurried towards McNamara and crouched down, pressed against the same side of the lockers. The Fed got to one knee and carried on shooting. This gave them time to reach him without catching stray shrapnel.

"This bunch your men?" commanded McNamara.

"Nope."

A bullet whizzed past, missing McNamara's ear by a hair's breadth and Mark spun round and fell to the ground. Blood poured out his neck. Mary Lou screamed and Frank grabbed Mark's gun. He gritted his teeth and fired back at Anthony and Mickey. The only way to escape those two was to kill them.

The cover offered by Frank gave McNamara the opportunity he needed and he ran to the end of the aisle and burst past the corner to get a better line on the snipers.

Frank kicked his holdall forwards. He and Mary Lou perched at the edge of the lockers and watched as McNamara put a bullet straight through Mickey's heart. Clean shot. Then he reloaded his pistol as they gave him cover. Anthony was staying his ground: he knew he was so close to the money, he could almost taste it.

Alarms were spitting out high volume bells by now and the citizenry were running left and right behind Anthony, desperately trying to avoid the gunfire but too scared to think straight and run in the opposite direction and outside.

With fresh slugs in his handgun, McNamara took aim at Anthony, who raised up on his haunches to get a better chance of a hit. Slugs rained out of his piece and McNamara ducked. Then he kneeled back up and sent two bullets into Anthony: one in the gut and the other in his chest. Anthony's body hurled itself in the air and came to rest five feet further on. He screamed in agony, grabbing his torso. McNamara stood up to deal with the felon.

Mary Lou put her hand to her forehead to wipe off the sweat. When she took it away, her fingers were red. Strange, she felt no pain. Then she looked down and gazed at the bullet hole in Frank's upper body and realized his blood had ricocheted onto her, plastering her face with his vital fluid.

WITH A SCREAM of agony, Mary Lou let go her holdall and kneeled down to hold Frank in her arms. Tears lashing down her cheeks, she kissed him on the forehead, kissed him on the mouth and sat with his body hauled on her lap.

Tears, air bubbles of mucus and spit fell down onto his lifeless torso, mixing with the blood puddling out his corpse. Mary Lou sobbed and wailed, crying for the only man in her life who had ever shown her even a hint of kindness. She was alone in this godforsaken world and her honey was dead in her arms.

The alarms carried on ringing and she continued to cry, not caring what happened next. One of Frank's feet twitched slightly in his death throes. The knot in Mary Lou's stomach ceased to ache as the overarching pain of her situation engulfed her completely. Her world reduced itself to her throbbing head and the man she'd loved in her arms. And the pool of blood coalescing around her.

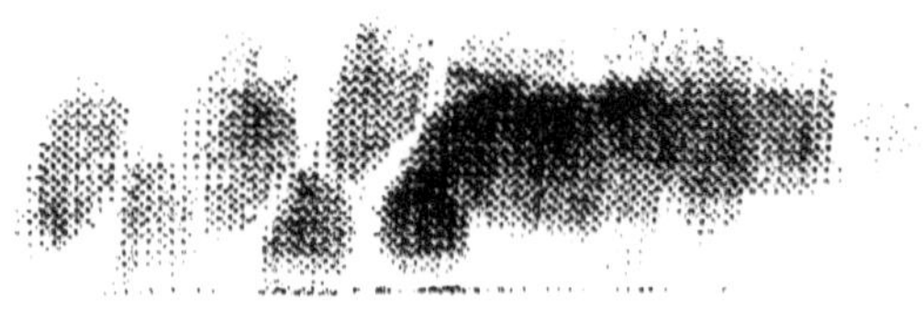

41

FRANK SENIOR WAS spending the last vestiges of the night pleasuring himself in the Kitkatt Club with a girl called May. He had plied her with vodka and fucked her in every available orifice. She hurt across the entirety of her body but knew better than to stop him. The receiving end of Frankie's ire was not a good place to be.

So she sat astride the moneylender, letting his half-erect penis flop near her bush. He was tired enough to be dozing and she was almost unconscious too.

Arnold Roach had received his instructions from Mary Lou by phone around lunchtime on Monday, June 16. The plan was simple and clear. Fifty per cent of the money arrived as requested prior to his task and she would send the rest on its completion.

Roach walked into the Kitkatt and ordered a drink at the bar. He kept his sunglasses on and the lapels of his coat pointed upwards, hiding part of his face. He leaned on the counter and watched the show on stage. Nothing special, just the relentless sight of semi-naked teenagers revealing their bodies in the hope of a Jackson in their G-strings.

He finished his watered down drink and left a dollar tip for the barman. Sauntered around the back edge of the seating area and arrived outside the private rooms. Arnold nipped into the first one but it was empty. Then into the second and closed the door behind himself.

Walked up to the bed where May had flopped on top of Frankie. Roach grabbed a pillow lying on the floor and pushed the sleeping girl off the moneylender. Cushion over his head before the guy could wake and react—and squeezed the trigger. Feathers flew into the air in a ball. Frankie's face was welded to the back of his skull.

May woke as she landed on the ground only to see white fluff. Before she could call out, Arnold stuffed the pillow over her mouth and pulled the trigger again. He didn't wait to check if she was alive because she hadn't seen his face either way. He walked out the room, out the Kitkatt and got into his car to drive off, knowing the second payment from Mary Lou was only days away.

HER PAIN WAS undiminished, but Mary Lou couldn't stay with Frank for an eternity. She pushed him gently off her lap and looked down at her bloody clothes, arms and legs. She wouldn't get far looking like that. This thought forced her to think about the world beyond herself and she saw the blood, the lockers, the terminal building and McNamara walking toward her, gun in hand.

If he got back to her, then there'd be handcuffs on her in less than ten seconds. She picked up one gun lying on the floor and took aim. A crack rang out and McNamara fell to the ground. She smiled as she hit her mark: the right leg. Mary Lou might ache with the loss of Frank but she was thinking clearly enough not to kill a cop.

She stuffed the gun into her waistband, grabbed both holdalls and exited out the nearest door. Mary Lou zigzagged in between the parked cars until she spotted a set of keys in the ignition of a green sedan. She jumped into the driver's seat and threw the bags next to her.

Out the lot and down the road. Tears still dribbling down her cheeks, she exhaled deeply and dragged the vehicle away from the air terminal, five miles an hour below the speed limit. The money sat in the footwell and Mary Lou's dreams lay shattered by the lockers back at Burbank Airport.

THE END

THANK YOU FOR READING!

Get a free novella

Building a relationship with my readers is the very best thing about writing. I send weekly newsletters with details of new releases, special offers and other bits of news relating to the Lagotti Family and Alex Cohen series, as well as information about my stand-alone novels.

And if you sign up to the mailing list I'll send you a copy of the Lagotti Family prequel, The Stickup. Just go to www.leopoldborstinski.com/newsletter-signup-book and we'll take it from there.

Enjoy this book? You can make a difference

Reviews are the most powerful tools in my arsenal when it comes to getting attention for my books. Much as I'd like to, I don't have the financial muscle of a New York publisher. I can't take out full page ads or put posters on the subway.

(Not yet, anyway).

But I do have something much more powerful and effective than that, and it's something that those publishers would kill to get their hands on.

A committed and loyal bunch of readers.

Honest reviews of my books help bring them to the attention of other readers.

If you've enjoyed this book I shall be very grateful if you would spend just five minutes leaving a review (it can be as short as you like) on the book's page. You can jump right to the page by clicking www.books2read.com/getaway

Thank you very much.

Leo

SNEAK PREVIEW

In the next installment…

Charlie Pentangelo accepted his mob money had floated into the wind. He was calm about not seeing the cash ever again, but he continued to fume at the people who'd taken the proceeds of the heist from him.

As he never held the cash, he was no worse off than before the robbery was mentioned. The Shylock, Frank Lagotti Senior, felt differently. He had the money almost in his hand before his step nephew snatched it out of his grasp. The real issue for Charlie was that people shouldn't steal from him. Rob from a bank? Knock yourself out. Take from Pentangelo? Not if you want to see your next birthday.

Earlier in the day, word reached him about a gunfight in LA and how the Feds had done for his boys while they were trying to get the money back. Details were scant, but he knew the proceeds were gone and two of his own needed a funeral.

Now he sat on his own in his favorite chair contemplating his next move. Frank Senior had been wise to let his step nephew take the First Bank of Baltimore and its half a million even though the man himself was a parasite on the carcass of the world.

The phone rang.

"Hello?"

The voice on the other end of the line spoke flat, no intonation. Just the facts with no comment.

"The money has left Burbank Airport. Our two are dead, the Shylock's men are offed as well."

"And?"

"Our FBI sources confirmed Frank Lagotti and one unknown guy are dead. The woman took the money and ran. She is still at large."

"Any good news for me?"

"Nothing to put a smile on your face."

"Keep me informed."

Charlie heard the click of the receiver as the call ended. That woman, Mary Lou, held his cash and would need to pay for her mistakes. The phone rang again - a different voice on the line.

"Bad news, Charles."

"What now?"

"There's been a death."

"Who?"

"Frank Lagotti Senior."

"The Shylock? How?"

"Bullet through his face."

A professional hit.

"Any idea on the perpetrator?"

"Not yet but we're working on it."

"Where did the deed take place?"

"In his cathouse. No struggle. The hitman walked in, plugged Lagotti, did for the girl sat on his dick and strode out. Too much of a coincidence for Lagotti's murder to occur the same day as the fracas in LA. Make some enquiries. I want to know more details."

Pentangelo waited ten minutes and dialed a special number - it was never written down but always memorized by those who used it. When serious men needed professional help to complete their murderous tasks, they contacted Murder Inc: the nickname for a unique group of killers who originally came out of Brooklyn. These fellas were the most dangerous the mob families knew. If anyone would take out a hit on someone outside their territory, these were the people to call.

Charlie booked a requisition on the head of Mary Lou and it was immediately sanctioned even with a specific request. He wanted the best man for this job: Arnold Roach. A killer's killer. An elite fiend with a knife or a gun. A relentless murdering machine. Once you hired him, he never gave up. Whoever he held a contract on always wound up demised.

As the sole survivor of the heist, Mary Lou must take responsibility for all that has happened: to the money, to the men and now to Frankie. Roach would track her down and slash her throat. Or cut her open from one side to the other. Whatever Charlie wanted.

The Getaway

Safe knowing Roach was on the case within a matter of hours, Pentangelo put on an aria on his record player and settled back down in his chair. Mary Lou was as good as dead.

To find out more, grab your copy of Powder now at www.leob.ws/powder.

OTHER BOOKS BY THE AUTHOR

The Lagotti Family

The Stickup (Free Prequel Novella)
The Heist (Book 1)
The Getaway (Book 2)
Powder (Book 3)
Mama's Gone (Book 4)
The Girl in the Striped Bikini (Sequel Short Story)

Other Releases

The Case
The Death and Life of Penny Pitstop

Alex Cohen

The Bowery Slugger (Book 1)
East Side Hustler (Book 2 - Due 2020)
Midtown Huckster (Book 3 - Due 2020)

ABOUT THE AUTHOR

Leopold Borstinski is an independent author whose past careers have included financial journalism, business management of financial software companies, consulting and product sales and marketing, as well as teaching.

There is nothing he likes better so he does as much nothing as he possibly can. He has travelled extensively in Europe and the US and has visited Asia on several occasions. Leopold holds a Philosophy degree and tries not to drop it too often.

He lives near London and is married with one wife, one child and no pets.

Find out more at LeopoldBorstinski.com.